A DISTANT LAND

Also by Alison Booth

Stillwater Creek
The Indigo Sky

Alison Booth
A DISTANT LAND

BANTAM

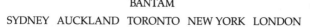

SYDNEY AUCKLAND TORONTO NEW YORK LONDON

A Bantam book
Published by Random House Australia Pty Ltd
Level 3, 100 Pacific Highway, North Sydney NSW 2060
www.randomhouse.com.au

First published by Bantam in 2012

Permission to reproduce words from the T. S. Eliot poem 'Burnt Norton', first published in 1935 and later in *Four Quartets*, courtesy of the publisher Faber and Faber Ltd, England. Permission to reproduce words from the Judith Wright poem 'All Things Conspire', from *A Human Pattern: Selected Poems*, published in 2009, courtesy of ETT Imprint, Sydney.

This is a work of fiction. Names, characters, places and incidents either are the product of the author's imagination or are used fictitiously. Any resemblance to actual persons, living or dead, events or locales is entirely coincidental.

Addresses for companies within the Random House Group can be found at www.randomhouse.com.au/offices.

National Library of Australia
Cataloguing-in-Publication Entry

    Booth, Alison.
    A distant land/Alison Booth.
    978 1 86471 194 3 (pbk.)
    A823.4

Cover images: tree by Jason Loucas, Photolibrary, courtesy of Getty Images; flora by dpaint, courtesy of Shutterstock.com; woman by Elena Yakusheva, courtesy of Shutterstock.com; sky by Iakov Kalinin, courtesy of Shutterstock.com
Cover design by Natalie Winter
Internal design and typesetting by Midland Typesetters, Australia
Printed and bound by Griffin Press, South Australia

Random House Australia uses papers that are natural, renewable and recyclable products and made from wood grown in sustainable forests. The logging and manufacturing processes are expected to conform to the environmental regulations of the country of origin.

Time present and time past
Are both perhaps present in time future,
And time future contained in time past.
If all time is eternally present
All time is unredeemable.
What might have been is an abstraction
Remaining a perpetual possibility
Only in a world of speculation.

T. S. Eliot, 'Burnt Norton'

For my family and in memory of PR

PROLOGUE
8 OCTOBER 1971

A green parakeet with a red beak swoops above the four men, followed a few seconds later by half a dozen more. Their harsh squawks rise and fall over the liquid notes of some larger bird, endlessly repeated. In response the jungle sighs and rustles. The air, heavy with humidity, is an almost palpable barrier that Jim has to punch his way through. To the side of the trail vines interweave the undergrowth, creating an impenetrable wall. The towering trees form a canopy pierced by spears of golden sunlight.

Jim's hands are shaking, his nerves lacerated. Adrenalin courses through his body, propelling him forward. Occasionally he pauses, to make sure the others are keeping up. Over the sounds of the jungle he hears, from barely half a kilometre away, the renewed hammering of automatic rifles followed by a series of explosions that have to be mortar attacks. The pounding of the guns recedes. The sun is shifting, altering the shapes of the shadows. Sometimes they seem to be black pyjama-clad people and at other times figures in military clothing. At last, as the sun is sinking, Jim finds a waterhole ringed by vines and the four men slake their thirst with the rust-coloured water.

When darkness falls, they halt in a small hollow to one side of the trail. As yet there's no moonlight and it's become increasingly difficult to see the way. Somehow they've taken a wrong turning in the rush to escape. But it's too late to go back, at least for a while; Jim can still hear the sporadic thudding of artillery in the distance.

Exhausted, they stretch out on the ground in the hollow, barely big enough for them all. The grumbling in Jim's stomach and bowels is from hunger, he tells himself, and not from the stagnant water he's just drunk. Tomorrow he and the other correspondents will find their way to the rear of all the action, and afterwards drive back to Phnom Penh. He longs to be at his desk in the wire-services bureau. Or better still, stretched out on the bed in his flat, listening to the whirring of the ceiling fan and the chirping of the geckos.

The others sleep while Jim keeps watch. Mark begins to snore and gently Jim rolls him onto his side. After a while the moon bobs into view above the clearing. Kim stirs and sits up, automatically reaching for his camera. Almost immediately he whispers, 'Voices.' A few seconds later Jim hears them too. 'Vietcong, I think,' Kim adds.

A group of murmuring figures passes, just metres away. By day the Americans and their allies control the air and can travel almost anywhere they want. At night the land belongs to the Communist guerrillas.

By the light of the moon Jim can make out the time: nearly two o'clock. The forest shifts and shudders as small creatures move through the undergrowth. Once he hears the sudden scream of an animal that's been taken, by a snake, perhaps, or a larger predator. His companions are as still as he is. Even the jungle is now quiet. He starts as a loud crash breaks the silence, followed by a rattling of leaves. None of them moves. After an eternity, Kim whispers, 'Just some bamboo trees falling, or maybe a sambar deer.'

The minutes pass, the hours pass. The moon moves across the sky like a drifting balloon and soon their hollow is in darkness again. At last Jim dozes. When he awakes, green light is filtering through the foliage. The others are already sitting up. They look startled, as if overnight they've forgotten where they are.

Jim's mouth is so dry he can hardly swallow. As he struggles into a sitting position, he sees on the lip of the hollow three pairs of feet. Three pairs of feet wearing sandals fashioned from rubber tyres and inner tubes.

Slowly he raises his eyes and sees three rifle barrels. Holding the rifles are three soldiers. They are not the allies. They are not the Cambodians either. These young men are wearing the belted green uniforms of the North Vietnamese Army.

Casually lifting his gun, the tallest soldier directs it at Jim. His stomach lurches and his heart begins to flap wildly. The youngest guerrilla motions the journalists out of the hollow and pushes them roughly into the centre of the trail.

The sharp pang of regret Jim feels is like a bullet piercing his chest.

PART I

September 1971

CHAPTER 1

It was only early September but the sun felt hot on Zidra's face. The centre of Sydney was cordoned off, the traffic diverted elsewhere, the streets occupied by anti-war marchers. It was a fantastic turnout, she thought; there had to be tens of thousands of people demonstrating. Narrowing her eyes against the harsh glare, she peered at the stream of bodies flowing towards the Domain, bodies holding up so many placards and banners that sometimes it was hard to make out the faces of the people carrying them. The messages were unmistakable though: 'Nurses For Peace'; 'Miners Against Massacre in Vietnam'; 'Youth Campaign Against Conscription'.

There was almost a carnival atmosphere, in spite of the violence at the last moratorium march, in spite of the gravity of the common cause. And in spite of the police presence: burly men arrayed like wooden figures in a game of table football waiting for the start of play.

After scribbling some words in the notebook she was carrying, Zidra's attention was caught by an enormous banner bearing the message 'End the Unjust War'. It was held aloft by five middle-aged women, all wearing pretty floral dresses and hats as if they were attending a formal garden party. The fabric of the banner billowed in the breeze, and a sudden gust filled it like a spinnaker and threatened to lift the women off the ground. Zidra nudged Chris but he'd already seen it. Snapping everything, he'd taken hundreds of photographs of the marchers, of the ranks of observers, and of the impassive policemen too.

Chris hoicked his camera equipment onto his shoulder and grabbed Zidra's elbow with his free hand. Their plan was to take a short cut through the side streets to reach the Domain, where the speeches were to be made. At that moment she heard someone call her name. It was her best friend, Lorna Hunter, marching only metres away. Wearing a T-shirt with the Aboriginal flag on the front and a red bandana tied around her shoulder-length black hair, she was at the front of the group under the banner of the Vietnam Moratorium Campaign.

While Zidra was waving back, her attention was caught by light reflecting off a telephoto lens on an expensive-looking camera. A rival newspaper, she thought, although she didn't recognise the man holding it. He was of average height with an unremarkable face: the nose was snub, cheekbones appeared absent, and his hair was so nondescript that you'd only describe it as mousy if you were being kind. A Mr Ordinary, whom she would never have noticed if it hadn't been for that shaft of sunlight glinting off his lens.

She watched him sidle along between the line of police and the onlookers on the other side of the road. He was keeping pace with Lorna. Photographing Lorna. The police presence didn't seem to stop the progress of Mr Ordinary, who was still taking snaps of the marchers bearing the Vietnam Moratorium banner.

'Get a shot of that man, Chris,' she said, pointing.

'Which one?'

'The guy with the telephoto lens, see?'

Chris obligingly snapped a couple of shots in the few seconds before Lorna was carried out of sight in the surge towards the Domain. Then he grabbed Zidra's hand and began pulling her through the crowd of onlookers, people peeling apart as soon as they saw the gear he was carrying.

'It's Zidra Vincent, isn't it?'

She stopped, while Chris loosened his grip on her arm and forged ahead. She recognised the voice. Hank Fuller was smiling down at her. Suddenly conscious of her dishevelled appearance – her curly brown hair was escaping from the ribbon she'd tied it back with and her face was devoid of make-up – she smoothed her crumpled dress. Better looking even than she remembered, Hank had the oval face and deep-set eyes of a saint from an early Italian painting. This was an illusion, she knew. The way he'd kissed her on the balcony at that cocktail party two weeks ago was far from saintly. Moments afterwards she'd gone inside and soon after left without saying goodbye. She'd felt wary about Hank the Yank after learning he worked for the American Consulate. And anyway he'd come on to her too fast. Yet she was pleased to see him in spite of that.

'Hurry up, Zidra. We haven't got much time.' Chris was yelling at her from several paces ahead and she could see that the crowd was already folding back over the opening he'd created.

'Are you with that big blonde guy with the camera?' Hank said. 'He's a man in a hurry.'

'Yes, we work together. I'm with the *Sydney Morning Chronicle*.'

'I know. You told me that when we met before. And I've read your articles.'

She stiffened. 'You can't know which are mine. None of the local news is attributed.'

'You cover anti-war marches,' he said lightly. Under the merciless sunlight she could see the mesh of fine lines around his eyes. He looked older than she'd first thought; probably in his early thirties. He added, 'And I know your style.'

'I don't have a style. I just observe and record.'

'In a particularly stylish way.'

She refused to be flattered. 'I can't stop now,' she said. 'We're covering the moratorium.'

'Would you like to have dinner with me tonight?'

She hesitated but only for a second. 'Yes, why not? Meet me at the Gladstone pub in Paddington at seven o'clock. I'm seeing some friends there, and you and I can have dinner after that.'

'Sure.' He shouted some more words after her but they were drowned out by the chanting of the marchers from the Rubber & Allied Workers' Union and she thought no more of him.

After stuffing her notebook into her shoulder bag, she ran in the direction that Chris had taken, although he was out of sight now. Pressing through the crowd, she emerged at last into an open space and glimpsed Chris disappearing down a side street near Sydney Hospital. Overweight though he was, and burdened with various pieces of camera apparatus, he still managed to maintain a cracking pace, and she struggled to catch up with him.

At the same time, she was mentally composing her article and filing, in another part of her brain, a different story, a story based on the conflicting messages of those various placards that she'd seen, a story that would win her accolades and a weekly column, if only she could get her editor to publish it.

Today everyone was united by their shared purpose, she thought, in spite of their different narratives. It was the waging of war on the warmongers. The marchers' battle was glorious, their zeal was almost messianic.

'Who was your mate?' Chris said when she was within speaking distance. They began to negotiate their way around the sea of bodies towards the platform at the far side of the Domain. It was a relief to be out of the unrelenting light and under the dense canopy of the Moreton Bay fig trees encircling the vast grassy area. Already the people who would speak were seated on the dais, six in a row, and someone was fiddling with a microphone in front of the lectern.

'Hank Fuller. He works for the US Consulate.'

'Yeah? He's CIA then. Be careful what you say.'

She'd had the same thought but she laughed at Chris. Though he was only three years older than she, he liked to pretend he was more. Liked to pretend he was in charge too, even though she was the official storyteller in this duo. His photographs were good, and sometimes so brilliant that they didn't need a story, the image told it all. 'Hank probably just issues visas,' she said. 'Anyway, you don't really think I have secrets, do you?'

He grinned. 'Nah, that's your problem. Too open. Apart from when you're bottling up a story – then you're like a clam. Got to be cagey with CIA types though. Why else do you think he'd be attending a moratorium march?'

'Observing, Chris. Like us. But there's a difference between spying and observing, you know.'

'Too bloody right,' he said and started unpacking his gear. 'I guess that camera he was toting was just for tourist snaps. Photos to show the folks back home rather than for work.'

'He had a camera?'

'Yeah, didn't you notice? I reckon you were too caught up in his handsome face.'

'Everyone watching the marchers has a camera. Didn't you notice?'

'I don't call a Polaroid Instamatic a camera. He had a Hasselblad. Bloody expensive, those things.'

'All that means is that he's rich. It doesn't mean he's using it for work. Maybe you're becoming just the tiniest bit paranoid, Chris.'

'We've got to be suspicious nowadays. You should know that more than anyone, my budding investigative friend. And anyway, why did you want me to photograph that other bloke, the one with the Leica?'

'Is that what it was? He was taking rather a lot of pictures of my friend Lorna.'

'A white bloke snapping an Aboriginal girl right under the banner of the Vietnam Moratorium Campaign, eh? He's either another journalist or police, I reckon. I took a couple of her myself. You can have copies of them if you want.'

'Thanks, I'd like that.'

Their conversation was interrupted by a piercing whistle from the amplifier on stage. When it had stopped, Chris said, 'If you want a nice-looking Yank, go to the Cross and pick up one. They're a dime a dozen up there and no strings attached. That's what I'd do. Not go fishing in the US bloody Consulate.'

'That's terrible advice, Chris.' It was a doctor who'd told her about the venereal disease infection rates, but she hadn't mentioned this when she'd interviewed a few of the American servicemen on Rest and Recreation leave. Some seemed like tough thugs you wouldn't want to meet on a dark night but others were traumatised vulnerable boys who needed to go home. She added, 'You want to be careful yourself. I've heard a lot of the soldiers have got VD.'

'Nah, they're all on penicillin. Not to mention other sub-stances. But as I always say, there's nothing wrong with a good old Aussie bloke.'

There's plenty wrong with a good old Aussie bloke, she thought, *especially when he doesn't live here any more.* Jim Cadwallader might have been in her heart but he wasn't in her country. Four years in Britain was four too many, and now he was in Phnom Penh covering the Vietnam War as it spilt over into Cambodia. Even though she'd loved him for years, even though they'd been writing to each other for years, none of that was enough to bring him home.

At that moment she was distracted from her reverie by the banner that was being stretched out across the back of the dais.

'Beaut flag, isn't it?' Chris said.

It was the Vietnam Moratorium logo, a white sunburst on an orange background. Chris raised his camera and began snapping. Zidra pulled her notebook out of her bag as the applause began and the first speaker, a Labor Party politician, stepped up to the lectern. She knew what he would say. He'd said it again and again and still it was worth repeating: 'Democracy begins on the farms, in the factories and in the streets, and if people will not, often at risk to themselves, stand up for their rights there will be no democracy.'

CHAPTER 2

The Paddington terrace house that Zidra shared with Lisa and Joanne was in darkness. None of its daytime shabbiness was visible. The street lamp faintly illuminated the best features of the terrace: the triple-arched windows to the living room and the intricate cast-iron lacework bordering the first-floor balcony. How fortunate, Zidra decided, that Lisa was staying with her boyfriend tonight and Joanne having an early night. She led the way up the stairs, past the first floor, where Lisa and Joanne had their bedrooms, and up to her bedroom on the next level. On the last half-flight, Hank put his hand on her backside.

'Gorgeous ass,' he said.

'I bet you say that to all the girls.' She was pleased none-theless.

I wish I'd made the bed properly, she thought as she opened her bedroom door, *but it's the papers I have to check first*. Quickly she gathered up the pages littering her desk and shoved them into the top drawer. There were certainly several things that she didn't want Hank to see, especially her opinion piece on the policing of the moratorium marches. In her typewriter was a sheet of paper on which were written a couple of paragraphs; she spooled the page out and put it away.

Meanwhile Hank had parked himself on the edge of the bed. After pulling the desk chair around to face him, she sat down. He didn't say anything, just stared at her – an intense stare that she found disturbing, though she gazed back anyway. After a few moments she got up and knelt on the floor in front of him. Reaching out her arms, she framed his face with her hands. He leant forward and kissed her. He tasted of whisky and something else, something that she wanted to get a lot more of.

———◆———

Zidra was paying the price for not drawing the curtains the previous night: the sunlight glared in at her, harsh and unforgiving. Her mouth was dry and her head aching. She rolled over and was hit by the lingering scent on the sheets, of Hank's aftershave or deodorant or God knows what else he anointed his body with. Not to mention his anointing of her own flesh. She sat up. The clock on her bedside table indicated that it was already eight. Hank hadn't wanted to stay the night and that had been a relief. She was never at her best first thing in the morning and she doubted he was the sort to bring her a cup of tea in bed, even if he had been able to locate the tea things in the kitchen.

The sound of music drifted up from the floor below: Leonard Cohen, Joanne's current favourite. For a moment Zidra wished she was at Ferndale, her parent's property near Jingera, which she still viewed as home. From her bedroom there you only ever heard the distant crashing of the surf and the birds calling, or the wind sighing through the trees, and maybe clattering from the kitchen signalling delicious things for lunch. In two weeks' time she'd be heading south to Ferndale for a week's holiday. She could certainly do with a break.

She threw back the sheet and slipped on a kimono. Her nightgown was in the laundry basket, along with a host of other things. The sheets would need washing too, she decided – she didn't want to carry Hank's scent with her for days. It was disturbing that in appearance he reminded her of Jim. Although Jim didn't have those deep-set dark eyes, he had the same olive skin and straight brown hair. Yet she had to move on from this, just as Jim had.

The effort of fastening the kimono worsened her headache. Throbbing temples, dry throat, flashes of light. She shut her eyes. After feeling her way to the window, she pulled the curtains across. Funny to think that she'd known her two best friends, Jim and Lorna, for over two-thirds of her life. She'd first met them when she was only nine, soon after she and her mother had moved to Jingera. They'd befriended her and shielded her from those taunts of being a *bloody reffo* or the daughter of a *commie bastard.* And Jim had protected her from the predatory interest of the publican Mr Bates too. She'd imagined, as she was growing up, that she and Jim would end up together. A wrong assumption. By the time she'd gone to university, he was in third year and in a different league. He'd become involved with beautiful Lindsay and had little time for her. Not that beautiful Lindsay stayed with him for long. Barely six months later she'd taken up with a rich lawyer ten years older and Jim had won the University Medal as well as a Rhodes Scholarship. Once he'd gone to Oxford, Zidra had embarked on a series of unsatisfactory relationships with unsuitable men.

Of course not everyone would view Hank as unsuitable.

In the bathroom she gulped down several glasses of water and swallowed two paracetamol. After a quick shower she ran damp fingers through her hair; it was no good combing curls like hers.

She and Jim had continued a close friendship by post. Sometimes it seemed to her that their relationship had deepened through the many letters they'd exchanged over the years. Letters giving details about their lives and their thoughts, if not about their romantic exploits. Jim was a part of the fabric of her life, even though he wasn't in Australia.

Inspecting her reflection in the bathroom mirror, she decided she looked terrible; this is what too little sleep did to you when you were approaching twenty-four. Carefully she patted face cream onto her skin. Surely that wasn't a line appearing on her forehead? No, it was just the skin creasing from her raised eyebrows. Facial immobility was the thing if you wanted to stay youthful – that's what the women's page editor had told her in all seriousness. Maybe she'd have to stop raising her eyebrows and revert to wearing a fringe. She laughed and then grimaced at her reflection. Last night Hank had told her she was beautiful, but some people will say anything to get you into bed.

As she passed Joanne's room, the door opened. 'Who was that guy?' Joanne said. In her too-large pyjamas, she looked more like a twelve-year-old boy than a woman in her mid-twenties.

'Hank Fuller. How did you know he was here?'

'I heard you talking on the way up.'

'Sorry. I thought we were whispering.'

'Stage whispering, Zidra. I heard all about your *gorgeous ass*. Is he still here?'

'No, he left early this morning.'

'Pity. I'd like to meet him. Cute accent. Is he the one for you?'

'Oh, Joanne, I don't know what that means.'

'Darling, don't spoil my illusions. I like to think there's a unique partner for each and every one of us.'

'I've never heard such nonsense in my life.' Zidra was now starting to feel slightly ashamed of using Hank as she'd done last night.

As she opened the front door of the house, she heard the telephone ring and then Joanne's voice as she picked it up on the kitchen extension. 'Yes, Zidra's here but she's just about to go to work . . . You're calling from where? . . . Just hold on a moment.'

Joanne put her hand over the receiver and shouted, 'Some guy from Phnom Penh.'

'Phnom Penh,' Zidra repeated. It had to be from Jim, though calls from him were a rarity – in fact he'd phoned from Cambodia just once before, on her birthday. As she took the receiver, she noticed her hand was shaking. 'Hello?' There was only static at first and then Jim's voice uttering her name. She waited a few seconds, until she could hear that Joanne was well on her way up the stairs, before saying, 'How are you? It's been a long time.'

'Did you get my letter?'

'I got one dated the end of August.' It was in the top-right-hand drawer of her chest of drawers, in a shoebox with all his other letters.

There was silence. The slight time delay made a natural conversation almost impossible. Her voice had mingled with his along the telephone wires; their exchange was either a duet or a pause in which all she could hear was the hissing of static.

At last she heard him say, 'I wrote another one a week ago.'

'I haven't got that yet. The post from Cambodia's sometimes a bit erratic.'

'I'm coming home for a visit.'

'Fantastic.' He would go to Jingera, though, and she might barely see him, for she'd already promised her editor she'd work over the Christmas holiday period. She said, 'Is that for Christmas?'

'No, much sooner. I'm arriving on Sunday the twenty-sixth, early in the morning.'

Startled, she said, 'You mean the twenty-sixth of *September*?'

'Yes.'

'What a coincidence.' Abruptly she sat down at the kitchen bench. Her heart had begun to bang against her ribcage and her hands felt clammy. 'That's when I've arranged to spend a week at home at Ferndale.'

'I know.' Jim laughed, but his voice sounded slightly embarrassed. 'Your mother wrote and told me.'

'How long are you staying?'

'A week.'

'Your parents will be overjoyed.'

'Yes.'

'I could collect you at the airport and we could drive straight on to Jingera.'

'That's terrific. Could we get there in a day?'

'Easily.' She paused. 'Unless you wanted to take it more slowly?'

'No, I just thought it might be too much driving for you.'

She would love to do it over two days. They could stop off somewhere such as Ulladulla, have dinner together and stay in a motel – separate rooms of course – and then potter on through those sleepy coastal towns.

She was about to suggest this when Jim said, 'A story about Sydney's fourth march was picked up by UPI. I knew it was yours.'

'That's the last march ever,' Zidra said, smiling at the phone receiver. That Jim had recognised her unattributed piece was almost as pleasing as learning it had been picked up by the wire service, in spite of its poor positioning in the *Sydney Morning Chronicle.*

'That's what they said about the previous one. But anyway, the troops in Vietnam have been told that most of them will be home for Christmas and won't be going back. Do you know how they heard?'

'On a radio broadcast in the middle of August over the American network. It was all over the papers here. Your parents must be thrilled that your brother's coming home at last.'

'Yes. Nui Dat's a mess if ever there was one. Andy'll be glad to get out of that.'

'Do you ever see him?'

'No.'

'Who'd have thought when he went to the Army Apprentices' School that he'd end up serving in the Third Battalion?' Zidra knew from her mother that Andy's parents, George and Eileen Cadwallader, lived in fear that he wouldn't come home, lived in fear that neither of their sons would come home. She added, 'How are things going up there?'

'Bad, but maybe we won't talk about it on the phone. You take care, Zidra.'

Suddenly she felt shy. The moment had gone when she could suggest stopping off somewhere on the drive south. There was a pause before Jim said, 'Have you got a pen? I'll give you my flight details.'

'I'll get one.' She put down the receiver and burrowed in her handbag for a pencil and paper. Carefully she wrote down the flight number and time, and then could think of nothing more to say. Somehow the conversation had to reach a conclusion, even though she wanted it to go on forever, if only she could overcome her awkwardness and speak as she used to. Though at times she felt his face was permanently imprinted on her memory, now it became elusive and for an instant she couldn't conjure up his image at all. Then he broke the silence and the memory restored itself.

'Well, I mustn't keep you any longer,' he said.

She laughed tentatively and was relieved when he joined in, though she couldn't have said what amused her, unless it was simply an impression that her future was altering its course.

'It's okay,' she said.

At last the conversation was over and she was replacing the receiver in its cradle. She was alone again, yet not as she had been. She felt lighter; some burden that she hadn't known she'd been shouldering had been lifted from her. For a few moments she continued sitting at the kitchen bench, smiling at the fruit bowl as she listened to the morning shrieking at her through the open window.

CHAPTER 3

Zidra was surprised when her boss, Joe Ryan, rang her extension. Though she wanted to see him, she certainly didn't expect to be summonsed by phone. Why on earth ring rather than simply appear in the doorway to his office and bellow to her across the newsroom, the way he usually did?

'Come and see me in ten minutes,' he said. 'There's something I'd like to talk to you about.'

And I to you, Zidra thought. *Like why the hell you shoved my piece on the moratorium march to page seven.* To add insult to injury, one of Chris's photographs had appeared on the front page of the issue, a picture of the well-dressed women with the banner 'End the Unjust War'. He'd caught the instant when the fabric had filled like a spinnaker, and the angle of the shot lent the illusion that two of the women had been lifted right off the ground. Underneath the photograph was the headline 'All a Lot of Hot Air?'. Below this was a report on what a Liberal Party parliamentarian had said about the marches and the speakers.

'Something up?' said Dave Pringle, the foreign editor, who was passing by as she banged down the receiver. He was thin and overgrown, as if he'd been reared in a dark place and had to struggle upwards to reach the light.

'Not really.' She liked his habitual kindly expression, although this could have been partly the result of poor eyesight. He'd worked in the Department of Foreign Affairs for fifteen years before becoming a journalist and was well informed about everything. 'Joe wants to see me, that's all.'

'Don't be late,' Dave said. 'He can't abide unpunctuality, unless it's his own.'

Precisely ten minutes later Zidra was at Joe's door. Through the open doorway she could see him sitting behind his paper-strewn desk, his glasses on the top of his head like a black plastic bridge over that shining pink scalp. A fringe of thick white hair around the perimeter of the dome gave him a monastic appearance. Indeed, Joe had started training for the priesthood before his life had taken another direction. Now he was married to both his newspaper and Bridget, and was the father of seven strapping sons, each over six feet tall. How this had come about seemed on occasion to mystify Joe, who was himself a mere five feet eight inches, although in the four years that Zidra had known him the inches had been accumulating around his girth, and the waistline of his trousers dropping lower and lower to accommodate the ballooning stomach.

She knocked. Joe looked up at once and motioned her to the seat opposite him. It was too high and her legs dangled, only her toes reaching the floor. She'd rather have both feet firmly planted on the ground before beginning the speech she'd been preparing.

'Well, Zidra,' Joe said, rocking his chair backward and forward while resting his hands behind his head. 'There are a couple of things I'd like to talk over with you.'

'Me too,' she said. She took a deep breath in readiness. The story she'd written to accompany Chris's photograph had been

23

much too *pertinent*, she was going to say, to be relegated to the bottom of page seven. Why the words of the Liberal Party parliamentarian should displace her story was beyond her, although in her calmer moments she had to admit that the headline was great and the article's positioning certainly illustrated how empty was the rhetoric of Bob-the-Shoveller Barrow.

'I've been thinking,' Joe said, giving the lopsided grin that, together with his bright blue eyes, was one of the more attractive features of his doughy face. 'I've been thinking about what to do with you.'

Her mouth suddenly felt dry and her stomach tightened with anxiety. Maybe Joe was about to sack her or, almost as bad, shift her back to the women's pages, where she'd started at the *Sydney Morning Chronicle*. Would he really do that? It had been he, after all, who'd spotted what he termed her potential, after she'd written a humorous piece about correlations between fashion trends and business-cycle fluctuations the week the women's page editor was away. Had he regretted his decision to give her a trial on the news section two years ago? Surely not. He'd regularly encouraged her and frequently invited her to Sunday lunch with his family and some other journalists. Over the years she'd come to view him as her mentor. But had she become too partisan of late? She found herself grimacing nervously at this possibility. She was supposed to be a journalist, reporting the truth from all perspectives. Was it possible she'd overstepped the mark?

'Yes,' said Joe. 'I've given it a lot of thought and I've talked it over with the deputy editor as well. And, after due deliberation, I've decided to give you a bit of headway to do some more investigative journalism. It's not a job change as such, or much of a change of duties either, although we're taking on a couple more cadets, which will free up your time. I want you to think of it more as an expansion, to give you time to explore issues in depth. That Fourth Moratorium March, for instance. That was a beaut piece you wrote, though not really front-page stuff. It was too reflective for that. Maybe you could revise it and we might be able to put it out as an opinion piece. And I want you to do more along those lines. If you get a bit more freedom, you might come up with something hot. What do you reckon? Willing to make a start when you get back from your holiday?'

Laughing was the only way to express her delight, Zidra decided, when she couldn't really dash around the desk and plant a kiss on his shiny pate. 'I reckon that's the best thing I've heard all week,' she said.

And to think that, only a few moments ago, she'd believed he was trying to get rid of her. She leant back in the chair and swung her legs and suppressed the questions that had sprung into her mind. Questions such as are you sure? Am I really awake and not dreaming this? 'Thank you, Joe,' she added. 'I won't let you down.'

'I know you won't,' he said gruffly. 'And now be off with you.'

She half-expected him to clap his hands and say 'Chop chop', as she'd seen him do when telling the Ryan family cats to shift off the sofa, but he didn't. He simply gave her that asymmetric smile that on good days made him look almost boyish and on bad days as if he were recovering from a slight stroke. Today was a good day, no two ways about it.

CHAPTER 4

Zidra spotted Jim as soon as he emerged from the immigration and baggage hall, one of the stream of people flowing through the swing doors. She waved but he didn't notice; a party of giants had somehow managed to squeeze in front of her, even though she'd been there long before them.

Jim strode past a large family, the parents pushing trolleys that had minds of their own and an older couple, probably grandparents, marshalling four or five recalcitrant children. For a moment Zidra feared he might stride past her as well, although she was waving and calling his name. His straight brown hair was shaggier than it had been when she'd last seen him, and he looked older too, as you'd expect after nearly two years. It had been that long since they'd last seen each other. Long enough to fill a shoebox with letters.

As soon as he caught sight of her, he grinned and waved. She ran behind the crowd of waiting people and reached the end of the barricade at the same time as he did. There he dropped his bag and, bloody hell, undemonstrative Jim was hugging her! She put her arms around him and rested her face against his chest. How she loved this smell of cotton and clean skin; somehow he'd managed to wash and shave before getting in this morning. Yet he could have arrived travel-stained and stinking and she wouldn't have cared. They stayed like that for a moment, before the press of people propelled them forward. Then they let go of each other but still he was smiling, and so was she. There was such a lot to catch up on but they'd never learn each other's news, not if they were both talking at once. She stopped speaking at the same time as he did, and then they began to laugh. *You go first. No, after you. We've got all day to catch up with each other, and then there'll be time in Jingera too.*

She led him out into the oblique sunlight of the Sydney morning, still only seven o'clock, although she'd been up for two hours already. Jim didn't have much luggage; he never did – everyone she knew who'd been to a boarding school seemed to travel light. Yet it was still a bit of a squeeze in the boot of her car because she had a lot of stuff. That was the thing about driving, she found: you could just chuck things in and not have to worry about capacity, even with a car as small as her red Mini.

It was one of those perfect spring days. Cloudless, and the air crystal clear, cleansed by overnight rain and a westerly wind that had blown away the haze of pollution. As she drove, she barely noticed the ugliness of the inner-city streets, the industrial area around the airport, and then on through the interminable suburbs and eventually out of the city altogether, and still they were talking and laughing.

After a couple of hours they stopped for coffee. When they were getting back into the car, Jim spotted the book she'd forgotten she'd left on the floor in the back; her reading matter for Ferndale. Though Hank had lent it to her days ago, she hadn't got any further than the title page and table of contents. Jim picked up the book and opened it. '"The library of Henry Fuller",' he read from the inscription inside the book. It was written on a nameplate embellished with curlicues. 'Ha,' said Jim. 'Have you read this yet?'

'No,' she said.

'I have. It's a rather self-serving justification of US involvement in Indochina. I'm surprised you'd want to read it.'

She suspected that his reaction to this find was emotional rather than logical. He'd taken against Hank on the basis of the sticker and the book. 'Well, Jim,' she said, 'I'm surprised you actually finished reading it if it's such terrible trash. On the other hand, you only learn something's rubbish from reading it all, don't you think? What's that old saying? You can't judge a book by its cover.'

There was a silence. She thought the topic finished with and was struggling to think of some way of bridging the gulf that had opened between them when he said, 'Who *is* Henry Fuller?'

She replied, more impatiently than she'd intended, 'He works for the US Consulate.'

'What does he do there?'

'I don't know precisely. Maybe he issues visas or stamps passports. And he's always going to cocktail parties so I guess he pushes US commercial interests. Anyway we don't talk about his work.'

'Do you see much of him?'

Taken aback by this question, she used the excuse of overtaking a truck that was labouring up an incline to delay replying. She didn't see much of Hank, she might have said, although this last week they'd several times made *wild passionate love*, as a trashy novel that she'd picked up on a railway station described it. Maybe wild passionate sex was a better description of what they had actually got up to, but she wasn't about to explain this distinction to Jim. She thought of Jim and Lindsay's love affair in Jim's final year in Sydney; she'd bet there was lots of wild passionate sex there. Lindsay was beautiful, and Zidra felt a pang of the jealousy that she thought she'd got over years ago. Somehow Jim's first lover had been the worst. She hadn't cared about the ones afterwards, although she had felt a twinge or two recently when a French photographer called Dominique had begun to appear in his letters.

'Do you see much of him?' Jim repeated.

'Not really,' she said. That was a noncommittal reply that covered a lot of possibilities. Perhaps it was because she was concentrating on her driving that it took several more minutes before annoyance with Jim's probing began to set in. It was none of his damned business whom she saw or how often.

'Do you tell him much about your work?'

She took several deep breaths before answering. 'No, I'm not stupid, Jim. I tell him nothing.'

She unnecessarily changed down a gear and then up again. It was silly for her to feel agitated by the conversation but she did. 'My job's terribly dull, Jim,' she said. 'No one could possibly be interested in it.' She surprised herself with these words. They'd erupted from some hidden depths, where they might have been bubbling like molten lava for many months, perhaps ever since she'd turned down a traineeship with United Press International in Saigon only weeks before he'd accepted a posting to the bureau in Phnom Penh.

'Dull? Your job sounds really interesting from what you've been telling me.'

He was humouring her, surely. Her life must seem to him pedestrian, her reporting even more so. No adrenalin rushes, no danger, no feeling of being on the front line with important events unfolding right around you. Then she thought of good old Joe Ryan and the new freedom he'd offered her. It was up to her to make of that what she could.

'Zidra, my job might sound glamorous,' Jim said slowly, 'but it's not. It's a mix of news and checking legal contracts. Sure, the news is exciting at times, but not in the way you might be thinking. A lot of it's the same old things happening again and again. Same old news headlines, day in, day out. Week in, week out. Bombing raids, forces from opposing sides fighting back and forth, bits of jungle being lost and then regained. And so it goes on. Nothing conclusive. The only certainty is that it's going to get bloodier and more deadly.'

She thought about what he'd said. Bloodier and more deadly. She wished Jim out of all that. They drove in silence for several more kilometres before she blurted out, 'Do you ever hear from Lindsay?'

'Only indirectly.'

It was clear he didn't want to say anything more but she persisted. 'What's she doing?'

'She's been married twice. Each one a lawyer. Moving up the hierarchy.'

'You mean like barrister, judge?'

'Yes, exactly. She divorced the barrister when the judge's wife died.'

'Isn't she a bit young to be married to a judge?'

'Not when he's got a farm in Kangaroo Valley and a mansion in Vaucluse.'

She laughed. While longing now to ask him about Domin-ique, she thought her voice might wobble and give her feelings away.

'Lindsay was years ago, Zidra.'

'I suppose I was jealous of her. Lots of us in Women's College were. She was the most gorgeous girl on campus. Funny how these things stick. I saw her recently in Woollahra with someone I took to be her father but he was probably the judge. She didn't recognise me, though I don't think I've changed that much.'

'No. You don't look a day over sixteen.'

'You never have been able to take me seriously, Jim Cadwallader.'

A few more kilometres passed in silence. Wattle was still blossoming in the bush on each side of the road, the flowers lingering later here than in Sydney. She wound down her window and inhaled deeply. She was about to question Jim regarding the safety of his job when he said, 'When I asked you about Henry Fuller, I was just trying to see if he's good enough for you. It wasn't prurient interest.'

She laughed at Jim's choice of words. He was so formal and old-fashioned sometimes. 'Hank Fuller,' she said. 'So you weren't trying to establish the degree of hanky-panky then?' She would have preferred that he was jealous.

'Think of it as brotherly love. I've known you ever since you were nine, after all. I've had to rescue you many times.'

'Only twice,' she said. 'And you know I'll never forget that.'

'That's what friends are for.'

'Yes, that's what friends are for.' She didn't understand why she felt a twinge of sadness as she angle-parked in the main street of the little fishing town where they'd decided to stop for lunch. Quickly she dismissed it. She was tired, that was all. The day was much too lovely to be spoilt by any introspection.

They bought soft drinks and fish and chips from the shop next door to the fishermen's cooperative and drove up to the park on the promontory to eat them. When they'd had enough,

Jim carried the leftover chips a hundred metres away. Standing on the vivid green grass, surrounded on three sides by deep blue sea flecked with whitecaps, he hurled the chips into the air. For an instant he was lost behind the seething sphere of screaming seagulls and then he emerged laughing like the boy she'd met at Jingera all those years ago.

Why tears should spring to her eyes she couldn't fathom. She stood up and felt the stiff sea breeze whip her hair across her face. Turning away from the wind, she found Jim standing behind her. She looked up at him: his skin was glowing, reflecting the sun's rays back at her. She resisted the temptation to reach out and touch his face. Instead, she said, 'Time to go.'

After they'd settled into the car again, she turned on the ignition and then the radio. Tina Turner belting out 'River Deep – Mountain High' instantly took her back to the days not long after she'd started university. As she put her palm on the gear stick, she felt the touch – the accidental touch – of Jim's hand as he reached for the map. A current passed through her, like a small electric shock. At once she withdrew her hand, before looking at his face, just a few inches from her own. He was staring at her. Surprised by the intensity of his gaze, she looked back, deep into those eyes that she'd always thought of as olive green, the colour of the bush or the Jingera lagoon on a dull day. Now she could see that they were flecked with tiny streaks of brown.

For a moment she thought he might kiss her, but she was mistaken. Turning away, she put the car into gear. It was odd how you thought you knew everything about someone when you really knew only a little.

She didn't even understand herself all that well and she certainly couldn't trust herself to speak.

CHAPTER 5

Zidra, starting to feel exhausted, was the first to glimpse the township of Jingera and its collection of cottages clinging to the hillside. Below the road lay the river, widening into a lagoon connecting to the ocean beyond. While negotiating the first of the hairpin bends, she said, 'Perhaps you'll come to dinner at Ferndale.'

'Yes, your mother's already invited me,' Jim said. 'For the night after tomorrow.'

'Oh? I know you write but I didn't know about the dinner invitation. That's great.'

As they turned into the little square that lay at the heart of Jingera, he said, 'Two years since I was last here and nothing's changed.'

She laughed. 'That's one of the nice things about Jingera.' She drove by the hotel, shut for Sunday, around the war memorial, past the road leading down to the lagoon and turned left just before Jim's father's shop, Cadwallader's Quality Meats.

'Progress has passed the town by and gone to Dooleys Beach,' she said. 'And look what a hellhole that's become. Suburbia by the sea. Kerbed subdivisions, all the trees knocked down, and nothing of the old character left. God, I'm starting to sound middle-aged, but it's true. I don't mind them building new houses as long as they keep the trees.'

She stopped the car outside the Cadwalladers' cottage. Since she'd last visited, it had been painted a pale blue, and the window frames and picket fence a glossy white. So glossy that she suspected they'd been painted recently, possibly even for Jim's homecoming. The corrugated iron of the roof and the awnings over the windows hadn't been painted for years, though, and she was glad of this; the rusty patina added to the charm.

As soon as she switched off the engine, Mr and Mrs Cadwallader appeared at their front gate. They were dressed for an occasion. Mrs Cadwallader, in a red and white floral dress, a string of red beads and tightly permed hair, had slightly spoilt the effect by forgetting to take off her stained pinafore. Mr Cadwallader was in neatly pressed trousers and what looked like a brand-new tweed sports jacket.

Not wanting to intrude, Zidra stayed in the car while Mrs Cadwallader embraced her son and shed a few tears. When it was his turn, Mr Cadwallader shook Jim's hand and patted him on the back while saying, several times over, 'Good to see you home again, son.'

Mrs Cadwallader bent down to smile through the open car window. 'Hello, Zidra. Won't you come in for a cup of tea? It's been a long drive.'

'No, thanks, Mrs C. My parents will be waiting. Only another few kilometres to go and I'd like to get home before it's dark. I'll come and see you again though. I'll be at Ferndale for the best part of a week.'

'Come for tea then. I'll give your parents a quick call to let them know you're on your way.'

Zidra got out of the car to open the boot and, once Jim had removed his bag, he gave her an awkward hug. Afterwards they stood looking at each other intently in the fading light. He began to say something but she couldn't make out the words, for at the same time Mrs Cadwallader called out, 'Better let Zidra get on, Jim. She wants to get to Ferndale before dark.'

Zidra climbed back into the Mini. Her back was starting to feel stiff and her eyes tired, and she unexpectedly felt disappointment sluice over her. One day spent with Jim was nowhere near long enough and it would be another two days before she'd see him again.

Though the street was so narrow that it was little more than a lane, she executed a three-point turn without damaging either her own paintwork or that of the pristine picket fence. In the rear-vision mirror, the waving Cadwalladers became progressively smaller. So intent was she on this sight that she might have missed Mrs Blunkett if she hadn't heard her voice. And there she was, waving from the garden outside her cottage.

'How are you, Mrs Blunkett?' Zidra said, stopping the car. Though the old lady had retired five or six years ago from running the post office, she hadn't moved far, only fifty yards or so across the square to the little place next door to the school mistress's house. From this vantage point, she was able to maintain her vigilant watch of the town and its inhabitants.

'I'm good, love. Mustn't complain about my hip,' said Mrs Blunkett, her voice a solo trumpet against an accompaniment of distant surf breaking and seagulls wailing. 'Glad you stopped, never know when I might see you again. You young things are always coming and going, mostly going I reckon. There's not much for young folk around here unless you want to work in the fishing or timber industries.' She paused for breath, before continuing, 'So Jim's just got in from Vietnam, has he? Bad luck to have two sons there, that's what I said to Mrs Cadwallader this morning. Oh, it's Cambodia you say? Same difference, dear, they're both in a war zone, and that never does you much good, does it? Andy's supposed to be back by Christmas, Mrs Cadwallader said. Lucky he's not in the Fourth Battalion, she said. That got picked to stay. That'd be terrible luck, wouldn't it?'

'Terrible,' Zidra agreed. The last time she'd seen Andy was two years ago, when he'd come home to Jingera for Christmas on Jim's last visit, and just before his first tour of Vietnam. The only reason he'd wanted to enter the army was to get a proper apprenticeship. There must have been a fair few young men in that position. Andy's dream of running a joinery works in Jingera or Burford had stayed exactly that. Before his nine-year indenture was up, Australia was at war.

'Well, I mustn't keep you, love,' Mrs Blunkett said. 'It'll be dark soon and I know your parents'll be wanting to see you.'

Zidra headed north again, this time on the winding coastal road leading to Ferndale. Fingers of shadows were creeping down the hills from the Great Dividing Range, and one by one stars began to appear. The fading sky blazed golden towards the west, until abruptly the sun sank behind the escarpment. *Such a long day this has been*, she thought, *and I need time to absorb what's happened.*

But now she was almost home. In the vanishing light she could see the state forest on her right giving way to the paddocks of Ferndale, which rolled, in undulating green billows, down to the ocean's edge. Mrs Cadwallader had been true to her word, and her parents were waiting, with a torch and the dogs, at the open front gate. After turning the car off the road, she got out, leaving the engine running. While the dogs danced around her feet, she threw her arms around her mother, whose freshly washed hair smelt of lemon-scented shampoo, and then leant up to kiss Peter's cheek, feeling the slight graze of his stubble that you would never notice otherwise. At the end of the long driveway, she could see the homestead sheltering in its semicircle of pine trees, with all its windows illuminated.

CHAPTER 6

Over the years Peter's face had been pared down by a combination of weather and endurance. His smooth brown hair was streaked with white, more so than on Zidra's last visit. At some point soon there'd be a tipping point and it pained her to think that then you'd have to describe him as silver-haired rather than brown.

Her mother's once fair hair had darkened with the passing years, until she'd been persuaded by the hairdresser in Burford to try blonde highlights. After that, so overwhelmed had Ma been by the compliments that she'd chosen to lock herself into a four-monthly cycle of torture by aluminium foils. Maybe she'd had her hair done specially for Zidra's return yesterday, but Zidra didn't want to think of that. There was no denying that she looked lovely tonight, however irritated Zidra was with her going on and on about Jim for far too long. Her usually pale skin glowed as she ran through the litany of Jim's virtues. About how bright he was, how brave and intrepid too.

By now Zidra had lost all appetite. She put down her knife and fork. Through the kitchen window she could see the whitening sky above the ruffled ocean. Tiny birds weaved through the low scrub defining the cliff edge. If she concentrated on them, rather than her mother's appearance, perhaps she could block out the incessant talking that, together with the drive down the day before, was whipping up her emotions into a toxic brew. If she didn't get out of this room soon, she'd hurl a plate, or bang her head on the table, and how shocked her parents would be at that.

While Peter was looking at her with some concern, her mother was still prattling on, caught up in her soliloquy of Jim's merits: virtues that in her daughter would be unwelcome; virtues that in her only child would cause distress. All at once Zidra lost control of her emotions and spat out – there was no other way to describe it – her anger. 'You're so bloody two-faced! I can't believe you're saying this, you of all people. One rule for girls, another for boys, that's what you really mean. It's okay for Jim to be in Phnom Penh but not me, that's the implication. In spite of all the rhetoric about independence and having a career that you've been blathering on about for years.'

Startled into silence, her mother stared at her.

'Yes, just you reflect on that, dearest Mama.'

Her mother flinched at the sarcasm in the endearment, and a part of Zidra was pleased with this reaction. She continued, 'Think about it. When I got offered that traineeship in Saigon, what did you tell me? It was too dangerous, you said. But also that you were against war. As if my actions should be based on your opinions!' She laughed, an angry sort of bray with no mirth in it. Although she recognised she was being childish, she couldn't stop herself. 'I understand your views about war. I know where you're coming from. How could I be allowed to forget it?'

Even as she spoke, she knew that this was completely unfair. Her parents never mentioned the World War that they'd somehow managed to survive, her mother enduring the horrors of a concentration camp and her adopted father, Peter, of a prisoner-of-war camp. She hadn't learnt about that war from her parents; she'd learnt about it from studying history. She might almost have thought the war didn't exist in her parents' minds if she'd judged it only by their silence on this topic, rather than by her interpretation of what that silence meant.

'We never understood why you wanted to go to Vietnam,' her mother said at last. Though her voice was calm, she started running her hands through her hair, a sure sign of distress. 'That's one war Australia should never have got itself involved in. It was just blind toadying to the US.'

'Toadying to the US? What nonsense, Ma.' Although Zidra agreed with her mother and would put the same argument to anyone who would listen, she wasn't about to admit this. 'Prime Minister Menzies genuinely thought we were at risk and the bulk of the population supported him.'

'If Menzies had waited a year or two, he might have seen that all the capitalist states of South East Asia could have formed a reverse domino effect. A counterbalance.'

'It's easy to be wise after the event,' Zidra said crossly. 'Anyway, I wasn't proposing to *fight* in the Vietnam War, for heaven's sake, only to report it. To seek out the truth and to record it, just as Jim's doing in Cambodia. The simple fact of the matter is that you don't want me to take risks, and never have.'

'That's not true at all,' her mother said. Her face by now was looking quite flushed. 'Anyway, Jim's taking major risks partly because he's an expert on Cambodia. And he'll be returning home soon to write a book about it.'

'Returning home? Who told you that?' To disguise the skipping of her heart, Zidra took several sips of water.

'Eileen Cadwallader. He's been offered a job in the Human Rights Centre at Sydney University. Didn't he tell you?'

'No.' Zidra put down the glass with a slightly unsteady hand.

'That's odd. What on earth did you talk about on the drive down?'

Zidra didn't reply but picked up her table napkin and began pleating it. Perhaps she hadn't given Jim the chance to tell her his news. She'd talked a lot about her job and Sydney and old friends; but so too had he, until falling asleep for a couple of hours in the late afternoon. The truth was that he'd had every opportunity to inform her but hadn't wanted to. That was the only explanation.

Yet he was coming home at last. He was coming home for good.

Looking up from her napkin, she caught her mother exchanging glances with Peter. She hated it when they did that; it made her feel so excluded. Anyway, what did this complicity signify? Puzzlement that Jim hadn't told her? Hope that she and Jim would get together? Relief that they'd distracted her from banging on about Saigon or, more likely, her accusation about risk-taking?

Jim's omission now began to make her feel even more irritated with her mother than before. She had to fight her influence; she had to learn to make her own way. She was surely old enough to make choices without worrying about her parents. Coming back to Ferndale was all very well, for a few hours at any rate, but after that all those old conflicts came flooding back. Their expectations versus her own, the distance between them widening over the years. She stood and began to clear the table. Her mother rose too.

'You relax, Mama,' Zidra said. 'I'll do this.' This wasn't altruism, though; she just wanted to be alone at the sink. Sometimes scraping the dishes afforded a type of therapy, and it certainly gave her time to think.

But her mother wrestled the plates from her. 'Sit down,' she said. 'This is your holiday and we've been looking forward so much to seeing you again. And we haven't eaten dessert yet.'

'I'm not hungry. I'll walk the dogs.'

'They don't need walking. They're working dogs, for heaven's sake,' her mother said.

'Let's all have a glass of wine,' Peter said soothingly.

Before he'd quite finished this sentence, Zidra was on the back verandah, deciding only at the very last instant not to slam the door behind her. She ran across the home paddock to the cliff edge. Spotless Spot, an ancient kelpie dog, followed her but only as far as the steps leading down to the little beach below. Though the surf here was too treacherous to swim in, she'd always found soothing the endless thudding of the breakers on the white sand. The ocean had got into her somehow, into her bones, so that she could never bear to be too far away from it. Whenever she needed to reflect, she sought it out.

After taking off her shoes and socks, she sat cross-legged on the beach. *I only assert myself through avoiding close relationships,* she decided. *If you choose the right person, you can get company when you want it and sex when you want it, without running the risk of being told what to do. Get close to someone and what happens? They tell you what to do like Ma, or they don't tell you what you want to know, like Jim.*

But she was deluding herself. She'd chosen this way of living because of other things that had happened in her life and because of those flaws in her own character. If she were stronger – or loved her mother less – she could decide what to do herself without factoring in her mother's opinions. Ma's opposition was the real reason she'd refused the traineeship in Saigon.

Anyway, who was she really annoyed with: her mother or Jim? Both, she decided. Jim simply hadn't bothered to tell her his news, in spite of their friendship.

She knew she should have been delighted he was coming home, instead of this simmering irritation with everyone. Certainly, now that she'd had time to absorb the news, she could admit to being pleased about his removal from danger. But didn't that make her just like her mother, unwilling to see anyone she loved taking risks?

She walked down to the water's edge. The tide was advancing, breakers surging around the jagged pinnacles of rock before crashing down on the shore. She dipped one foot into the water and then withdrew it quickly; it was as cold as if it had come straight from the Antarctic. Soon it would be hard to see her way back to the homestead; the light was fast fading.

After climbing the steps, she strolled across the home paddock to the back verandah. The band of cloud that had veiled the moon drifted northwards, and moonlight washed over the paddock. The pine trees, shifting in the breeze, cast dancing shadows on ground that looked almost white.

At the tap under the rainwater tank, she splashed cold water over her face and was afraid of what she might have said at dinner. She'd given too much away, or perhaps it was too little, and she hated herself for hurting her mother.

In the kitchen, her parents were illuminated like actors on a stage, awaiting the return of the prodigal daughter. An apple crumble, in a Pyrex baking dish on the table, was untouched. A glass of red wine had been placed on the tablemat in front of her chair, and the wine bottle in front of Peter was half-empty.

43

Something unfamiliar in her mother's stance, something timeless in her attitude, made her catch her breath. Ma might be a statue hewn from pale marble and remain forever in this pose.

'Sorry about that,' Zidra said as she opened the back door.

'No worries,' said her mother, her Latvian accent as usual more noticeable when she was upset. She added, 'Some American man called Hank rang when you were out.'

'Oh,' she said, surprised. 'Did he leave his number? I'll phone him back.'

'No. He said he'd try again in a day or two.'

There were many reasons to admire her mother, Zidra thought. She never pried, would always wait to be told, and even now was averting her eyes. She said, 'Hank's a man I'm seeing a bit of. Nothing serious, just a friend.'

'It's good to have lots of friends. Not to put in one basket all the eggs.'

Ma's face was so relaxed that she couldn't possibly mean anything by this remark, Zidra decided. It was just one of those aphorisms – appropriate or inappropriate – that her mother liked to introduce into any conversation.

'I'd love some crumble,' she said. 'Thanks for waiting.' She picked up the glass of wine and held it up. 'Here's to you both. It's really great to be home.' And it was. This place, and her parents, meant more to her than she could ever express.

CHAPTER 7

It had been a good idea to push the desk under one of the dormer windows in her attic bedroom, Zidra decided the following afternoon. Seated on the desktop with her legs stretched out in front of her and her back resting against the wall, she could read and keep an eye on the driveway into Ferndale at the same time. But only the far end, she thought, peering through the pine trees. Beyond where the drive met the Jingera Road, the folds of the hills rose to the distant mountain range. The sky was littered with clouds and the air felt humid and heavy.

Jim would have to stop the car to open the first gate. If she looked every few minutes, she should easily be able to spot his arrival.

Although her position on the desktop was comfortable, she was beginning to feel restless. After reading the same paragraph three times, she still couldn't remember what it was about. It wasn't that she was tired, for she'd slept for almost ten hours the night before.

At that moment she saw the Cadwalladers' cream Holden pull into the driveway. At once she closed her book and dashed down to the front door. If she could intercept Jim out of sight of her mother, she could interrogate him before her parents were even aware of his arrival.

She reached the car when it was almost at the last gate into the home paddock. Jim could have been Hank before a haircut if she didn't know better. It was a physical type that you were attracted to, not an individual, she thought. But then Jim opened the passenger door for her and began talking, and she knew she was wrong.

'Don't drive on yet,' she said. After climbing in, she added, 'There's something I wanted to tell you.'

'Sure,' he said, switching off the engine. 'There's something I want to tell you too.'

'At last,' she said. 'Why on earth didn't you tell me the day before yesterday? I had to hear it from Ma, who got it from your mother. You and I had the whole day together on Sunday, with endless possibilities to talk, so why didn't you let me know then?' She was shocked by the hostility she experienced.

When she felt his arm around her shoulders, she angrily shook it off. Only later would it occur to her how hurtful this might have been.

'I didn't know, Zidra. Honestly I didn't.'

So ridiculous was his denial that she began to laugh. 'How come your mother knew then?'

'She didn't know. No one knew until today.'

'That's nonsense. Of course I should be congratulating you. It's terrific news and it's going to be fantastic having you back in the country. But why on earth didn't you tell me?'

'Are you talking about that human-rights job?'

'Of course, what else?'

'Zidra, that's just an offer. I haven't made up my mind yet if I'm going to take it. Mum's decided I should and that's why she's blabbing about it to everyone, but she's getting a bit ahead of herself.'

Now that he'd provided a believable reason for not telling her, she began to feel even more annoyed with him for not accepting the job. She took a deep breath, astonished at how emotional she was being. Coming home to Ferndale was making her revert to childish ways.

'There's something else I want to talk to you about. Something that's got nothing to do with all that.'

'What's that?'

'I got a phone call after lunch today, from my boss in Saigon.' He frowned and tapped his fingers briefly on the steering wheel. 'John Federico, one of our Phnom Penh correspondents, has gone home. His mother's dying, apparently. The Phnom Penh office is really short-staffed, and so I've got to go back early.'

'But you've just got home.'

'I'm flying back on the first of October.'

'That's Friday. So you've only got two more days here?'

'One more, tomorrow. And Mum wants me to take her into Burford. She wants to go shopping and I promised to buy her lunch afterwards. Then I'll go up to Sydney on Thursday.'

She looked out the side window, not wanting him to see her regret. The sun had gone behind a cloud and the pine trees looked forbidding. 'I'll drive you up to Sydney,' she said.

'Thanks, Zidra. I'd really like that, but Dad's going to. Mum's coming as well.'

'I see.' Of course his parents would want to drive him, after his time with them had been so curtailed. She would stay on here until Sunday morning and head back on her own.

'I'm so sorry, Zidra.'

'It's all right. I was coming home this week anyway.'

———

Sensing that Jim was feeling down – and to conceal her own intense disappointment – Zidra tried to keep the conversation light during dinner. It was her father who turned the discussion to Indochina once the dessert bowls had been cleared away.

After Jim had explained what was going on, Zidra said, 'How much of Cambodia is Communist now?'

'Around three-quarters of the countryside, they reckon.'

Zidra noticed that her mother was frowning. 'And you want to go back to all of that,' she said, 'when you could be writing your book at Sydney University?'

'Yes, Ilona, I do. Maybe I won't stay there much longer. I know I'll be sick of it soon. But for now I have to go back.'

'It's a hopeless war.'

'I understand that. No battle's ever decisive. It's hard to see any resolution ever being reached. But I can't let the UPI down.'

The conversation drifted on to other things. When the clock struck eleven, Jim got up to go. After wishing him well – a handshake from Peter, a lengthy embrace from Mama – Zidra's parents stayed on in the living room. Once upon a time, Zidra told herself, they would have gone out to the front of the house to wave him off. She recognised that this new reticence was to give her time alone with Jim.

Outside she might have hugged him if she hadn't felt that anything physical was beyond her. It was an effort just to stand beside him on the gravel drive and continue breathing. Above them the pine trees sighed and the distant surf beat relentlessly on the shore. Inside her mother began to play Shostakovich on the piano.

Eventually it was Jim who broke the silence. 'You'll write, won't you?'

His speech was prosaic and it seemed to her that they'd said these words to each other too often over the years. Tears filled her eyes and she blinked rapidly to disperse them. Jim, frowning at his own thoughts, didn't seem to notice. 'Of course I'll write,' she said. 'I always do.'

The telephone in the hallway began to ring, and she heard her father's footsteps clattering over the floorboards as he hurried to answer it. It would be Hank, she thought, picking his time to call.

A moment later her father appeared at the front door. 'It's Lorna,' he said. 'She's ringing from a public phone box so you can't call her back.'

Zidra gave Jim a cursory hug that was more a bumping of shoulders than the warm embrace she longed to bestow. 'Keep safe,' she said and felt his lips brush her forehead. Then she ran up the few steps to the front entrance.

———❖———

After shutting the door behind her, Zidra took a deep breath before picking up the receiver from the telephone table.

'Can we meet when you get back?' Lorna said, once the preliminaries were over. 'There's something I want to talk to you about.'

'Sure.' Zidra could hear Jim start the engine of the Holden and the sound recede as he drove off. She wondered how long it would be before she saw him again.

'Are you okay, Dizzy?'

'Yes, fine. A bit tired maybe. We can talk now if you like.'

There was a pause. Lorna's phone line was almost certainly tapped after her arrest in the Third Moratorium March last June, Zidra thought, but ASIO were bugging so many people involved in the marches that she doubted they'd have time to process all the data.

Lorna said, 'I was just phoning to check you got there safely. It's a long drive. You have a rest, you sound exhausted. Holidays do that to you – that's why I never have one.' Lorna's voice was becoming tense. Almost certainly she was working too hard, finishing her honours degree and still managing to find time to be involved in various political groups.

Yet Zidra had an uneasy feeling that something wasn't quite right. Perhaps if she hadn't been so distracted by Jim's departure she might have been able to think of a clever way to elicit the true reason for Lorna's phone call. She said, 'I'm coming back to Sydney on Sunday.'

'Are you coming up the coastal road?'

'Yes. The same way I came down.'

'There are some beautiful sights, you know.'

'Yes.' Zidra resisted the temptation to say she'd been up and down the coastal road so many times she could navigate it blindfolded.

'Bermagui, Ulladulla, Gerringong.'

At last Zidra understood the purpose of the phone call: Lorna wanted to remind her to see her people at Bermagui and the Wallaga Lake Reserve. It was home to Lorna's family but not to Lorna. After leaving the Gudgiegalah Girls' Home years ago, Lorna had spent only a couple of months at Wallaga before moving to Sydney. Waitressing in the day, studying for the Higher School Certificate at night, she'd eventually won a scholarship to university.

'Of course I'll stop,' Zidra said. 'I intended to anyway. I know you worry about me driving long distances without a break. Ma does as well.' Then she heard the warning pips indicating that Lorna's cash was about to run out. 'Thanks for ringing,' she added quickly. 'See you when I get back.'

'I'll call you,' Lorna said, and then the connection cut out.

———❖———

After her parents had gone to bed, Zidra was on the way up to her bedroom when the telephone rang again. She dashed downstairs and picked up the receiver.

'I hope I didn't get you out of bed,' Jim said.

'No.' Her throat was suddenly dry and her voice came out as a croak. 'I'm glad you called.'

'We didn't really have a chance to say goodbye.'

'I know. It's all been so sudden. I thought we'd have the rest of the week.'

'Yes, so did I. And that we'd drive back to Sydney together.' There was a pause that stretched and stretched. Zidra was beginning to wonder if he was still there, when he added, 'There's something else I wanted to tell you tonight but somehow I just couldn't. I was struggling to when Lorna rang. On the drive back to Jingera I decided it would be better to put it down in writing. It's a long flight from Sydney to Saigon and I'll have time to write you a decent letter. Anyway, that's why I didn't say goodbye properly.'

'Can't you tell me now?'

'No, it's a bit difficult.'

'What's it about?'

He laughed. 'You'll see,' he said.

'Some things are easier to say in writing,' she said. 'Especially for journalists like us.'

'I don't think I'm going to be a journalist for much longer.'

'Is that what you wanted to tell me?'

'Just you wait and see.'

She guessed now that he was going to take the Sydney job. 'I'll look forward to getting your letter. I always do, you know.'

'Goodnight, Zidra. It's been terrific seeing you again.'

She put down the receiver and went up to her room. The curtains were undrawn. She stood in front of the dormer window facing east. As she watched, the gauzy cloud moved from the face of the moon and the paddocks turned silvery.

Only now did it occur to her that perhaps Jim wasn't going to take the Sydney job and that maybe he was trying to tell her something quite different. That he was going back to Britain, for instance, or about to announce his engagement to someone he'd met in Phnom Penh – Dominique probably.

CHAPTER 8

The aircraft lumbered along the tarmac and at last rose slowly upwards – an engineering miracle that never failed to evoke Jim's wonder. He peered out of the window as the plane banked over Botany Bay and continued rising, higher and higher. The ocean appeared solid, like a piece of frosted glass patterned with fine ripples. The few ships dotted about might have been squashed flies on its surface.

Soon Sydney's bays and beaches and buildings were hidden by a thick layer of cumulus clouds. Now that the excitement of becoming airborne was over, he felt a growing sadness. Why was he leaving Australia so soon? It had been less than a week since he'd arrived, and it might be months before he could return. Was his sense of duty so misplaced that he put obligations to his employer first, rather than obligations to himself? Or was it a sense of duty to his friend John Federico, whose mother was so ill?

At this point the seat-belt sign was switched off. The middle-aged man sitting adjacent to the aisle immediately put his briefcase on the vacant seat between him and Jim. Though the metal corner knocked against Jim's thigh, he barely noticed. His frown was directed inward.

The passing air hostess stopped next to his row. Leaning over the man in the aisle seat, she asked Jim, 'Are you feeling all right, sir?'

'I'm good, thanks.' Jim rapidly converted his scowl into a smile.

'We're wondering when dinner will be served,' said the man in the aisle seat.

'After the bar service,' the stewardess replied. 'The drinks trolley will be coming around shortly.'

Jim turned his face towards the window and stared at the white towers of vapour arising from the undulating cloudscape. Of course he'd felt he had to return early because of Federico's sudden departure. But if he'd declined, what would they have done? Hired someone else, that's what. There were queues of qualified people willing to take this job, yearning for this job; people who'd do it every bit as competently as he would. And he wasn't even sure this was what he wanted. He'd only ever viewed working for UPI as an interim experience, a way of garnering local knowledge first-hand before moving on to a career as a human-rights lawyer. Instead he was behaving as if it were his career path and forgetting where his real interests lay.

It was impossible to deny that those few days at home had clarified things for him, had helped him to reorder his priorities. Now he knew that he was ready to leave Phnom Penh and the UPI. All he had to decide next was where he would go.

And there was that difficult letter to Zidra that he had to write.

Yet he delayed starting on this for several moments more, his thoughts turning instead to his parents. In the end he'd been glad they'd insisted on driving him up to Sydney. It had given them another day together, though it would have been easier for everyone if his mother hadn't been fussing so much. They'd stayed at a guesthouse in Rushcutters Bay and had got to the airport far too early, in spite of the wrong turns that his father had taken. Caught up in a snarl of traffic in the streets of Kings Cross, they'd seen the rash of steakhouses and hamburger bars, and the gaggles of American soldiers on R&R leave, unmistakable in their crew cuts and determination to have a good time. By now his parents would be negotiating their way out of Sydney, perhaps quarrelling over which route to take, his mother in charge of the Gregory's road map and issuing belated instructions as his father sailed past the correct turn-off.

Smiling at this thought, and at another air stewardess who'd appeared with the drinks trolley, he unfolded the tray table in front of the empty seat next to him. On this he placed the beer and packet of salted nuts the stewardess handed him. At the airport his parents had insisted on staying with him after he'd got his boarding pass. They had a long drive ahead of them and yet they'd sat with him for two hours more in the bar, long after they'd exhausted all topics of conversation. His mother was wearing her best frock, as if it were a special occasion she was witnessing. His father, smartly dressed in a tweed jacket and trousers that were too new to look casual, had insisted on buying Jim another beer, although he hadn't wanted it. Watching his father limp away to the bar, Jim understood this as an escape from the emotional charge electrifying the atmosphere around his mother.

At last the Saigon flight had been called. After the farewells were over, he'd looked back once and seen his parents waving. United in this activity, you would never guess how shaky was their union, a misalliance even after more than a quarter of a century of marriage. He'd felt a moment of shame for not loving them more, although heaven knew he'd do almost anything for them. Anything as long as he could live his life the way he wanted to.

He took a sip of beer before removing from his briefcase a fountain pen and a few sheets of paper. After releasing the catch on his own tray table, he began his letter to Zidra. He'd only written half a page when the middle-aged man in the aisle seat opened his mouth wide and a stream of words poured forth. For the first time since their initial greeting Jim looked at him properly. Military or business? It was hard to guess. Short hair, but probably too portly to be military, unless it was well behind the lines. 'Ben Spark's the name, marketing's the game. I see you're writing a letter. Planes are good places to catch up on things, I always say. Letters. Reading newspapers. Drinking. A bit of a snooze. Can't find a better place than six miles high. No distractions, you see.'

After five minutes had passed and the man was still continuing with his monologue, Jim sighed and shuffled his sheets of paper so that a blank page was on top. This was going to be a hard letter to formulate – the words had to be carefully crafted – but his concentration was now completely shattered. Of all the people he might have sat next to, it had to be this man with his barrage of conversation. Jim tried shutting his eyes but this had no effect. Probably Ben Spark was used to people closing their eyes whenever he spoke.

Only after dinner and a couple of brandies did the soliloquy cease, supplanted by regular snoring and the occasional twitch that was fortunately never severe enough to interrupt his sleep. Again Jim began to draft his message to Zidra.

Although the letter ended up being only a couple of pages long, and he'd rehearsed many times in his mind exactly what he wanted to say, it took several hours to finish. He had to write it out twice; the first draft was marred with frequent crossings-out, and he decided to keep this for himself. When he'd read the second version through several times, he put the pages into an envelope and addressed it carefully, writing Zidra's address in a ballpoint pen that he borrowed from the stewardess. Having been in the tropics for a while, he'd developed a bit of a phobia about fountain-pen ink being washed out by rain. He would post the letter at Saigon airport while waiting for the connection to Phnom Penh, and she'd have it within the week.

Events were out of his hands now.

CHAPTER 9

The first thing that hit Zidra when she opened the front door of the Paddington terrace was the racket from the television, and the second was the strong scent of lilies. In the living room Joanne and Lisa were watching an episode of *Dr Who*. Although Zidra knew this was an activity that brooked no interruption, she stuck her head around the door. Joanne was curled up in an armchair, looking smaller than ever. Lisa, stretched out on the sofa, was twisting her silky blonde hair with one hand the way she always did when concentrating. Though handfuls of it had regularly to be extracted from the floor waste in the shower recess, the hair on her head never seemed to look any thinner.

'Flowers for you,' Joanne said. Without looking away from the screen, she waved an arm towards the back of the house. 'From that guy with the cute accent, probably. The one who likes your *gorgeous ass.*'

'Shhh . . .' hissed Lisa.

On the kitchen bench was a huge bunch of pale pink lilies. Their stamens, oozing nectar, looked obscene. For an instant she wondered if they might be from Jim. She ripped open the small envelope attached to the cardboard base and pulled out the card. 'Let's get together again. Kisses from Hank.'

She inspected the bouquet. Maybe this was an American thing. The Australians that she knew, unromantic lot that they were, kept bought flowers for weddings or hospital visits or funerals, and an idea for an article on this theme presented itself in her head.

Of course the flowers were designed to soften her up. She wondered why she had become so cynical. Who wanted a man when you could have a career instead? Reporting was her life and it was a good one, although she had to admit that she did enjoy being fancied. That always made you feel good about yourself.

She put the lilies on the coffee table in the living room. The television program was just ending, the credits scrolling down the screen.

'They pong,' said Lisa, who had recently developed an aversion to perfume.

'They're gorgeous,' said Joanne. 'But you might put them in the dining room. Lisa never goes in there. Perhaps you'll get carnations next time. Such a practical flower.'

'None of us goes into the dining room. I'll take them upstairs.'

'Don't forget to remove them from your room at night,' Joanne said. 'Like they do in hospitals. God knows why.'

Zidra picked up the flowers again and went into the hall.

'Lorna Hunter rang,' Lisa shouted after her. 'She wants you to phone her back tomorrow morning. From a phone box.'

'From a phone box? Did she say why?'

Lisa smiled and stretched; standing on tiptoe, she could just touch the rice-paper light fitting. 'No,' she said. 'It was at the start of *Dr Who* so we didn't talk for long. She said it was important though.'

'I guess I'll find out soon enough tomorrow.'

———•◦•———

Lorna picked up the phone on the third ring. 'Dizzy, I hoped it was you. Where are you calling from?'

'A phone box,' Zidra said. 'That's why there's all this background noise, not to mention a ghastly stench of urine. Lucky that can't travel down the wires.'

'I've got something that might interest you. Can you meet me today? Usual time and place.'

'Okay, but I won't have long.'

'That's fine. This won't take long. See you soon.'

Just before twelve o'clock, Zidra parked her car in Darlinghurst and hurried to the corner pub where she and Lorna often met. There was no one around but she could hear a racing commentary, from either a radio or television, blasting through the side door of the bar. Lorna, pacing up and down the pavement with the grace of a natural athlete, didn't see Zidra at first. She paused to take off her jacket, and Zidra saw how much thinner she'd become since they'd last met only two weeks ago. At this moment Lorna caught sight of Zidra and smiled. But it was more a grimace, Zidra decided, than a smile, and it was immediately replaced by a slightly furrowed brow and a biting of her lower lip.

'You look worried,' Zidra said.

'I am. Let's go somewhere else. There's a place about a quarter of a mile away.'

'Why the cloak and dagger stuff?' Zidra said as she followed Lorna into a side road, in which rows of shabby single-storey terraced houses confronted one another across an expanse of bitumen. Above them was the dome of the cloudless azure sky. The pavement was littered with bits of paper and dead fronds from the palm trees lining the street.

'I'll tell you when we get there.'

Walking fast, Lorna took several more turnings before they reached another pub, a modest-looking establishment with the inevitable yellow-tiled walls outside. 'We'll go to the Ladies' Bar,' she said. 'That's us, Dizzy, we're ladies.'

Inside there were rather more tables than customers. Two elderly women were sitting near the door. They each had in front of them a bowl for the peas they were shelling and what looked like untouched shandies in middy glasses. Zidra might have smiled at this sight, and the women's aprons and slippers, if she hadn't been concerned about the tut-tutting sound that one of them made when she caught sight of Lorna.

'It doesn't matter,' Lorna whispered. 'I get it sometimes, though not from those two. They're not here at night. I reckon it reflects badly on them, not on me.' She led the way to a table in the far corner of the room and sat with her back to the women and the door. After pulling a tweed cap out of her bag, she pulled it down over her hair and grinned. 'You keep an eye on the door. I'm incognito now. If I can't see them, they can't see me, right?'

Zidra laughed. 'I'll get us a drink each. We have to blend in.'

'Lemonade for me,' Lorna said.

Zidra leant through the hatch opening into the main bar next door. After a few seconds the barman served her two lemonades and she carried them back to Lorna. Before she'd had time to sit down, her friend began to talk.

'Did you manage to get to Wallaga Lake Reserve?'

'I did, and your mother was there.'

'How is she?'

'Fine. She sends you her love.'

'Did you see my kid sister?'

61

'Daisy? No, I didn't. Your mother said she's staying with one of your aunts.' Zidra had found the meeting with Lorna's mother, Molly Hunter, slightly strained. This was in spite of the fact that she'd felt close to the Hunters ever since helping arrange a reunion between Lorna and Molly when Lorna was at the Gudgiegalah Girls' Home.

'Have the police been sniffing around at Wallaga Lake?'

'No. Why should they be?'

'What about Welfare?'

'Your mother didn't say. Why do you ask?'

Lorna took a gulp of lemonade before saying, 'A funny thing happened last week. I was walking across Railway Square on my way to uni when a man in a black bomber jacket and jeans came up to me.' Lorna placed her glass on the table with a hand that was shaking slightly. 'He said his name was John. He was probably in his early thirties and for a moment I thought he was trying to pick me up. But then he told me he was from intelligence at the New South Wales Police. I stopped myself from saying "Ho ho, that sounds like an oxymoron", which was what I was thinking. Anyway, after a bit of small talk he said he had an offer to make. It turned out that he wanted me to spy on what he termed "your fellow activists in the Vietnam Moratorium Campaign".'

'Do you mind if I tape-record this?' Zidra interrupted. 'It's easier than making notes. More accurate too.' She paused, wondering if she was overstepping the boundaries. She was a journalist but she and Lorna were old friends. Lorna picked up a beer mat from the table and began to turn it over and over. Zidra said gently, 'You do want me to run with this, don't you?'

'Yes, that's why I wanted to meet you today. And I'm more than happy for you to record it.'

Zidra reached into her briefcase and turned on the recorder she always had with her. 'Just repeat that first bit, would you?' she said.

Lorna did so, before carrying on with her story. 'John said that if I did what he wanted, he could arrange to have all those charges against me dropped. You know, when I was arrested in that march in June, for doing nothing apart from being there. This was the carrot he was offering.' She hesitated for a moment to take another sip of lemonade before continuing. 'I told him I wasn't interested. He turned nasty then. Said that if I didn't cooperate they'd get my kid sister welfared. That was the stick, Zidra, and a whopping big stick too. He said he didn't think I'd want Daisy taken away after my own experiences at Gudgiegalah.'

Zidra knew that the years Lorna had spent at the girls' home hadn't given her much of an education but they had politicised her. Lorna often said that the Aborigines' Welfare Board hadn't succeeded in grooming the blackness out of the girls at Gudgiegalah. By treating them so harshly, they'd sealed it in, and inculcated in the girls a common bond against the AWB.

Lorna continued. 'I told John that Daisy's too old to be welfared. She's nearly fourteen and what's more she has model parents who are both Aborigines, so she's not a half-caste like me. But he said, "Oh no, that's not too old, and anyway she can still be welfared, you ought to know that, even with *apparently* model parents. Plus there are worse things we can do to her, believe you me."

'Then I told him that I didn't think he could be from the New South Wales Police, because they wouldn't make threats like that. Of course I knew that they would, but I was buying time so I could mull over what he was saying. He carried on talking in a threatening sort of way for a while, so eventually I said that

63

I thought the police weren't involved in intelligence. I meant it as a joke but he didn't get it, and maybe that's just as well. I added that I thought it was the Australian Security Intelligence Organisation that did that sort of thing.

'"Oh, you mean ASIO," he said. "They haven't got any powers of arrest, see, so they have to coordinate with the state police."

'I said, "Oh that's really interesting. I didn't know intelligence was so complicated."

'He looked at me then a bit oddly, like he couldn't make out if I was being smart or just plain stupid, so then I thought I'd better string him along a bit.'

Lorna stopped talking and again picked up the beer mat from the table. Restlessly she began to spin it, and when it rolled onto the floor she drummed her long fingers on the tabletop instead.

'Go on,' said Zidra. 'Tell me what else happened.'

'I reminded John that those police charges against me weren't all that serious,' Lorna said. 'About thirty of us were arrested for not doing anything much at all. But he said, "It's amazing how charges can escalate, especially against you lot." That really upset me. At first I wasn't sure if he meant Aborigines or activists, and then I figured out he meant both. So I told him that I was starting to get the picture, and that I needed to go away and get my head around it all. It was a lot to take in and very frightening, and maybe he could meet me again soon. "Perhaps for a drink," I said.

'But he said, "No, we could meet all right, but no drinks."

'I'm to go to Railway Square in a week's time and give him my answer. I told him okay, and in the meantime perhaps he'd be able to think of all my friends he wanted me to do the dirt on, only I didn't put it quite like that. I was trying to seem agreeable by that stage.'

She put her head in her hands. 'Dizzy, what on earth am I going to do? I more or less told him I'd go along with what he wanted, although of course I won't. But I'm really worried about my little sister.'

'So am I. And I'm worried about you too.' Zidra concealed the anger that was simmering within her at the injustice of Lorna's treatment. She hated the thought that the authorities would harass someone like her, a bright woman, a brave woman. And one who was managing to make a way for herself in spite of the unfair way she'd been treated all of her life.

'We've got to get this into the public domain,' Zidra said. 'I'm going to let you have my tape recorder. It's a tiny little one.' But she knew that, even though it was small, there was always some chance John would notice it. Was she asking too much of Lorna to wire herself up? It was surely far too dangerous. She was allowing her judgement to be clouded by her eagerness to help; she might end up making things worse, not better. She added, 'But maybe you don't want to do this. It could get you into a lot more trouble.'

'I'll do it.'

'Are you sure?'

'Well maybe you'd better tell me a bit more of what you have in mind first.'

'You'll go to Railway Square all wired up, but with no bag. If you have a bag, it might make John suspicious. Just carry a few books. You often do that. Then get him to repeat what you told me, or most of it. After you've got the recorded evidence, I'll run it as a story in the paper. I've got some other bits and pieces I can include too. My editor will jump at it.' She hesitated, before adding, 'What do you reckon?'

'I'll do it.'

'What can you do about getting Daisy somewhere safe?'

'She *is* somewhere safe. That's why you didn't see her with Mum. As soon as I could after meeting John, I called one of my aunties who lives near Bermagui, and she got in touch with Mum. Daisy's staying with my aunty for a bit. There are lots of other places Daisy can go too. It's best that you don't know about those. Mum's got quite a network going with all those kids from Gudgiegalah Girls' Home passing through, and aunties and cousins everywhere.' Lorna smiled rather grimly. 'I guess I'm going to have to string this John along a bit, aren't I? We've got the makings of a terrific story here. I knew you'd jump at this!'

'I never can resist a good story,' Zidra said. 'I wonder if this John is the same bloke who was taking photographs of you at the last march.'

'Photos?'

'Yes. I didn't have a chance to tell you. I asked Chris to take some pictures of a guy who was snapping you. He was weaving along the road next to your group. Chris is a great photographer, but you couldn't see much of that man's face. I've got copies in the office. I'll bring them next time we meet.'

'The thing is, John's so plain-looking he's nearly invisible.'

'Hmm. That man was pretty anodyne-looking too. Mr Ordinary is what I christened him. See if you can have a few more meetings with him. When your story comes out, it won't look good for the police. Intimidating students. Intimidating Aboriginal students in particular. Won't look good at all.'

'Of course I'll have to give John something,' Lorna said. 'Harmless material. It'll help that he already thinks I'm a bit stupid, even though my exam results must be tucked away in a file somewhere. Being a black female can be an advantage.'

Zidra removed the tape recorder from her briefcase and depressed the off button before ejecting the tiny tape. She replaced this with a blank spare and showed Lorna how to operate the machine. 'Put it in the pocket of your trousers and run the wire up under your shirt. Better wear a jacket or blazer on top, and keep it on. The one you've got is perfect. It covers your pockets so the little box won't be visible. And for God's sake don't forget to turn the thing on!'

Lorna laughed and saluted. 'Yes, miss.' She tucked the recorder into her bag.

'Bossy, aren't I?' Again Zidra wondered if she was taking advantage of Lorna to get a good story, rather than thinking only of her friend's best interests. Quickly she dismissed this doubt. She was doing the right thing, and Lorna had agreed on that. She added, 'Maybe we should arrange our next meeting now. It's probably better if we don't use the phone for a bit.'

'What about here at the same time the day after I see John?'

'When's that?'

'Thursday of next week.'

'That's perfect. You and I can meet on the Friday. This story of yours is going to be really good. I'll bring you a couple more blank tapes. If you've got anything more on John, I can take it away.'

'Thanks. I knew I could count on you.'

As they left the Ladies' Bar, Zidra heard one of the women shelling peas saying, 'They shouldn't let Abos in here.' She turned and would have spat out the angry words burning her throat if Lorna hadn't whispered, 'Cool it, Dizzy. We're coming back here again, remember? No scenes.'

Zidra allowed Lorna to guide her outside. 'I thought you were a protester,' she said when they were standing on the pavement.

Her heart was pounding; was there no end to what Lorna had to put up with?

'I am, but you have to pick your audience. You know that as well as I do. That's why you're a journalist.'

'I'm not sure journalists pick their audience.'

'You think it's more the other way around? Maybe you're right. But the *Chronicle* is one of the more liberal newspapers. And its readership has been growing, I read the other day.'

'In the *Chronicle*, I'll bet.'

PART II

Early October 1971

CHAPTER 10

Only four days after arriving in Phnom Penh, Jim was already feeling as if he'd never been away. This morning he'd awoken late, hot and sweating, and with the mosquito net in a tangle around his feet. The ceiling fan, clicking at each revolution, was doing little to reduce the humidity, which dampened everything, even though it was the start of the dry season.

Would Zidra have received his letter yet? Almost certainly not, he told himself as he took a shower. Even with the hot tap turned off, the water still felt tepid. The postal service was so slow that it could be a week yet before she'd get his letter. Assuming she wrote back right away, it would be at least another week after that before he'd get an answer. He cursed his timidity in not being able to tell her face to face. *You wimp*, he told his reflection in the bathroom mirror as he shaved. *You bloody pathetic wimp.*

Now he was sitting on the petal-strewn balcony of his flat, in this once-grand house built by the French fifty years earlier. Shaded by a pair of flowering trees that glowed purple in the sunlight, he sipped his first cup of coffee of the day. It was impossible to mistake these purple flowers for anything other than bauhinia, he decided, inhaling deeply; you could identify their heady scent even with your eyes closed.

He was glad he'd finally decided to stay in Cambodia for only another two months. Though in many ways he'd loved his time here, it was really just an interlude while he determined where to go next. And there never seemed to be enough time for reflection. His days were full of UPI work. In the evenings, when he wasn't in one of the hotel bars picking up intelligence about potential news stories and pumping the other correspondents, he worked sporadically on trying to finish his book. He had a contract with a British publisher; all he needed was the time to complete the redrafting. The revision was going far too slowly; at times he thought he'd never find the uninterrupted time to finish it. There were too many distractions in Phnom Penh.

He was running late but took the usual morning detour on the way to the office, down to the riverfront and Sisowath Quay. The day already felt hot. The opalescent surface of the river flickered; it might have been a vast fish undulating past the city. What would he remember of this place when he moved on? The pavilions and pagodas and stupas of the palace. The sparkling white spire of the Buddhist temple. The thronging markets. The confusion of apartments and shanties. The murmur of voices speaking in the Phnom Penh dialect, with its elisions that he would never master.

And everywhere the refugees streaming in from the country-side that was ravaged by fighting. Families who'd been driven into the city, their rural livelihoods destroyed. There would be more and more of them, at least until this futile war ended. What hope did these people have for the future? What power vacuum would be left behind in this beautiful country, after the bombing was over and someone had won the war? Day by day the vegetation was being denuded and rice crops were dwindling, and a legacy was being created that would travel across generations.

Yet the morning was glorious and it was good to be alive. He strolled past makeshift stalls set up under umbrellas, pots of food being cooked, bicycles weaving through the crowds, beggars reaching out to him, desperate for the rapidly devaluing riel that he distributed each morning on his walk to the office.

By the time he reached the UPI bureau, Khauv, his assistant, and Dominique were already there, laughing at him for being ten minutes late, when usually he was the first to arrive.

'Put it down to jet lag,' he said. His nights since his return to Phnom Penh were interrupted by periods of insomnia. Last night he'd tossed and turned in bed for ages, before getting up for a large slug of whisky, which had brought him a few hours' sleep. He was on the way to becoming the stereotype of a correspondent in the tropics. All he lacked was a crumpled cream linen suit and a willingness to take up smoking.

'For you, *mon chouchou*, there is no excuse for jet lag,' said Dominique, a freelance photographer who made this office her base when she was in town. Small and dark, she had a nose with a pronounced turn to the left; it gave her an air of restlessness, as if she were about to follow its direction at any moment. 'You have only been through a few time zones. Not like me when I flew here from Paris.'

Clutching his second mug of coffee for the day, Jim stood in front of the detailed map of Cambodia that was pinned up on the office wall, while he and Khauv discussed what had been happening, as they did every morning. The South Vietnamese forces were trying to recapture Chup, a rubber plantation north-east of Phnom Penh. The Communists and the South Vietnamese were fighting up and down a mountainous ten-mile stretch of

Highway Four, a fuel supply route linking Phnom Penh with the port of Kompong Som.

Nothing much had changed in the week he'd been away apart from Federico's departure. The battles raged up and down the same old stretch of road, people died or were wounded every day, refugees continued to throng into Phnom Penh. The bureau could have carried on without him for a day or two more, and he inwardly cursed his boss. Khauv was up to running it for a short time, and the contracts that Jim had needed to look at weren't even ready on his return and hadn't arrived until two days after he got back.

After a while the freelance cameraman Kim arrived, grinning and bowing as he always did. His boyish stature belied his thirty-four years. Somewhere he had a wife and two children, whom Jim had never met. Like many Cambodians and Vietnamese, Kim made Jim feel too large, with huge hands and feet, and shoulders that got in the way. Kim was a talented photographer, good at spotting something that might tell a story, although so far he'd found nothing to capture the imagination of the world as Eddie Adams' photograph had done. Adams' picture of the Saigon police chief shooting a Vietcong prisoner in the head during the Tet Offensive had appeared on the front pages of newspapers all around the globe. Kim sometimes talked of how he wanted to get an image like that. It wasn't so much that he was aiming to make his name, he said, though there'd be no harm in that. But it was more that he wanted the war to stop. A dramatic photograph that somehow conjured up all there was to say about the horror and the pointlessness of war wouldn't do that, but it could help galvanise support against it.

'Where've you been?' Jim said. 'You look like a cat that's got the cream.'

'Ha, ha, very good,' said Kim. 'Cat that got the cream, yes, that's me.' He explained that he'd been to one of the briefings given by the military. There he'd learnt of a new offensive that was about to take place some fifty miles south-west of Phnom Penh, along Highway Four. 'I will go there,' he said in his heavily accented English. 'I'll take the car. I wish to see how far the paratroopers have got. Maybe get good photos. Big fighting. Human interest.'

Jim sighed. He doubted there was much point in going out there for a few more photos of wounded soldiers, or dead soldiers. 'I don't think it's worth it,' he said.

'I'm going anyway,' Kim said, smiling. He brushed a small speck of dust off the front of his maroon polo shirt, before checking the pockets of the black trousers he always wore in spite of the heat – the automatic gesture of the heavy smoker.

For a moment Jim hesitated. Kim usually had an excellent intuition for what to run with. Clearly he'd heard enough at the military briefing to make him think the risks were justified. 'Okay,' Jim said. 'I'll come with you.' The little squirm of excitement in his stomach made him realise how restless he'd been feeling in the office the last few days.

Dominique looked up, disapproval blazing from her deep blue eyes. 'You have just said you didn't think it was worthwhile,' she said. She took another cigarette out of the packet on the desk and lit it from the one she hadn't quite finished.

'Just for a quick reconnaissance,' he said. 'There and back in a day. We won't bother to take much. Only Kim and his Leica. And my notebook of course.'

After checking his wallet for his press card, Jim collected a bottle of water. He thought about taking a pack of C-rations but decided not to bother. On the way out he glanced at the wall-clock. It was just after nine-thirty. Today had been earmarked for dealing with the latest contract for the sale of news services, which had arrived at last. It would take at least a day to go through, but tomorrow would do to make a start on that.

———◆———

This is madness, Jim thought. *Madness for me to be walking down Highway Four alongside a lunatic photographer who's already used up a whole roll of film taking shots of the burnt-out trucks. Madness to be heading towards the front lines, when we really should be going the other way, back towards the rear base, back towards the car we left there only twenty minutes earlier.*

The midday sun beat down on Jim's head and shoulders. He rolled up the sleeves of his dark blue shirt and wished he'd worn shorts instead of trousers. Sweat beaded his face and trickled down his neck and between his shoulder blades. He became aware that the gunfire had ceased and the highway seemed strangely deserted. That there were no peasants around was understandable; this had been a battle zone less than an hour ago. That there were no soldiers apart from the dead and wounded – Vietcong mainly – seemed odd. There was no evidence of any South Vietnamese Army people, who must all have been up ahead. Amazing how soon you got used to seeing dead bodies. The trick was to avert your eyes and, if you were too late, pretend you were seeing dead livestock, the carcass of a sheep or cow, rather than a human body. That didn't stop the images turning up in your nightmares though. Nothing could prevent that.

Jim watched Kim pull a packet of cigarettes from his back pocket. He lit one, letting it dangle from his mouth as he changed his film. It was while he was stowing the plastic canister in his shoulder bag that the silence was torn apart by gunfire so close that Jim jumped with the shock of it. From the jungle on the left he could hear the M-16 rifles of the South Vietnamese Army screeching on full automatic, and from the other side the slower pounding of the North Vietnamese Army's AK-47s. After this came the unmistakable popping of a grenade round followed by the thudding of the explosions as they landed. Jim dived for the ditch next to the road, pulling Kim down with him.

Someone began screaming. More gunfire, before the sound suddenly stopped and there was silence. Even the birds had stopped calling. Jim's ears began to ring and his heart was pounding, a metronome measuring out his dwindling mortality. Painfully, in short sharp gasps, he struggled to get air into his lungs. Lifting his head, he could see the dry red dirt forming the banks of the ditch and, a few feet away, the bloodied twitching leg of a wounded NVA soldier. No more than a boy, fourteen or fifteen perhaps, he lay on his back with one hand over his eyes. Cautiously Jim stood up just as the AK-47s began another burst. In the instant before he dropped down again, he saw the bullets stitching through the dust along the side of the road.

After this came another silence, broken at last by the chirrup of a cricket. Red dust drifted through the air before settling over patches of darkening blood and the mangled bodies that had been lying there for hours, he guessed. His stomach churned and he swallowed the excess saliva. Turning onto his elbow to look behind, he saw only centimetres away a brown arm that had been cut off just above the elbow. At once he retched, and spat onto the ground a trickle of yellow fluid and traces of his breakfast croissant, before wiping the back of his hand across his lips.

Yet this was no time to be squeamish. He gestured to Kim and mimed his plan of worming a way along the bottom of the ditch. They needed to get moving north-east, back to the rear base, along the channel running parallel with the road.

Kim sat up and brushed red dust off his camera lens before putting on the lens cap; you might have thought he was unperturbed if you hadn't seen the shaking of his hands. Pulling out his cigarette packet again, Kim raised an eyebrow at Jim, who shook his head and pointed to the NVA soldier a few feet away. Kim removed two cigarettes from the crumpled pack and lit them both before giving one to the wounded boy.

'We need to get out of here fast,' Jim said. 'Back the way we came.'

'*Di di di*,' said Kim. The words you heard everywhere in this crazy war. Hurry hurry hurry.

A slight movement attracted Jim's attention, a figure in a white shirt and tan shorts crawling along the ditch and around the bodies bloating in the sun. This man's longish red hair and pale freckled skin were unmistakable. It was Mark McFadden, a correspondent for a Canadian newspaper.

'What's going on down there?' Jim said.

'*Ils sont morts*,' Mark said, glancing at Jim with glazed and unrecognising eyes, before resting his face in the dust. Even from three metres away Jim could smell the reek of fear and sweat. Behind Mark was another man whom Jim knew slightly, a Japanese freelance photographer, Michio Tanaka. In his mid-thirties, Michio was one of Kim's friends – and his competitor. Normally a dapper man, he looked as dishevelled as Jim felt. One lens of his gold-rimmed spectacles was cracked, his white linen shirt was ripped along a side seam and his black cotton trousers dusty and torn.

'What's happening at the front?' Jim asked.

'Same as here only worse,' Michio said. 'We've got to get out.'

'Couldn't agree more,' Jim said. 'The SVA might have invited us here but the NVA sure as hell haven't.'

Jim began to lead the way along the ditch, in the direction from which they'd come that morning. Soon the ditch became a gully that seemed to be veering away from the highway although broadly parallel with it. The air felt thick and heavy. Sweat stung his eyes the way salt water could when you were surfing. He felt desperately thirsty and his lips were beginning to crack, and he thought with longing of the bottle of water he'd stupidly left in the car.

Occasionally he paused, to make sure the other three were still behind. Mark had looked as if he might go to pieces but he was still there, crawling after Kim and in front of Michio. Behind them, probably half a kilometre away now, came the renewed hammering of the AK-47 automatic rifles and the answering screaming of the M-16s, and then a series of explosions that had to be mortar attacks. The sun was shifting overhead, altering the shapes of the shadows cast by the jungle. The pounding of the guns receded as they half-ran, half-crawled along the gully. Sometimes the deep shadows seemed to Jim's fevered mind to be black pyjama-clad people, and at other times he imagined them to be figures in military clothing. But mostly he could see them as they were, flickering patches of darkness and light.

When it was too dark to see their way along the gully, they rested in a hollow off to one side. Jim found sleep impossible, disturbed by his fears and a miscellany of strange sounds, of rustling as insects and animals made their way through the jungle, and once the voices of people walking along the trail. Guerrillas of course; at night this forest belonged to the guerrillas. And in the small hours, renewed artillery fire.

At last, after the firing ceased, Jim dozed. When he awoke, he saw green light filtering through the foliage and his three companions looking stunned, as if overnight they'd forgotten where they were. His mouth felt so dry he could hardly swallow, and his body ached from lying on the hard ground. Only as he struggled to sit up did he see the reason for the startled expressions of the others.

Three soldiers stood at the edge of the hollow, three soldiers wearing the belted green uniforms of the North Vietnamese Army. The casual way the tallest guerrilla lifted his rifle made Jim hold his breath, and his heart began to flap within his chest. With his AK-47, the youngest soldier motioned Jim and his companions out of the hollow and pushed them into a row in the centre of the trail. Jim felt a rifle butt knock his thigh, or perhaps it was the sandalled foot of one of the soldiers. He shut his eyes and muttered a quick prayer.

———•——

Cautiously Jim opened first one eye and then the other. The three NVA soldiers gestured with their rifles, miming that the journalists should drop everything they were carrying – cameras, binoculars, wallets and even their watches. Jim removed his wallet and put it on the ground in front of him. He struggled to loosen his watch strap, his hands like clumsy tools over which he had little control, his breathing so rough it seemed to rasp the walls of his throat. With an unsteady hand he placed the watch next to his wallet.

'*Nha bao*,' Michio said, pointing to the three cameras and making scribbling movements with one hand, as if he were writing in a notebook held in the other hand. 'Journalists. *Nha bao.*'

The soldiers kept their rifles trained on the four while speaking rapidly among themselves in Vietnamese. They looked little more than boys, Jim thought. Too young to be making decisions about who should live and who should die. Eventually the unusually tall Vietnamese – whom Jim mentally christened The Leader – said, 'American?'

'*Canadien*,' Mark said, tapping his chest. '*Anglais*,' he said, gesturing to Jim. '*Cambodgien*.' He pointed to Kim, and then to Michio. '*Nippon. Japonais*.'

He'd spoken in French rather than his fluent Vietnamese, and Jim wondered why. It could have been fear or it could have been that he didn't want to be identified as working with the South Vietnamese. He'd identified Jim as English too. Jim was travelling in Indochina under the British passport he'd acquired under patriality while a Rhodes scholar. They'd agreed earlier that it wouldn't make sense to mention his Australian nationality given Australia's involvement in what many of the Vietnamese called the American War.

'*Nha bao*,' Michio repeated. 'We are journalists.'

Ignoring him, one of the soldiers pulled a rubber poncho out of his pack and spread it on the ground. He arranged the journalists' possessions in the centre and then rolled them up. *Like Dad wrapping a pound of sausages in Cadwallader's Quality Meats*, Jim thought as he watched the boy attach the bundle to the bottom of his pack. *We won't see these things again.*

'*Nuoc*. Water,' said Kim, smiling.

There was something special about Kim, Jim thought, that allowed him to smile in the most adverse circumstances, while he could only grimace and run his tongue over his parched lips.

'*Nuoc*,' Kim repeated, still smiling. '*Nha bao*.'

The soldiers conferred briefly before giving the captives tin pannikins full of water. It was warm and had a metallic flavour to it. Jim tried to swallow down his dread with the liquid but it refused to go away.

A bullet in the head and a shallow grave in some jungle clearing wasn't the future he'd planned for himself. He thought of the Phnom Penh hotels thronging with journalists dispatching telegraphs and starting rumours. He and the others would be the subject of those now.

He'd known this could happen and yet he'd been prepared to take the risk. To face danger, to face death. But now it seemed like such a bloody stupid way of going when there was so much else he wanted to do with his life.

He shut his eyes. Images of Zidra progressed through his mind, as if he were flicking through a photo album. Zidra driving him up to the park on the promontory to eat lunch not quite two weeks before. Zidra sitting on his jacket on the vivid green grass, surrounded on three sides by deep blue sea flecked with whitecaps. Zidra laughing like a schoolgirl as he'd hurled the uneaten chips high into the air for the seagulls to eat.

Zidra whom he'd loved for half his lifetime now.

CHAPTER 11

Wispy beard, bandana tied around his head, he had to be labelled Jimi Hendrix. Naming him was a distraction from the pain, as the soldier yanked Jim's arms behind his back, forcing the elbows together. The Leader barked out instructions, suddenly older, his smooth skin acquiring lines commensurate with his responsibility. The youngest soldier grabbed hold of Jim's shoulders and fastened him with ropes to Kim.

'This man Fourth Brother,' Kim muttered. 'Does what he's told. He'll tie us all up, you'll see. Human column.'

Fourth Brother shoved Kim hard enough to quieten him. Jim winced as the ties bit into his arms.

'*Di di di*,' The Leader hissed. Hurry hurry hurry.

Marching feet, humming insects forming an aura around them, trail rising as they stumbled on. Passing minutes, passing hours, how much time was left? Jim's toes hurting. Heels rubbed sore by the leather shoes. A leech on his right ankle, growing fat on his blood. Impossible to brush it off with the heel of his left shoe. And impossible to brush off the fear. It was embedded too deep in his heart.

Later the pain faded into insignificance as thirst took over. Count your paces: how many seconds to a step; how many steps to a kilometre? Concentrate hard, keep your apprehension at bay. The path rising more steeply now, and his concentration going, replaced by a vision of a bottle of iced water, beaded with condensation.

Cold clear water.

They could have shot us right away, he thought, remembering Hué and the mass graves. Thousands of South Vietnamese civilians executed during the Tet Offensive. They could have shot us right away but they didn't. First they'll cross-examine us and then they'll shoot us. He shivered, in spite of the heat blanketing him. Would he be courageous under interrogation? Or torture? He didn't know. It was easier to be brave when looking after others than when looking after yourself.

In the late afternoon the party stopped to rest. Jimi Hendrix unfastened the ropes binding the journalists together, his nose wrinkling at the stench of sweat and fear. Jim stretched out on his side, against the bank of red earth at the edge of the clearing. A feast for leeches, but he was too tired to care. *We look like four corpses*, he thought. *Like those on Highway Four yesterday.*

The Leader and Jimi Hendrix headed off along the trail, leaving Fourth Brother in charge. '*Nuoc*,' Kim said loudly. 'Water.'

Fourth Brother ignored him and moved a few metres away. Squatting on the ground, he lit a cigarette, all the while keeping his rifle trained towards them. Mosquitoes were starting to bite. Jim felt several of them pierce the fabric of his trousers and there was nothing he could do about his exposed neck. He watched a black ant labouring up the bank, over small stones and twigs, around leaves. Heading for the underbrush. It knew where to go.

Darkness; forgetfulness that was suddenly invaded by strange dreams. Upwards, onwards, pursued by who could guess? Demons from the past, demons from the present. Forcing an escape, he woke and felt something knocking into his leg. Ten or so figures in miscellaneous military garb formed a semicircle around them. One soldier directed another kick at his thigh. *We are exhibits in a zoo*, Jim thought, *and scarcely human*. He looked around. The Leader and Jimi Hendrix were nowhere in sight. Fourth Brother was still squatting on the ground but he'd put down his rifle.

'American,' the soldier accused, and aimed a kick at Mark as well.

'English,' Kim said in French. 'Canadian. They're not American. We're not soldiers. We're international journalists and *not* Americans.'

The soldier kicked Jim's feet hard, and two more squatted down next to him. They yanked off his leather shoes, not bothering to untie the laces. Guffawing, they passed the shoes from hand to hand. Were they so funny, his brown leather shoes? Wrong for the climate, wrong for the jungle, wrong if you were wearing rubber Ho Chi Minh sandals. And what about the other journalists? What did they have on their feet? The soldiers laughed as they wrenched off their leather sandals. Only Mark tried to stop them, his reward a blow on the chin with a rifle butt.

'American! American!' one of the soldiers taunted.

'Canadian, Canadian,' Mark said.

'English,' Kim said, gesturing to Jim. 'Canadian,' he added, nodding in Mark's direction.

The soldiers began tossing the shoes and sandals, one to the other, as if they were playing Frisbee or some game of catch. *They look like high-school kids on an outing*, Jim thought. *But they are not.* His heart began to thump painfully as he remembered the small boy he'd found at school years ago pulling the legs off a live cicada. The look of pleasure on his face. What other sport might these soldiers turn to, once this game had palled? How long would it take before their hilarity turned to cruelty?

A soldier noticed Michio's spectacles and pulled them off his nose. Putting them on, he stumbled around the clearing, an old man who couldn't see where he was going. Another threw a sandal high into the treetops, where it caught on a branch and clung there like some strange bird. The others cheered, and soon they were all playing toss-the-footwear.

After being hurled into the air a number of times, first one of Jim's shoes and then the other became entangled in the highest branches of the trees. His heart sank, together with his hopes of having them returned. He'd be walking in socks or bare feet from now on.

Or perhaps this clearing was his final destination. If they were forced to carry on marching, they would be shot when their feet gave way. In war anyone who couldn't keep up would be shot.

'*Dừng lại!*' shouted Kim, as his sandals became lodged in the treetops. 'Stop!'

'*Dừng lại!*' came another shout. The Leader and Jimi Hendrix stood at the edge of the clearing. Between them hung a rubber poncho, slung from two branches and brimming with water. A few curt words from The Leader and the soldiers were absorbed back into the jungle.

One by one the prisoners knelt in front of The Leader, while he poured water into their open mouths. *A communion of sorts*, Jim thought. As he raised his face to accept the offering, he saw a fleeting expression of what might be pity on The Leader's face. Did he know they would soon be dead? Was this compassion, or anxiety about the water supply? Impossible to tell, and an instant later it was replaced by an emotionless mask. Smooth, impassive, he was a young man again.

Di di di. Time to move once more. Without shoes, Jim stumbled along the rough path. Tripping on a root became an overwhelming injustice. So too did having his heels trodden on by Michio, and he had to bite his lip to prevent an angry outburst. Although his feet were sore, his socks at least gave them some protection; the others had nothing. He could see that Kim, walking in front of him, was increasingly finding the going difficult, and his arms were becoming swollen with the tightness of the ligatures.

When it became dark, Jimi Hendrix and Fourth Brother turned on torches until the moon hove into view. It was Sunday night. The UPI would be worrying about them by now. At some point Zidra and Jim's family and friends would hear the news. He remembered with painful clarity his parents' faces as they waved to him at the departure gate at Sydney's Kingsford Smith Airport. His mother's sadness, his father's pride. He couldn't bear to think of how his capture would affect them. Or his death.

Hours later, when it surely must have been early morning, they stopped in a small clearing. More soldiers appeared, holding oil lamps: small glass bottles with a wick poking out of the top of each. Jim inhaled the oily stink of the burning wick as one of the soldiers, a thin man with lined skin, held up a lamp to his face. The man nodded at Jimi Hendrix, who untied the wires restraining the arms of each of the journalists.

Fourth Brother pushed Jim's head low as he shoved him forward. Down, down into a tunnel with sides of compacted mud. He collapsed onto the ground, the others beside him.

Within seconds he was asleep.

CHAPTER 12

'They'll have got counterinsurgency agents here by now,' Mark said. It was early morning and through the opening to the bunker Jim could see guards squatting around a fire. 'They'll be wondering about our intelligence value. What they can learn from keeping us alive.'

'They'll learn nothing,' Kim said. 'We know nothing more than what we heard at the military briefing in Phnom Penh before we got captured, and that's days old.'

One of the guards squatting around the fire was stirring a blackened iron pot from which steam was rising. Hunger gnawed at Jim's guts. His mouth began to salivate at the smell of rice cooking.

'They don't know that,' Mark said. 'They think at least two of us are with the CIA: me and Jim. Michio's okay but Kim could be with the South Vietnamese Army.'

'We've got our press cards.'

'*They've* got our press cards,' Mark said. 'They've still got that bundle with their backpacks.'

'Here they are, look. And they've got food.'

The Leader and Jimi Hendrix stood at the mouth of the bunker, with a steaming basket of rice and a pot of tea. *Drink slowly, eat slowly*, Jim told himself, as his stomach contracted with the first mouthful. He ate no more until he'd finished the mug of fragrant tea and his stomach settled.

———•—•———

After breakfast, The Leader beckoned the prisoners out into the clearing. Dazed by the early morning sunlight, Jim peered around. So dense was the jungle surrounding them you might almost think that there was no way in or out, although if you looked more closely you could see the trail at the far end, concealed by loops of vines. His head began to swim and he would have fallen if The Leader hadn't seized hold of his elbow. He murmured some words that Jim had difficulty understanding. Only at the second repetition did he realise they were in French. 'Visitor from high up to ask you questions. Come with me.'

Jim followed The Leader across the clearing. Past the curious faces of the soldiers they went, towards the path at the far end. Where the narrow trail began, The Leader held back a swag of vines. Jim inhaled deeply to steel his nerves; best not to think of what lay ahead. Best to keep calm, to focus on the leafy litter covering the red earth, the dense understorey, the tall trees with mottled grey and white bark and buttressed roots, the cooing of a pair of green pigeons.

———•—•———

They arrived at another clearing. Uniformed soldiers sat in a semicircle facing Jim. It was as if he were in court: a kangaroo court, a military tribunal, an interrogation – he didn't know which. A frail-looking old man sat at a low table, and on each side of him sat others, all on upright wooden chairs. The old man wore a dark green uniform and a blank expression, and a pistol in a holster on his belt. The Leader motioned Jim to sit on a log facing them in the full sun. To one side of the clearing, a slender youth began to take photographs of him with a Nikon camera.

The old man said something to the man on his left, who started speaking in halting French-accented English. His thick-lensed spectacles gave him an appearance of focused intensity. 'You are in the hands of the Liberation Armed Forces. You must answer some questions slowly and clearly. What is your name, age and nationality?'

'James Cadwallader, twenty-six, British.'

'What is your rank?'

'I have no rank. I'm a journalist. I'm a civilian.' While Jim spoke, he noticed that the old man didn't look directly at him. Instead he appeared to be doodling on a piece of paper in front of him. On his other side, the third man was writing in a notebook.

'What is your rank?' the translator repeated.

Perhaps the translator hadn't understood his responses, or maybe he was trying to catch him out. He replied, 'I don't have a rank. Journalists don't have ranks.'

'What is your title?'

'I don't have a title. I'm a journalist. No, I'm not with the military. *Je suis un correspondant.*'

Again Jim wondered how much of what he was saying the interpreter understood correctly. It was becoming apparent that the old man was growing restless. He spoke impatiently to the interpreter, who next began to ask questions about Jim's salary. How much it was, where it was paid, who paid it, how long he had been in Cambodia, why he was a journalist. And why was he going down Highway Four? To find out what was happening.

Why was he with the Lon Nol troops? He wasn't with them, he followed them.

The interrogation continued for another twenty minutes and then the panel stopped for tea and talked in low voices. Jim was handed a half-coconut shell of palm-sugar juice. He took a sip. It was too sweet and made him feel nauseated again. Behind the interpreter, he could make out a fig tree of some sort. Its mottled grey roots appeared to trickle like lava down a crumbling cliff face that, now he was seeing properly, was not a cliff at all but some ancient building that was disintegrating under the weight of the strangler *ficus*. The lava roots were advancing down the stones, advancing across the clearing, and might soon consume him too if he stayed there long enough. He had to keep alert; he needed to get some fluid inside him. Slowly he took another sip of the sweet liquid.

After the break the questions continued. What did he think of the war? He thought it was too long. Why did he think it was too long? Because the different groups of people couldn't agree; they believed different things were important. How long had he spent in Cambodia? Ten years? No, that wasn't correct. It was only one year. *Seulement une année.* How often did Jim go to the American Embassy in Phnom Penh? How many Americans were in Phnom Penh? What were they doing there? Jim answered as accurately as he could. All that he was saying had already been written in reports; everything written by the journalists at UPI and the other wire services was monitored by Radio Hanoi. They had no secrets.

'Why did you go down Highway Four? What did you write about it?'

'Nothing. I didn't get back to Phnom Penh.'

'Whose victory do you think it was?'

'It looked like yours but I didn't see the end of it.'

'Why did you run away?'

'Because I didn't want to die.'

'Why didn't you stay with the Lon Nol troops?'

'I didn't come with the troops.'

'Why did you go there?'

'To find out what was really happening.'

'You are a very brave man. You go down Highway Four in a battle zone for only one reason, to get at truth. This is very hard to believe. Very hard.'

'I went down the highway to find out what was happening. It's the only way to find out. How else would I know?'

'Can you not listen to what your government tells you? Do they not tell you the truth?'

Governments don't tell the truth, Jim thought. *They may tell an approximation of the truth, but it's one that suits them, and the approximation may be very imprecise.* He said, 'The government gives one version of the truth. You give another version.'

He held his breath, wondering if they would get angry at this. Anything he said that was more than one sentence seemed to take a long time to be interpreted. When the translator had finished rendering Jim's words into Vietnamese, there was no change of expression on the old man's face. Jim continued, 'Because of that, we correspondents need to find out for ourselves what's really happening. That's what we're paid to do. That's our job.'

'Who pays you to do this? Does the government pay you?'

'No, the government doesn't pay me. The press agency pays me. It's a private company, quite independent of the government.'

'But United Press is American, is it not?'

'Yes, it's based in America.'

'So you must work for the American Government.'

'No, I work for United Press International. It's independent and it broadcasts all over the world. It broadcasts in Hanoi and Peking. You know that, I'm sure. Its reports tell listeners what's happening, not journalists' opinions of what's happening. That's why I went down Highway Four. To find the truth about what's happening.'

Now the cycle of questions began again, back to his salary, back to his reasons for being a journalist. Again and again the questions were repeated, as if the interrogators believed nothing of what he'd said, or hoped that eventually he'd be caught out and tell them what they wanted to hear. He tried to speak clearly and to answer consistently; it was vital not to make a mistake. Fearing his trembling hands betrayed his anxiety, he sat on them. He knew that as an employee of an American wire service, he would be viewed as more in the enemy camp than the other journalists, but at least he'd been travelling on his British passport.

The old man now spoke to the soldier taking notes, while the translator sat quietly. Even if Jim had been able to understand Vietnamese, he couldn't have distinguished what they were saying; their voices were too low. He felt faint. The sun was getting hotter and beating down on his head.

Eventually the translator told him to stand up. The old man also rose to his feet. Slowly he ambled around the back of the table and towards Jim, whose heart began to skitter and palms to sweat. Though the old man stopped in front of Jim, he didn't make eye contact. Instead he inspected his forehead, his hair, everywhere but his eyes. He was an object being sized up, and not a human being. Heart pounding, sweat now streaming down his face, he willed himself not to faint. At last the old man finished his inspection. Turning to one side, he started to walk around the log on which Jim had been perching.

Jim begins to breathe deeply. In for ten seconds, out for ten seconds. In and out. *Don't lose your nerve. Don't turn your head. You don't want to know what's happening behind you. Look in front, at the strangler fig tree. Look up now. Look up at the circle of clear blue above the clearing and at the infinity beyond.*

Over the hammering of his heart, he hears the chirring of insects and the *plod plod plod* of the old man's feet as he marches around the log.

Now the footsteps stop behind him.

He hears the unmistakable rasp of metal on leather as the old man pulls out his pistol. Even now it is being directed at his head. *Give me some time*, he thinks. *Please give me some time. Time to put my life into perspective, time to write to my family, time to tell them I love them.*

Hearing the clicking of the pistol's safety catch being released, he takes another deep breath. He is floating now, floating above himself, floating out of this clearing, out of this jungle, out of this country. He is going home. Home to his beloved Jingera. The surf is beating on the beach. His family is with him and Zidra is by his side.

All that remains here in the clearing of the Cambodian jungle is the shell of a young man, a shell that is waiting for the pistol shots to ring out.

Breath held, resigned to his fate, he is counting out the seconds.

PART III

Mid- to Late October 1971

CHAPTER 13

O nce the others in the newsroom had departed for a counter lunch, Zidra made herself a mug of coffee. She sipped it while distractedly staring out of the window at the street below. There were still a few days to go before Lorna met with Mr Ordinary, and she needed to get hold of some more material to augment the storyline she was developing. This afternoon she'd make a few phone calls to her contacts in political groups to see if they could offer any suggestions.

Joe Ryan was talking on the phone again and even through his closed office door she could hear his voice. Outside, shafts of rain were being driven onto the pedestrians. Only some were shielded by umbrellas; others, caught without protection, darted about like ants before a storm. The wind changed direction abruptly. Raindrops now hit the windowpane at an acute angle and slid down the glass, as if reluctant to leave its surface and join the pool of water on the sill. With her forefinger she traced the path of one of the drops, and then another. She breathed on the glass and used a tissue to wipe away the smudge left by her fingertip. Methodically she continued polishing the entire pane until the tissue was black with grime.

On the way back to her desk, she passed the foreign editor's workstation. A wire-service bulletin from the United States lay on Dave's table. She stopped, her attention caught by the large letters.

'MISSING UNITED PRESS INTERNATIONAL CORRESPONDENT REPORTED DEAD IN CAMBODIA.'

In her haste to pick up the cable, she stumbled on the wastepaper basket and dropped her empty coffee mug. As far as she knew, the only UPI reporter missing was Tom Anderson, and that was months ago. But could his body have been found recently? Or perhaps the bulletin was referring to someone from the UPI bureau in Saigon. There were a number of correspondents there, she knew. She picked up the sheet of paper and began to read:

Yesterday afternoon the body of a United Press International correspondent was found in south-western Cambodia. The body is believed to be that of the United Press International bureau manager in Phnom Penh, who disappeared three days ago, James Cadwallader.

The body of James Cadwallader? They must have made a mistake. Jim wasn't missing. He was in his office in Phnom Penh, not in south-western Cambodia. It had to be someone else they'd found. The press in Indochina was often getting things wrong. That's what happened when the reporting was done from a bar in Phnom Penh or Saigon, Jim had said. Yet she experienced a fluttering sensation in her chest and began to feel faint. She might have fallen had she not been clutching at the desktop. She read on, heart pounding so much she could hear the blood beating in her ears:

Cambodian troops found several bodies in the area, including that of a Caucasian man. Two Cambodian army officers examined the body of the man and subsequently identified it as Mr Cadwallader, 26 years old.

Zidra's hands were shaking so much that she dropped the sheet of paper onto the desktop. 'No, no!' she shouted. Tears blinded her, and she began to feel the peculiar numbness and dissociation that was shock. Her throat felt so constricted that she could scarcely breathe. After wiping the back of her hand across her eyes, she picked up the bulletin and read on:

Mr Cadwallader was covering a battle on Highway Four about 55 miles south-west of Phnom Penh in which Communist forces overran Cambodian positions. Cambodian army officers said that his body bore a single bullet wound in the head. His body was cremated on the spot in accordance with Cambodian military procedure.

The remains were brought to Phnom Penh and examined by a pathologist at Calmette hospital. Mr Cadwallader was appointed United Press International bureau manager in Phnom Penh in June this year.

The death of Mr Cadwallader brings to at least 14 the number of correspondents killed in Cambodia since Prince Norodom Sihanouk was ousted in March 1970. Nineteen are still listed as missing.

At this point the room began to swim and Zidra felt her legs give way. Just as a black screen began to roll slowly over her eyes, she thought she heard Joe Ryan's voice calling out her name. Relentlessly, remorselessly, the blackness scrolled down. By the time her body hit the floor, she was no longer conscious.

CHAPTER 14

Replacing the receiver, George felt only disbelief. He stood perfectly still, staring at the wall. They must have made a mistake. It wasn't his son they'd found but someone else. It was one of those other correspondents thronging into Indochina who'd been shot in the head, and not Jim.

It was this disbelief that allowed him to go back into the lounge room. Eileen was sitting on the sofa, her head bent over her embroidery, the lamplight illuminating her dark hair in which silver threads shone. She looked up at him, as she always did after he'd taken a phone call. The question was unstated but it was there just the same: *Who was that on the phone, George?*

Sitting in the armchair opposite her, George moved his lips but no sound emerged. He swallowed before croaking, 'It was someone from somewhere. I'm not sure where. Someone official.'

'What do you mean, someone from somewhere, someone official? Pull yourself together, George, and tell me what's up.'

He shut his eyes and took a deep breath. He wasn't going to be able to protect her from this news.

Her voice, high and shrill, sliced through his shock. 'Is it Andy?' she shouted. 'Speak to me, George.'

'Not Andy,' he said, his voice breaking. There was no gentle way he could break the news to her. 'It's Jim,' he said. 'Jim's dead. They've identified his body in Cambodia. He and some other journalists got stuck between the lines in a battle. He got shot.' He wouldn't tell her yet about the bullet in the head. It sounded like a cold-blooded killing, probably after the fighting was over. And he wouldn't tell her yet that the Cambodians had already cremated the body.

'No, George, that can't be right.' Eileen's hands were shaking, he observed with detachment, as if he were not a part of this tableau but instead someone else looking on.

He turned his head, and at once his eye was caught by the framed photograph on the mantelpiece. Jim at his graduation from Oxford, smiling at the camera. The scarlet gown suited his olive skin. They're a bunch of wankers here, he'd told his father once, laughing. It was the sight of this photo and the memory of Jim's words that were George's undoing. His shoulders started to shudder and his breath came in spasms. A strange bellowing sound seemed to be coming from his mouth. *No, no, no!* He covered his face with his hands, not wanting to expose his grief. If he exposed it, Jim's death would be real. If he could suppress it, Jim would be saved. Then perhaps the present could unravel, and they could begin again on some new trajectory in which Jim would return.

Yet that wasn't right, George knew. Within his chest he began to feel a frightful pain, as if a piece of himself were being wrenched out. This agony was far worse than anything he'd ever experienced and he didn't know how he could deal with the loss.

Jim was dead. His beautiful boy was dead. The person he'd loved unquestioningly ever since his birth. The person whom he understood best. *Had* understood best. It should have been him to die first and not Jim. He was two and a half decades older. George would willingly have given up his own life so that his son could survive. Such a waste of a young life; such a waste of all that brilliance. Jim's future gone, all their futures gone. The injustice and futility of it all.

Now he opened his eyes. Seeing Eileen's face close to his, he judged she hadn't absorbed the news. She was in shock, her reaction was yet to come, and he had to be ready for it. He wiped his hands across his eyes. A moment later she stood up. He watched her square her shoulders. He watched the colour drain from her face. He watched her walk across the room to the mantelpiece. She picked up the photograph of Jim and looked at it apparently calmly, though George could see that her hands were trembling still and her face that ghastly shade of white.

Slowly she raised the photograph above her head and then she hurled it into the fireplace. It landed with an almighty crack. The glass shattered, shards spilling everywhere. 'Gone!' she shouted, her voice breaking. 'Gone, gone, gone!'

Next she leant towards the porcelain vase in the middle of the mantelpiece. Although George could see what was coming, he was too slow to reach her. Already she'd picked up the vase.

'No, Eileen. You love that thing.'

She raised it above her head and hurled it across the room. 'My son isn't dead!' she shouted as the vase hit the window frame and shattered into tiny pieces. As she reached for the framed photograph of a smiling Andy in his army uniform, George seized hold of her wrists. Though she fought like a wild animal to be free, he put his arms around her.

And then, after a minute or so, it was over. Limp in his arms, all her fighting spirit had gone. He hugged her to him, this rag doll who was Jim's mother, and listened to the heart-wrenching sound of her sobbing.

CHAPTER 15

Zidra woke with a start and the impression that it would be preferable by far to remain in a state of unconsciousness. Quite why she couldn't remember. She felt woozy, as if her brain had been replaced by some spongy material, and her throat was so dry it was a struggle to swallow. Only when someone took hold of her hand did she open her eyes. Her mother's face was just centimetres away from her own; she could see the tiny pores around her nose and the fine lines around her eyes.

'Where am I, Ma?' She blinked; the light was so bright it hurt her eyes.

'Don't you remember, darling? I collected you from the hospital yesterday and afterwards we drove to Paddington to collect some of your clothes and then we came home. I forgot to pack your nightie though. That's why you're wearing one of mine.'

Zidra didn't care whose nightie she was wearing. She had no recollection of being in hospital. Shutting her eyes, she kept a tight grip on her mother's hand, its skin slightly roughened from so much outdoor work.

'You're in your bedroom at Ferndale, Zidra. The doctor pre-scribed some sleeping tablets. You took two last night when we got home. That was the recommended dosage, but perhaps that's one too many. You've slept for fifteen hours, can you believe? It's ten o'clock in the morning and I've brought you some tea.'

'I don't remember anything much.' The notion of tea was appealing but she felt too tired to sit up. Then a memory surfaced, a memory of the bulletin she'd seen lying on the foreign editor's desk. A memory that she had to suppress. It wasn't real; it hadn't happened.

She relinquished her mother's hand and rolled onto her side to face the wall.

'Do you remember what happened, darling?'

'A bit.' Her voice faltered.

'You collapsed at the *Chronicle*. Joe Ryan found you and called an ambulance to take you to the Royal Prince Alfred Hospital. Then Joe rang me, and Peter and I drove up to Sydney. You spent a couple of days in hospital. You were out to it for most of the time. You've been suffering from some sort of temporary amnesia, apparently. Plus the drugs they put you on in the hospital, I suspect.'

Now it all came flooding back, those two drugged days and nights in hospital. Pushing away food, unable to do more than gaze at the ceiling, lacking even the strength to weep, let alone to speak. Only when her mother had appeared by her hospital bed had she been able to cry and then she'd sobbed for hours. Fate had so cruelly taken Jim away and had cheated her of all hope. On the trip down to Ferndale she hadn't wanted to talk, hadn't been able to talk. All she could recall of the journey was lying on the back seat of the car and staring at the roof.

'Joe Ryan's called a couple of times to ask after you. He's said it's okay for you to take leave for as long as you need.'

'Thanks, Ma.'

'He's a kind man.'

'Yeah.'

'And that American man's been phoning too.'

'You mean Hank?'

'Yes, Hank Fuller. He said he'll call again.'

'I don't want to talk to him.'

'What am I supposed to say to him?'

'You'll think of something. Say I'm sick. Lost my voice. Got the flu. Any damned thing.'

———◆———

Zidra and her mother sat in silence on an ancient wooden bench in the garden and sipped their tea. The late-afternoon light angled through the trees, which cast long shadows on the rough grass. The air was becoming cool and Zidra pulled her kimono more closely around her shoulders. At the cliff edge, on the far side of the home paddock, seagulls were crying and wheeling in ever-widening circles. The light was so harsh that you couldn't escape it. You couldn't escape it but it clarified things somehow.

You've got to take one moment at a time, Zidra thought. *Focus on this moment. This nowness. Get through this moment, and then the next.*

Her mother said, 'I'll always be here for you. Always. Wherever I am.'

'I know that, Ma,' she said, lightly touching her arm.

CHAPTER 16

A day at a time. Take things a day at a time. That's what George told himself when he awoke each morning. After struggling to find the energy to sit up, he would lower his feet to the floor and take those few steps into the bathroom. There he would splash cold water on his face before going into the kitchen to boil the kettle for his and Eileen's morning tea.

Sometimes he'd forget where he was or what he was doing. Hands on the kitchen table to steady himself, he would let the torrent of memories flood over him. Recent memories hurt more than the past and the newest memories were the biggest torment. If he'd known that the hours at the airport were the last he'd spend with Jim, he would have worked harder to make them better, to tell his son how much he loved him. How he'd given his father's life meaning. That's what he should have done instead of allowing Eileen to fuss over trivial matters. Instead of going off by himself to the bar to get away from Eileen's anxiety, with that pathetic pretext of getting Jim another beer, though he'd said all along he hadn't wanted one. When the flight to Saigon had been called, Jim's schooner of beer had been hardly touched. This image haunted George. It was a symbol of something but he didn't understand what. Now, as he braced himself against the kitchen table and listened to the hiss of the gas under the kettle, the image of that glass of beer moved him to tears.

As the days dragged by, he forced himself to shift further back into the past and away from those recent times in which his own sins of omission seemed to overlay everything. Several afternoons he left work early, leaving the shop in charge of his assistant, whom he still thought of as The Boy although he was over forty. He never told Eileen of these lapses, nor of his need to wander alone around the edges of the lagoon, and up and down the beach. He experienced an urge to revisit all those places that had been a part of Jim's life when he was a boy, and a part of his own life too. But he no longer felt any desire to take out the dinghy; no desire to row upriver and drift down with the current; and no desire to dive into the depths of the celestial hemisphere on clear nights. His telescope remained untouched in the shed. Although he would sometimes pick up the little book on the constellations, he would never open it. He handled it only because Jim had given it to him the Christmas before he'd sat for his final school exams.

At times he felt he couldn't face those kindly people who came into Cadwallader's Quality Meats, offering their sympathy along with their money when he gave them their neatly parcelled rump steak and sausages.

Mrs O'Rourke was an exception. Her son Roger had been at primary school with Jim and Andy, and she'd been the first person into the shop after the news of Jim's death had appeared on the front page of the *Burford Advertiser*. 'I'm so sorry,' she'd said, her eyes brimming with tears. Thanking her, George had looked away to hide his own. Roger had been a National Serviceman, called up in the birthday ballot and packed off to army training. Later he'd been sent to Vietnam. The night before he'd left, there'd been a function in the church hall to celebrate; in those days people still thought the Vietnam War was a Good Thing. Several years later Roger was dead, killed in the Tet Offensive, his name added to the list on the war memorial in the centre of Jingera.

Worse even than the heartfelt but awkward words of some of the town's people was the absence of words, from those choosing the easy way out, choosing to say nothing in the face of his grief. Yet what could anyone do? What could they say?

You just had to take things a day at a time and hope that the pain would lessen as the weeks passed by.

After taking another afternoon off work and spending it wandering around the lagoon edge, George ended up sitting on the sand not far from the headland. Seaweed littered the beach, dumped by the storms of the previous night. Earlier that afternoon it had rained, and his clothes were still damp. He stared at the aquamarine breakers as they rolled inexorably in and felt the humidity rising in almost palpable waves. By late afternoon the sun had broken through the thick clouds and suddenly a fragmented rainbow appeared over the ocean.

Then he knew he had to pull himself together. There were things he had to do. He had to begin to talk to Eileen again. That morning, before he left for the shop, she'd told him they needed to discuss the memorial service. At the time he hadn't really absorbed the detail of what she'd been saying.

There would have to be a memorial service, he knew. Everyone expected it. Eileen wanted it; he wanted it too. It was to be a celebration of Jim's life. Watching the surf breaking on the sand, George remembered the afternoon of that terrible bushfire back in 1957, when the entire town had been evacuated onto the beach. Jim was only a boy then, and George had thought he'd lost him. Peter Vincent had eventually tracked him down, covered with ash. Even at that age Jim had done what he wanted, and afterwards it always seemed to be the right thing. He'd been lucky every time, until ten days ago in Cambodia.

George stood up, brushing the sand from his trousers. At the footbridge over the lagoon, he wiped his bare feet with a handkerchief before pulling on his socks and shoes. He was bound to have left some trace of sand somewhere, which Eileen would spot when he got home. He didn't care about the prospect of being roused on any more. Some things just didn't matter.

As he climbed the steps to the back verandah, Eileen called out, 'Is that you, George?'

'Yes.' After leaving his shoes at the back door, he trod heavily into the kitchen.

'I need to talk to you,' she said.

Sitting down opposite her at the kitchen table, he stared at the mound of empty pods and the bowl of shelled peas.

'St Matthew's Church,' she added. 'That's where the memorial service will be held.'

'Is that so? When?'

'Next week.'

'Shouldn't we wait until Andy gets back?'

'That's not till mid-November. That's much too long to wait, George. I just can't bear to let the days go by without any sort of service. We owe it to Jim. Weren't you listening this morning when I told you all that? You agreed, don't you remember? And anyway, Dr Barker's arranging to hold another memorial service in early February at Stambroke College. He rang you only two nights ago and you told him that was all right. Andy can come with us to that.'

'The army mightn't let him take leave again.'

'I've already checked. They will.'

'I see. You might have told me.'

'I did. This morning. For the second time. And I've asked the Reverend Cannadine to officiate next week.'

'So it's all signed and sealed. But perhaps you can tell me what on earth's wrong with the regular cove.'

'He only comes here once a month. He hardly knows us. That's why I asked the Reverend Cannadine.'

'He's from Burford.'

'I'm aware of that.'

'I don't know him and neither did Jim.'

'I do though. We became quite friendly after I got involved in the Aboriginal Housing campaign.'

'I see,' George said and looked at her closely. That pinkness in her cheeks might have been a blush or the heat from the oven behind her. More likely was that Eileen still had a crush on the good padre. George had suspected this for nearly a decade, though he'd never met the cove. It was certainly the case that Cannadine was very handsome, at least according to those photos that appeared regularly in the *Burford Advertiser*.

'He's already agreed to do it.'

'I see.'

'Don't keep saying "I see".'

He pressed his lips together. Perhaps Eileen's flushed cheeks were because she'd been crying again, just as he had only an hour ago. Curbing a sigh, he decided that it might be better to let her take over everything. It would be her release and he could get on with grieving in his own way. In spite of this he found himself saying, 'We could always try asking Professor Smyth.'

'Professor Smyth?'

'Yes. He's the one who encouraged Jim to enter for the Rhodes Scholarship.'

'We don't want him then. If Jim had stayed in Australia, he'd still be alive. Anyway, I've already asked the Reverend Cannadine and he's accepted.'

It's done and dusted, he thought, *and I have no say in the matter.* He stood up, and in his haste to get away he almost knocked over the chair. 'I've got to wash my hands,' he mumbled.

He shut the laundry door behind him and turned the tap on hard. He didn't wash his hands though; he just stood there clutching the side of the concrete tub. It was all he could do not to shout. What a relief it would have been to bellow at Eileen, to yell out 'He was my son too'. Yet there was no point getting angry with her. What he was feeling was simply a reaction to all the pain. Perhaps he'd never get used to the fact that his home and his life were changed forever.

Nothing would ever be the same again.

Afterwards, when tea was over, he remembered the cigar box of Jim's treasures hidden away in the garage. It had appeared on the top shelf when Jim was ten or eleven, when he would have had to stand on something to reach that high. Of course George had seen the box right away, imperfectly concealed behind half-used tins of paint; he knew the location of everything in the garage, even though it did look a bit of a tip. Yet he'd always maintained the fiction that he hadn't noticed the box, and had even put more tins of paint in front of it, to protect Jim's secret.

Over the years Jim had continued to use the box. Once George had come into the garage when Jim was putting something into it but he'd backed out again quickly, pretending that he hadn't observed his son standing in the shadows.

Now George removed the tins of paint and pulled out the cigar box. *You could just leave it here unopened,* he thought. *Leave it here forever.* And yet he desperately wanted to see what was inside. He desperately wanted to have a piece of his son. Something tangible, rather than these memories that haunted him day and night. *You should open it,* he decided at last. Gently he released the lid. Inside were some pieces of folded newspaper and a few rocks.

He unfolded the first of the newspaper clippings. It was about the radio telescope at Parkes. This had been a shared obsession between father and son over the years, and yet they'd never visited it together. The second was far older, a cutting about the US Navy ship sunk during the Second World War by the Japs off the south coast. George remembered Jim pouncing on that when his mother had been clearing out old newspapers lining some drawers.

George folded up the clippings again and took out of the box the three rocks. Not ordinary rocks at all but some of the fossils that Jim had found under Jingera headland years ago. As George put them back, he noticed in the bottom of the box a tarnished brass badge, with the rising sun above the imperial crown. His heart lurched. He'd given this to Jim years ago, and the boy had kept it. It was a relic from the Second World War, a relic from George's time in the military when he'd been stationed in the Northern Territory after the bombing of Darwin. He picked up the badge and rubbed it against his sleeve. For a moment he thought of putting it in his pocket, to keep with him always, a part of his son and a part of himself. Then he dismissed this impulse. It was better by far to keep the badge in the box, on the shelf, behind the half-used tins of paint.

A memorial to his son.

CHAPTER 17

Zidra was sitting in the living room trying to concentrate on the words of the book that lay open on her lap. They might have been in another language, these meaningless squiggles arranged in neat lines across the paper. A trapezium of sunlight shifted slowly across the Persian rug as the minutes passed by, and occasionally the grandfather clock chimed the quarter hour. When she heard the crunch of tyres on gravel, she stood and peered out the window: Mama was home from Jingera at last.

After she'd come inside, Zidra's mother said, 'A postcard from Lorna. She's definitely coming to the memorial service and she'll stay here a couple of nights. And there's an envelope for you, darling. A thick one, from Paddington. Joanne said she'd forward your post on to you.'

Without enthusiasm Zidra opened the envelope. There were some smaller envelopes inside: a bill, cards from friends and, last of all, an airmail envelope with Jim's spiky handwriting scrawled across it.

A voice from the dead. The shock of it took her breath away. She threw down the cards and bill and ran upstairs with Jim's envelope. After ripping it open, she pulled out two pages of airmail paper:

My dear Zidra,

There was something I wanted to tell you that night I came to dinner at Ferndale but the right opportunity never presented itself. And now I'm sitting on the plane flying from Sydney to Saigon and struggling to think of the appropriate words to use. Perhaps I should pick the simplest. I've been in love with you for years.

Zidra took a deep breath. *I've been in love with you for years.* Abruptly she sat down at her desk. Her hands were trembling so much that she lost her grip on the letter and it fell to the floor. She snatched it up and continued reading:

Why have I waited so long to tell you? I don't really know. When you started at university, I was in third year and you were a fresher and you looked so youthful and so innocent, and I thought that you were much too young to begin a serious entanglement. Too young for permanency. We were both too young for that. Soon after Lindsay turned up, and I never meant to hurt you with that relationship, although I suspect you were hurt, and I knew right from the start that it wasn't serious. Then I got the Rhodes Scholarship. Yes, of course, I know I had to apply to get it so I had thought of leaving Australia, but I never imagined I'd be successful. And by then, at the end of your first year, you'd become the darling of everyone in men's college. They all lusted after you – did you even notice? Although from what I heard you lusted after several of them yourself. Then I left Australia but I never stopped loving you, never stopped hoping that some day we could get together.

Dearest Zidra, I love you and I would like to marry you. I know you often say you don't want marriage, but I hope you'll consider it. I'll take that human-rights job and come back to Sydney if you think there is even some possibility that you might love me. You don't have to give me a decision apart from indicating if you might think about us getting together.

At my most optimistic I think you love me too and not just in a sisterly way. I will never forget that moment in your car the Sunday I arrived back, not even a week ago, when our hands touched, nor will I ever forget that intense look you gave me, and how much I wanted to kiss you. But you glanced away and you put the car into gear, and it was too late. I thought we'd have the whole week in Jingera to talk through these things but it didn't work out like that. And that was my fault.

I know you've recently become involved with Hank but is that really serious? Although I've never met him, I can tell you're not in love with him. Your voice gave it away when you were talking about him. Perhaps I'm being presumptuous in writing this and maybe even deluded about it. If so, please forgive me, and don't let it mar our friendship that means so much to me.

This is my second draft, and the letter's getting shorter as I peel away the bits that might put pressure on you. The main thing I wanted to say is how much I care for you and that I really want us to live our lives together, and I hope you might come to feel this too. If I had any literary talent I would find words to describe your beauty and your kindness and your intelligence and your courage. As it is, I can only write that you make me laugh, you make me weep, you make the sun shine, you bring glory to everything you do. You are the love of my life and you always will be.

With all my love,
Jim

PS I've written out a stanza that is all I can remember of a poem I learnt at school, by Judith Wright:

All things conspire to stand between us –
even you and I,
who still command us, still unjoin us,
and drive us forward till we die.

Zidra was crying now, fat tears coursing down her cheeks, and she felt her heart would surely crack in two, it was hurting so much. The letter was late, far too late. *If only you'd told me before you'd left. If only I'd taken the initiative and kissed you. If only I'd told you how I felt. Too late, too late, too late. You'll never know how much I loved you.*

After a time she wiped her eyes and blew her nose, and splashed her face with cold water from the tap over the corner basin. She read the letter once more. As she looked up from the pages, her vision sharpened and she began to see the room as if for the first time. Everything had meaning: the half-empty glass of water on the bedside table; a tiny spider lowering itself on a filament from the ceiling; the walls that she and her mother had painted gloss white several years ago, walls that were now reflecting radiance into the room from the sinking sun.

She read Jim's letter for the third time. As she finished, she realised that a tune was running through her head. It was the song that had been playing on the car radio that Sunday when Jim's hand had accidentally touched hers: Tina Turner belting out 'River Deep – Mountain High'. She wept again, deep choking sobs that she muffled into the feather pillow.

Later she recognised that the certainty of his love would stay with her. This new information would give her strength. There would be no more collapses, or not if she could help it. No more sleeping tablets. And no more being so drugged that the past became lost to her.

———•———

A day later Zidra stood on the footbridge that led over the lagoon and onto Jingera Beach. It had rained earlier. All colour had leached from the landscape. The lagoon water reflected the encircling grey-green trees, stabbed with pallid verticals, and the paler sky. Seagulls hung around the foreshore like teenagers on a Saturday night, with nothing to do, no place to go. *Shush – shush* went the waves as they fingered the sand at the lagoon's edge. *Give up. Give up your dreams and go home.*

A small bird with a green head hopped near her, then away again. Her grim expression might have dispatched it, or perhaps it was the sudden movement as she wiped her eyes on her forearm. Jim would have known what type of bird it was. Sometimes she'd teased him: 'Jim Cadwallader, the walking encyclopedia, you know the names of everything'.

You knew the names of everything.

Searching the landscape for a distraction from her grief, she noticed that the poles supporting the jetty had been recently painted. How she hated that white paint. Would progress leave nothing alone? It was the same thing with the cottage in which she and her mother had lived when they'd first moved to Jingera. It had been done up recently. The weatherboards had been painted cream and the window frames and verandah posts a dark green. She resented the owners for destroying the past. Did time have to alter everything?

She sighed deeply. No matter how hard she tried, it was impossible to forget that tomorrow was the day of the memorial service.

Such an awful finality.

Once it was over, Jim was as good as buried, even though there was no body, just a few handfuls of ashes scattered somewhere on Cambodian soil. One day, when the war was over, she would travel to the area where he'd died, and there she would conduct her own commemoration. But in the meantime there was the Jingera service to get through. She hoped she would be able to perform, without breaking, the reading she'd promised the Cadwalladers. 'Read something Jim loved,' Mrs Cadwallader had said. 'You knew him like one of the family. You'll know what to choose.'

Although she'd decided right away what to pick, she didn't know if she would have the strength to read it in its entirety. She took from her trouser pocket the piece of paper on which she'd written the words. Silently she read them once more. Then she took a deep breath, pulled back her shoulders and began to proclaim the words: to the bush, to the seagulls, to all those places around the lagoon that she and Jim had shared.

Her memories of these places would survive as long as she did.

CHAPTER 18

George sat next to Eileen on the front pew. They were early. Immediately behind them were the Vincents and Lorna Hunter, whom George hadn't seen for years. St Matthew's Church was small and rapidly filling up, with people and notes from the organ that Daphne Dalrymple was playing.

When Zidra and Lorna had greeted George just moments before, he'd been shocked at Zidra's appearance. Her face was caked with make-up. Bright-red lipstick and so much foundation that it would crack if she were to grimace. A mask behind which you could only guess at what was happening.

Some minutes into the service, it was time for Zidra's reading. George watched her walk slowly to the pulpit and climb the few steps. A remote young woman in her prime and a sleeveless black linen dress with white stitching around the neckline. She looked around the church, her face impassive, as if she were searching for someone, or perhaps it was only for silence. The organ music stopped and Daphne Dalrymple rested her hands on her lap. Zidra cleared her throat, took a sip of water from the glass in front of her and began to speak. She'd chosen, she said, a poem by Judith Wright that Jim had loved, and that he'd sent to her the week before he died:

All things conspire to hold me from you –
even my love,
since that would mask you and unname you
till merely woman and man we live.
All men wear arms against the rebel;
and they are wise,
since the sound world they know and stable
is eaten away by lovers' eyes.

All things conspire to stand between us –
even you and I,
who still command us, still unjoin us,
and drive us forward till we die.
Not till those fiery ghosts are laid
shall we be one.
Till then, they whet our double blade
and use the turning world for stone.

Zidra read it slowly, and apparently calmly, each word carefully articulated. Dry eyed, she exhibited a startling self-control. It was this that finally eroded George's own composure, and tears began to stream down his face. Surreptitiously he dried his eyes on his cuff and passed his clean handkerchief to Eileen. She needed it more than he did; her own dainty square was now a sopping mess, which he took from her and slipped into his pocket. Zidra, having finished her reading, walked the short distance back from the pulpit with her head held high. As she passed by, her eyes met his; something slipped into place and he recognised the pain she was battling to conceal.

The words of the unfamiliar service eddied around him, shifting him hither and thither, until he was beached on an unexpected silence. Only when Daphne Dalrymple began punishing the organ again, and Eileen nudged him sharply, did he realise what was required of him. Struggling to his feet with the rest of the congregation, he fought to find the right hymn. Flip-flip-flip through the impossible pages of the hymn book, his fingers not belonging to him; he might never have located the chosen words if Eileen hadn't done it for him. Only by the last verse was he ready to join in, ready to sing with the rest of the flock, 'I'll fear not what men say, I'll labour night and day, To be a pilgrim.'

After the final chord, the Reverend Cannadine was off again, preaching of God's will and some other stuff that George chose not to listen to. Instead he concentrated on the more important shaft of sunlight that was illuminating the white and green floral arrangement under the pulpit, imbuing it with a significance that he struggled to comprehend. If only he could understand that, he might be able to grasp the meaning of Jim's too early death.

In the meantime the padre's words flowed around the column of light that was perceptibly shifting.

Finally it became impossible for George to avoid noticing Eileen, who was leaning forward the better to catch Cannadine's precious words. To distract himself, George started reciting under his breath the hymn he knew she'd chosen for the end of the service: 'The Lord's my Shepherd, I'll not want . . .'

Yet how wrong that was for, in spite of his prayer, he *was* wanting. He was wanting his son. His son whom he would never see again.

Now Eileen jabbed him in the ribs, none too gently. Blinking, he focused again on the padre chap. At last he seemed to have finished his religious ministrations, and George's attention was caught by the cherished words: 'James Cadwallader'.

'We are gathered together today in remembrance of the precious life of James Cadwallader, who grew up in this town.' Cannadine looked down at the notes that Eileen had provided for him, and which he'd spread out on the lectern in front of him. Of course he'd be speaking from the script and not the heart, for how could it be from the heart when he'd never known Jim? In spite of George's anguish – and the detached part of his brain that was objectively analysing the words of this Cannadine chap for whom his wife had for years had a thing – he felt a glow of pride. Scholarships from aged eleven, a distinguished academic record, a brilliant career in the making, his first book nearly written, his independent reporting on the war in Indochina appearing in newspapers and wire services throughout the world. Nonetheless James Cadwallader was always modest, always affectionate, always brave even in the face of the extraordinary dangers that men and women foreign correspondents faced every day of their lives when reporting from war zones. Brave also in informing the world about what was really happening in this war, in which Australia and New Zealand should never have got involved.

At this point the Reverend put down his notes. Gripping the sides of the pulpit, he began to deliver his own unscripted oration. 'Permit me to explain why our involvement in the Vietnam War so saddens me,' he said. 'Permit me to explain why we should get out of this futile war. This American War, as the Vietnamese call it. This war that is claiming the lives of so many of our sons. Young men like James Cadwallader, not yet in the prime of their lives before being struck down. Young men like James Cadwallader who are still losing their lives unnecessarily in a war that should never have started.'

George flinched as if he'd been struck and might have cried out if he hadn't heard Ilona's words: 'He's forgetting where he is.'

'He's picked the wrong speech,' Peter whispered. 'This is way too political.'

Before the Reverend could continue, there was an eruption from the front pew on the other side of the aisle: Mrs O'Rourke had leapt to her feet, her face red and crumpled. Now she was struggling past the people sitting next to her and stumbling down the aisle towards the exit. For a moment the Reverend Cannadine looked puzzled. He inserted a finger inside his close-fitting dog collar, as if to remind himself he was a clergyman and not a campaigner, or perhaps the collar was simply too tight. Having recollected himself, he thanked God for the blessing of James Cadwallader's life.

Eileen stood. For an instant George wondered why she hadn't warned him, with the usual jab of her elbow, that he was supposed to get up. Then he realised that she was the only person on her feet. Purposefully she marched across the worn green carpet to the pulpit. She paused in front of the white and green floral arrangement, illuminated still by the shaft of sunlight. Surely she wasn't going to speak too. She hated public speaking and anyway the service was nearly over. George noticed for the first time that her black dress was too loose, and the way the ugly black hat sat skew-whiff on her head made him ache with compassion for her.

The Reverend Cannadine descended awkwardly, too large for the narrow steps. At the bottom he stepped to one side, as if to allow Eileen access to the pulpit. But she didn't mount the steps. Instead she stopped immediately in front of him. Swinging her black patent-leather handbag to one side, she drove it straight at the Reverend Cannadine's head, delivering a blow that would have coincided with his face if he hadn't turned the other cheek.

A soft thud, a quick intake of breath, a stunned silence before Daphne Dalrymple bashed again at the organ. Slowly Eileen turned, slowly she returned to her seat. In the meantime the congregation began to sing. George held Eileen's shaking arm with one hand and searched for the words of the psalm with the other. Only by the last verse were the Cadwalladers able to join in.

Goodness and mercy all my life
Shall surely follow me;
And in God's house forevermore
My dwelling-place shall be.

Both of them were crying now.

CHAPTER 19

No body. No ashes even; they were in Cambodia, never to be returned. Why that should still hurt so much Zidra couldn't understand. Jim's death was the ending, and where the remains were was of no importance.

He was dead; that was the inescapable truth and all that mattered.

The last words of the service hung heavy in the air and she struggled to breathe. Too much emotion, too many people. People who would be looking for chinks in her armour, generous with their sympathy when none was wanted. You had to be alone to come to terms with what had been lost, and this might take years.

Or a lifetime.

The exposed necks of Jim's parents in front of her were more than she could bear. Their vulnerable heads were bent to take the blow that fate had dealt them.

She wanted to skip the reception in the church hall next door. Skip the niceties.

And skip the post-mortem on Cannadine's misplaced words about the Vietnam War. Sure, it was a war they shouldn't have gone into, but there were boys from this area who'd died in

Vietnam, including Roger O'Rourke, and it was crass insensitivity to tell the town their sons had died for some futile cause. Her mother spoke highly of Cannadine, and so too did Mrs Cadwallader, but his comments today had been misplaced.

Yet who would have thought that Jim's mother had it in her to assault anyone, least of all a clergyman? Zidra's journalistic instincts might have seen a story there if her nerves hadn't felt so lacerated that she could have screamed with the pain. Opening her handbag, she pulled out the red lipstick and slashed it across her lips. If she left off the make-up, even for a moment, the wounds beneath would be revealed.

Aware of Lorna's scrutiny, Zidra avoided her eyes while whispering, 'I'm skipping the do in the hall. See you back at the car in an hour or so.'

'Where're you going?'

'To the beach. Tell Mama.'

'What's that?' Her mother leant forward.

'I need to get away for a bit. Just an hour or so.'

'Come to the wake. For George and Eileen's sake.'

'No.'

'Please, Zidra. If George and Eileen can do it, so too can you.'

There was no arguing with her mother when she was in one of these moods.

—◆—

Through the people crowded into the church hall, Zidra followed her mother. She was looking for Bernadette O'Rourke. Eventually they found her, sitting by herself on the outside stair leading from the kitchen to the back lawn. You might have thought she was supervising the children running around if you hadn't seen that her eyes were blinded by tears. Ma didn't say anything when she sat on the step next to her; didn't even look at her.

Zidra perched several steps above them and watched the children fly across the grass. One of them was the youngest of the O'Rourke tribe.

After a few moments Mrs O'Rourke clicked open her handbag and there was a trumpeting as she blew her nose. Then she said, 'I've been thinking of the day two men from the army came to tell me about Roger.'

Zidra had been at Jingera Primary School with Roger, had shared a desk with him one year, one of those old-fashioned desks with an inkwell and graffiti all over the top that they had to sand down at the end of each term.

'I'll never forget that loud knocking on the front door,' Mrs O'Rourke said. 'And when I opened it, I knew right away.' She hesitated and twisted the handkerchief in her fingers. 'I'd been expecting it for months, you see. Can you understand that, Ilona?'

'Yes, I can.'

'Every time I heard on the news that an Australian soldier had been killed, I imagined it was Roger. Every time there was a knock on the door, I thought it would be the army people. When they came, all I could think of to say was, "Have you got news for us?" As soon as I'd caught sight of them, I'd begun to shake like a leaf, but I invited them into the kitchen. Theresa, she's my firstborn, and the little ones were in the lounge room watching telly, and I didn't want them to hear. There was a stew simmering on the stove and I turned it off. "Yes, I have got news," the chaplain said. "Is it bad news?" I said. "Yes," he said, "it's very bad news." I sat down on a chair then. The chaplain said, "I'm afraid your son's been killed by a landmine."'

Mrs O'Rourke's voice broke and she blew her nose again before continuing. 'Theresa took the news worse than me. She'd come into the kitchen without my noticing and she immediately started screaming. I tried to keep calm so the kids wouldn't get upset. Theresa was screaming so loudly that I almost couldn't hear what the notification officer was saying. Then I saw the chaplain picking up the knife I'd left lying on the kitchen table after I'd cut up the vegetables. That brought the news home to me all right. You see, he thought we might damage ourselves. It was only then I noticed the words Theresa was shouting. "I'll kill them," she was yelling. "I'll kill them."

'The chaplain tried his best to comfort us. But how could we find comfort? Roger's passing left a great gap that can never be filled.'

At this moment there was a loud squawking as a pair of dark grey cockatoos flew over the backyard and swooped around the fir tree, their calls drowning out Mrs O'Rourke's words. A great gap that can never be filled. That was what Jim's death had left too. The pair settled in the topmost branch and their cries stopped as they began to crunch on the pine cones.

Mrs O'Rourke continued. 'After a few weeks, Roger's battalion commander wrote to us. We took a copy that we keep with Roger's things but I always carry the original with me.' She opened her handbag and took out an envelope. From it she extracted a worn-looking sheet of paper, which she handed to Zidra's mother.

'Shall I read it out?'

'Yes.'

'"It is not a duty obligation which occasions me to write to you but a knowledge of the great sense of loss you must feel. To say that your son was a good soldier would be far from sufficient.

The degree of esteem in which he was held by his friends has been movingly demonstrated. His loss to them had a dramatic effect. I realise words alone cannot ease the pain of this tragedy for you. However I would ask you to accept the heartfelt sympathy of the members of the Fourth Battalion." Ilona paused before saying, in an octave higher than normal, 'It's a beautiful letter. About your beautiful son.'

There was an ache in Zidra's chest and she hoped she wouldn't cry again.

'It means a lot to me.'

Ilona cleared her throat before saying, 'I can understand that.'

'I thought you would, you losing your parents and all.'

'Those words are from the heart, Bernadette.'

'You think so? I do too. But my hubbie thinks they're from a book.'

How many such letters had the battalion commanders had to write? Hundreds, Zidra had read somewhere.

Now Mrs O'Rourke took back the letter and folded it carefully before restoring it to the zippered compartment inside her handbag. Then she adjusted her hat and said, 'I should go and wash my face. I look a mess and I don't want to keep you both from Eileen. I know you're good friends with her, Ilona.'

———————

Zidra hesitated. Somehow Ma had managed to breach the barrier of sound obstructing the entrance to the hall. Words from the mouths of fifty or sixty people ricocheted like bullets off the hard walls and ceiling. Zidra took a deep breath but it was no help. Feet glued to the floor, she remained immobile, until Ma returned and placed an arm around her shoulders, propelling her forward. 'There's Eileen,' she shouted. 'With the Reverend Cannadine, on the other side of the hall, see?'

Grim-faced, Mrs Cadwallader was nodding her head while the Reverend appeared to be talking continuously.

'We must rescue her, Zidra. You get two glasses of wine and so will I. Eileen usually never touches a drop, but I'll bet she can use some today.'

Conversations surged around them. Zidra took little notice of what was being said until they reached the group of men in which Mr O'Rourke was standing. Pausing to let someone pass by, her attention was caught by the words of Ian Harrison, who worked for a logging company and had the shoulders to prove it.

'The brown envelope,' he was saying. 'I'll never forget that day when the brown envelope arrived. Bob was nineteen when he was called up for National Service and when he opened it he was really pleased, like he'd won the lottery. The funny thing was, I was pleased too. I thought of it then as a career rather than a ticket to Vietnam.'

Zidra knew that even the army had been against conscription when it was introduced in 1964, but the government had gone ahead anyway. Few people had guessed how the difficulties in Indochina would escalate.

'My son Roger was balloted in a year later,' O'Rourke said.

There was a moment's silence for Roger O'Rourke. The death of Roger had turned his father's hair white. You'd never guess now that the O'Rourke children had inherited their lustrous red hair from him.

Mr Harrison coughed, before continuing. 'That's eight boys from this area conscripted so far.'

Shuddering, Zidra remembered how she'd always thought Jim was one of the lucky ones who hadn't been called up. He'd led a charmed life in every way until that awful day in Cambodia.

'Only seven went off to Vietnam, but.'

'Only seven! That's a bloody lot when you think of a town this small.'

'It was more than that from Burford.'

'No, it was less, and Burford's a lot bigger than Jingera.'

'What's happened to the Cadwalladers' second son, do you know?'

'Andy? He's still with the Third Battalion. Those boys'll be on their way home soon.'

At this point Ian Harrison noticed Zidra and her mother standing by his elbow. 'Oh, sorry, didn't see you two standing there. Do you want to get by or would you like to join us? That was quite some service, wasn't it? You read that poem nicely, Zidra. It moved the ladies to tears.'

'Thank you.' Zidra took a large gulp of wine from one of the glasses she was carrying.

'Mrs Cadwallader put on quite some show,' Ian Harrison continued. 'I'll bet the Reverend got a bit of a shock, eh?'

'Eileen is very upset,' Ilona said. 'I've got this wine for her.'

'She doesn't normally drink but who knows, she might be glad of it today. Must be pretty bloody hard to take – oh, excuse me, Mrs Vincent – pretty tough on both of them. And Jim such a brilliant young man, by all accounts.'

Yes, such a brilliant young man, Zidra thought, choking slightly after too large a swig of wine. *A brilliant man whom I'd hoped I would one day marry.*

'Follow me,' her mother bellowed so loudly into Zidra's ear that she jumped. 'Eileen has already been alone with the Reverend too long.'

'I'm so pleased to see you both,' the Reverend said as soon as Zidra and her mother reached him and Mrs Cadwallader. 'You read that Judith Wright piece beautifully, my dear.' A beacon of benevolence, he twinkled at Zidra, and for a moment she thought it would be impossible to escape a benediction. Instead he turned to her mother and said, 'Now, Ilona, I've just been conveying my deepest apologies to Eileen. I don't know what came over me. It was really insensitive. I got carried away with my anti-war sentiments, without thinking about how offensive that was on this occasion.'

'I'm sure Eileen will understand,' Ilona said soothingly.

Zidra glanced at Mrs Cadwallader. Forgiveness wasn't one of the emotions flitting across her face. A quivering vulnerability, a trembling of the lips, a tic around the right eye, all replaced by a grim expression when she glanced at the Reverend Cannadine.

'I've brought you something to drink, Eileen,' Ilona said. 'It's only wine. You might enjoy it.' She handed the glass to Mrs Cadwallader, who knocked it back as if it were a soft drink.

'Would you like this?' Ilona offered the second wine glass to the Reverend Cannadine.

'Thank you, but I'm just about to leave. There's a service in Burford that I have to attend.'

At this moment Zidra felt a touch on her elbow and turned to see Lorna. 'Go for a walk on the beach if you've had enough. You look drained.'

'I've had more than enough.'

'I'll come and get you in half an hour.'

'We'll see you both back at the car in an hour or so,' Zidra's mother said. 'I think that might be long enough for us all.'

'Drop in to see us before you go back to Ferndale, Zidra,' Mrs Cadwallader said. 'And now I'll take that second glass of wine if you don't want it, Ilona.' A bright pink spot decorated each of her cheeks and her eyes were glittering. 'And perhaps, Zidra, I'll take that spare one you're holding too.'

——•+•——

After chatting with Peter Vincent, George had spent the past hour wandering through the crowd, a word here, a word there. Never too long with anyone, although these were all folk he knew well: customers and old friends, or children or parents of old friends. He nodded and smiled and felt he was just about succeeding in holding himself together. The kindness on people's faces comforted him; the pity did not.

There were folk of all ages here: elderly, middle-aged and young. There were no kids inside though; they were all out the back of the hall, doing what kids always did at such functions, be they funerals or memorial services or weddings or christenings – running wild.

He'd noticed the Reverend Cannadine talking to Eileen and was glad of it. He'd warmed to the cove after he'd sought him out earlier to apologise. Although Eileen was mortified by what she'd done with her handbag, and in a church of all places, George felt proud of her.

At last people were starting to take their leave and the hall was emptying. By the time George caught up with Eileen, she was just finishing a glass of wine. 'This is my third one, George,' she said, her words slurred. She handed it to Ilona, as if she were the waitress positioned next to her for that very purpose. 'And now I want you to take me home, and I'll make a pot of tea.' Several plump tears trickled down her flushed face. 'I'm afraid alcohol doesn't agree with me. It's starting to affect my solar plexus.'

She will go to pieces in a moment, George thought, *and so will I.* Nodding to Ilona, he took Eileen's arm and led her out the side entrance of the hall.

CHAPTER 20

Zidra, watching the smooth breakers from the dunes behind Jingera Beach, felt that the architecture of her future had been destroyed. All that was beautiful existed no more and she was left only with a bare structure in which to live an infinity of minutes, of days. The awful enormity of this struck her like a blow. Rolling onto her stomach, she clutched at the strands of silvery grass binding the sand dunes, as if they might attach her too to the spinning earth.

How she regretted all their lost days. 'You were much too young to begin a serious entanglement,' Jim had written. 'Too young for permanency. We were both too young for that.' And because of that stupid good sense they'd never been together.

She pictured his face the last time they'd met, outside the front door at Ferndale, the pine trees sighing around them, her mother playing Shostakovich in the living room and his skin drained of all colour by the moonlight. And later that night his telephone call. 'We didn't really have a chance to say goodbye . . . Goodnight, Zidra. It's been terrific seeing you again.'

The last words he'd ever spoken to her.

Clinging to the grass, she cried for all that she'd lost, the physical closeness they'd never known and the tender friendship that had lasted over half her lifetime. Learning what Jim would make of everything was no longer an option. There'd be no more talking. No more rehearsing of what she might tell him. No more letters. No more fantasies.

No future.

She was on her own now.

Unless you counted Hank, who'd been phoning her for days, leaving messages that she would never return.

But she didn't want to think of that. Instead she concentrated on the pounding of the breakers, the ocean muffling all other sounds as it pushed and pulled insistently at the sand, never letting the shoreline alone.

———•—•———

Later she lay exhausted, face resting on the sand dampened by the tide of her tears. The sun continued to beat relentlessly down and she burnt, how she burnt. Sitting up at last, she brushed the grains from her face and neck, and found an inadequate handkerchief in her handbag. After pulling together what remained of herself, she walked uncertainly towards the footbridge. On the step facing the beach, she sat down to brush off the last grains of sand from her feet before wriggling them into the impossibly frivolous sandals she'd bought to go with her dress. The black linen dress had become funereal and she would never wear it again, or the sandals.

'Dizzy, you're here!' Lorna stood silhouetted above her. She sat down at Zidra's side and brushed a few specks of sand from her bare shoulders.

If Zidra's tears hadn't already been spent, she might have wept at the tenderness of her touch. Instead, she said, 'Has it finished?'

'People are beginning to go. There'll still be a few hardy souls hanging on though, working around the caterers in order to finish the beer.'

'Did anything else happen after I left?'

'Well, Rod Bigelow, the bloke from the *Burford Advertiser*, turned up. Late, fortunately, and without a camera. He wasn't there for the service, which was a good thing. Mrs Cadwallader's obsessed by what she did in the church but at least that's taken her mind off her loss. Your mother's fantastic. All the time moving around smoothing down feathers and quashing gossip, the odd word here and there – you know how well she does it.'

'I'll see the Cadwalladers before we head back to Ferndale.'

'Go on your own though, Dizzy. They'll be home by now, I reckon. It'll be good for you to talk to them without me. I'll sit on the dunes for half an hour – I could do with a bit of staring at the waves – and then I'll meet you back at the car.'

Slowly Zidra trudged over the footbridge spanning the lagoon. On the town side, a waterbird with spindly legs and a curved black beak cocked its head at her approach and sauntered away along the sand, as if that had been its intention all along. She sighed. Her memories of Jim were firmly attached to her past here – and to her childhood. Jingera was Jim's as well as hers and there was a connection there. Yet that connection ended today with the service celebrating his life.

Halfway up the hill, she glanced back and saw that Lorna was standing on the footbridge looking in her direction. Her friend mimed blowing kisses, her gestures exaggerated, arms extended. So leaden had Zidra's limbs become it was an effort to wave back. And an effort to carry on plodding up the steep road, when she knew she had to face the Cadwalladers' grief again. Avoiding the war memorial in the centre of the square, she turned left into the narrow street leading to their house.

Mr Cadwallader was standing in his front garden smoking a cigarette. 'I'd given up these things,' he said. 'But it looks like I'm going to have to give up all over again.' He stubbed the cigarette out on the brick paving and stowed the butt in the pocket of his suit. 'Come in, Zidra. Eileen was hoping you'd drop by, and so was I.'

She followed him along the path to the front door, and he held open the screen door to let her pass. 'Eileen, Zidra's here,' he called.

Mrs Cadwallader was standing in the doorway to her bedroom, in her stockinged feet and her too loose dress. 'Thanks for coming, Zidra,' she said. 'You read that poem beautifully. It was a bit too intellectual for me, but that was Jim for you. Perhaps you'll let me have a copy.'

'Sure. You can have this.' Zidra pulled out the folded piece of paper on which she'd copied the poem and handed it to Mrs Cadwallader.

'Would you like a cup of tea?' With unseeing eyes Mrs Cadwallader looked at the paper before slipping it into her pocket. 'George's just made a pot.'

Zidra followed her into the kitchen and accepted what she was offered. For a few seconds they sat in a silence that was punctuated only by the sipping of tea. The scent of lilies, in a cut-glass vase on the table, filled the air. *My least favourite flower*, Zidra decided and put her hand over her nose.

'Those lilies are too much,' George said. He picked them up and took them out to the back verandah, before shutting the door and resuming his place at the table.

'There's something I wanted to ask you,' Mrs Cadwallader said at last.

Zidra braced herself against the chair back. 'What's that?' she said, trying to sound relaxed.

'What was in Jim's last letter apart from the poem?'

'It was a love letter.' Zidra wanted to make this clear. She wanted to make something concrete out of this, something she could hold on to. Yet at the same time she didn't want to be asked to show it. The words were too private, although their intent was not.

'We never had a letter after he left here.'

'He wrote it on the plane, on the flight to Saigon. He and I never had a chance to say goodbye properly.'

'None of us did. No one ever does.'

'He asked me to marry him.' The futility of revealing this hit her hard, but at the same time it was something that she was proud of. She looked at the swirling patterns of the green and brown linoleum floor, not wanting to see the reaction of this couple who might have been her parents-in-law. 'I would have said yes.'

'He didn't tell us,' Mrs Cadwallader said.

'She's told us now, Eileen.'

Mrs Cadwallader looked worn out and Zidra could see that this extra news, though not necessarily unwelcome, was almost too much for her to bear. Zidra stood up. Mrs Cadwallader rose at the same time and leant forward to kiss her cheek. 'You'll keep in touch, won't you, dear?'

'Of course I will, Mrs Cadwallader.'

'Oh, by the way, Zidra, there's something else I wanted to say.'

'What's that?'

'Don't call me Mrs Cadwallader any more, dear. It's Eileen.'

'Goodbye, Eileen.' Zidra put her arms around her and felt how thin she had become.

'And now George will show you out,' Eileen said, as if it were a mansion in which they were living and Zidra might not be able to find the exit on her own.

On the front verandah George hesitated, as if uncertain of where he was or what was expected of him. Zidra's heart turned over as she looked at him, the father of the man she'd loved. She gave him a quick hug before kissing him on the cheek and bolting down the path. At the front gate she turned. He was smiling at her now. She was glad that she'd dropped in, and even gladder that she'd told them she'd intended to marry their son.

—◆—

Zidra stood at the dormer window of her bedroom at Ferndale. Not the one facing west; she couldn't bear that outlook any more and had moved the desk away so she wouldn't be reminded of Jim's last visit. A wave of exhaustion swept over her. She could easily become irritable.

Yet it was far too early for bed. Downstairs her parents and Lorna were clearing away the dinner things. The meal had been subdued, in spite of the bottle of wine and Lorna's valiant attempts to keep the conversation going. Clutching the window frame, Zidra leant out and inhaled the cool night air. It tasted salty on her lips, which meant the sea was up. To the east was the smudged horizon where the ocean met the sky, and overhead the band of stars seemed so close you could almost reach out and touch them.

Jim had gone. She thought of the passage of the seconds, the minutes, as if they were almost tangible. Time was not suspended, but she was suspended in time, caught like an insect in amber, in a state of disbelief. She found it hard to believe, she found it difficult to accept, that she would never see Jim again.

She gave a low moan. Even now she found it impossible to admit that her mother had been right about the risks of working as a journalist in a war zone. Only a few weeks ago she'd been envying Jim his job. 'A lot of it's the same old thing,' he'd said. 'Bits of jungle being lost and then regained. And so it goes on. Nothing conclusive. The only certainty is that it's going to get bloodier and more deadly.'

How right he'd been. Neither of them had mentioned at the time the fourteen journalists who had died in Cambodia and the nineteen who'd gone missing. This information had appeared in the papers again and again after his body had been found.

But could you live your life always avoiding danger? You could but it was no way to exist. It was the way to survive but not to live. Before you decided to take some action, you worked out the probabilities of failure and of success, and proceeded based on that information. What happened afterwards could never affect that initial decision. After the event had been realised, you couldn't turn back the clock.

Anyway, taking risks wasn't all there was to worry about. Getting things done, exposing what was wrong here in Australia was where she could make a contribution. Jim had been right about her job at the *Sydney Morning Chronicle*. It was interesting, and becoming more and more so, as she gained experience and the trust of Joe Ryan.

She shut the window and ran downstairs. The living room was empty; she could hear the others crashing around in the kitchen still. The curtains hadn't been drawn and a half-moon was visible through the top sash. Completely framed by one of the panes, it looked as if it were stuck there, immovable.

It was when she was searching for the Monopoly box – Lorna had put it away the night before and it wasn't in its usual place – that she opened the door at the far end of the sideboard. Normally she never looked there. It was where her mother's sewing things were kept and she had no use for sewing. The Monopoly board was there all right, on top of the sewing basket. But her attention was caught by the file that lay on the shelf underneath, the file with the neat black lettering on the cover, in her mother's writing: 'Zidra's press cuttings'.

She pulled out the file and flicked through the pages. Everything she'd ever written for the *Sydney Morning Chronicle* was there, both the attributed and non-attributed pieces. She blinked rapidly; her damned eyes were watering again. That her mother loved her had never been in doubt. But she hadn't guessed until now how proud her mother was of her.

Hurriedly she put the file away. After a few moments she went to the window. She placed a hand on a pane of glass and felt its welcome coolness. The half-moon had shifted slightly. It illuminated the garden and cast deep shadows on the ragged lawn.

At this point she heard her mother's and Lorna's voices approaching. She set her face into a mask. When they opened the door, she was kneeling by the coffee table, unpacking the Monopoly board.

'I shall play Chopin while you girls fight over London, if my music is not too rowdy for you.'

'Noisy, you mean, Ma.'

'Noisy, rowdy: it is all the same.' Already her mother was shuffling through her music and pulling out a book. 'But that is

145

academic, for I have decided on a quiet piece,' she said. 'The third movement of Chopin's second piano sonata. It is lento. Do you remember it?'

'No, you know I'm not musical.'

'Of course you are musical but you do not listen.'

Zidra smiled and Lorna snickered.

'To music only I meant, for you always listen to your mama. Though sometimes with gritted teeth.'

Lorna laughed, in that way of hers that made it impossible not to join in. When her mother started to play the Chopin piece, Zidra said to Lorna, 'When are you seeing John again?'

'Your Mr Ordinary? I don't know. I didn't have any way to reach him before coming down here. But I expect he'll contact me when I get back.'

'What about Daisy?'

'Mum's moved her again, out west with another one of the aunties.'

'You'll phone me once you've seen John?'

'You bet. And you can show me those photos Chris took. I'd like to know if John is the same man that you saw snapping me at the last moratorium march. Now, how about you get on with distributing the Monopoly money. You're the banker tonight, don't forget.'

'I am. And I'm determined to stop you putting hotels on both Park Lane and Mayfair again,' Zidra said.

And once the game was over, she would go to bed and fall into a deep and – she hoped – oblivious sleep.

PART IV

Early November 1971

CHAPTER 21

Zidra woke reluctantly. Through the open window sunlight filtered, and Sunday church music from next-door's radio. Even after eight hours' sleep, she still felt lacerated by her encounter in Oxford Street the day before with a casual acquaintance, Michelle. Yet her words were thoughtless, nothing more, Zidra told herself.

'Terrible about Jim Cadwallader,' she'd said. 'The awful thing about people you know dying is that it forces you to face your own mortality.'

But that isn't it at all, Zidra had wanted to shout. *That devalues Jim's life and reduces it to nothing!* Yet she'd felt so flayed by the woman's words she'd only mumbled some response before hurrying on, pretending she had an urgent meeting. Anything, anything to get away. Still those words lingered in her mind. She held on to them as a focus for her anger, as if they were to blame for the direction her life was taking.

But really, she had to get a grip on things. Stand not the unshaken brave to give thee confidence? That's what one of her secondary-school teachers often said, and the words were a small comfort. Lorna was the unshaken brave. Lorna grew in the face of adversity, and so too must she.

After a time she got out of bed. She gathered together all her dirty clothes and stuffed them into one of the laundry bags her mother had sewn for her, from Marimekko fabric patterned with zebras and elephants. Slinging a bag over her shoulder, she ran downstairs and collected an apple from the fruit bowl in the kitchen before double-locking the front door behind her.

What was she doing, and where was she going? The street looked familiar but she was a stranger in it. There was hardly anyone about, just the odd jogger and a car or two. A cyclist speeding down the hill shouted a salutation, the words reaching her only after he'd passed: 'Lovely day!' With this, her feeling of disorientation trickled away, and she turned into the golden dazzle of the morning.

Her walk took her past a small park that was bordered by a row of contorted plane trees. This park was frequented by the homeless, but only one at a time, a floating population of singles. Today an elderly man, possibly of southern European origin, was scrabbling about in the garbage bin. His collection of paper carrier bags was arranged on one of the concrete tables. The smallest bag rested on an ancient leopard-skin coat. After some effort, he extracted a half-eaten apple from the bin and tottered with it to the bubbler on the far side of the lawn. While he washed it under the thin stream of water, she placed her own untouched apple on the edge of the leopard-skin coat. The man didn't appear to notice, nor did he look up as she passed by.

Several hours later she walked down the hill again, past the serried ranks of terrace houses facing one another across the street. Some were glorified dosshouses with half a dozen names at the front door. Others were newly renovated with expensive cars parked outside. The area was becoming fashionable; where once people had wanted to shift to the suburbs as soon as they could afford to, now some were moving back to take advantage of the proximity of Paddington to the city centre, whose jagged skyline was visible to the west.

What had attracted her to the area was its mixed population, and the luxuriant way plants grew here, even in the tiniest pockets of soil. Frangipanis, for instance, that started flowering in the late spring. You would never find those in Jingera. She put down her bags and paused for a moment next to a tree covered with creamy white flowers with delicate yellow centres. She picked up one of the blooms from the pavement and inhaled its sweet perfume before continuing down the hill. The sun seemed less unforgiving now that a gentle breeze had arisen to take the heat out of it. The park where she'd seen the elderly man earlier was deserted, although a supermarket trolley had been deposited there since she'd walked by.

As she opened the front door of the house, she thought for a moment that she heard Jim's voice. So sharp was her shock that her heart began to race, until she realised the voice was only from the television that Lisa or Joanne must have left on.

'Is that you, Zidra?' Joanne emerged from the kitchen and darted into the living room to turn off the television. 'Typical Lisa, she leaves everything on when she goes out. The iron, the TV, the radio, sometimes even a tap.'

'I'm getting that way myself. I sometimes even forget where I am.'

'You've got an excuse for that after all that's happened. Are you okay? Your hands are shaking.'

'I'm good, really I am.'

'I've got something for you. A letter. It got caught up in my mail and I only noticed it when I sorted through my stuff first thing this morning. Sorry about that. Thought it was all bills but I was wrong.'

Zidra followed Joanne into the kitchen. 'Not important, I hope,' Joanne said. 'But anyway it can't have been here for more than a couple of days.'

Zidra took the airmail envelope. Jim's letters used to come once a week, month in, month out, year in, year out. She inspected the envelope. No sender's address on the back but there was a Vienna postmark so she guessed it was from Philip Chapman. In the days when her mother taught the piano, Philip had been her prize pupil, and he had become the first person in the world to record the Talivaldis Variations.

Little things brought back the past so vividly. A letter, a connection. A sharp pain as all that was lost came flooding back. Her biological father had composed the Talivaldis Variations not long before he died. She'd never really missed him; she'd never really known him. Philip playing her father's music seemed much more real to her than her father ever had, but it was Philip's connection to Jim that made her eyes fill with tears.

Though her vision was blurred, sounds impinged on her with great clarity. The creaking of the staircase under her weight; the slap of her heels against her leather sandals each time she put a foot down; a bird calling from the shrub outside the back door; the telephone on the landing outside her bedroom stuttering into life before being picked up downstairs by Joanne.

She stretched out on her bed. The envelope was so light that there couldn't be more than one sheet of paper inside. She retrieved a nail file from the bedside table and slid it under the flap. With a quick jerk she slit the envelope open and removed from it the single page.

Dear Zidra,

You will be back in Sydney by the time you receive this. I was devastated to hear this morning about Jim, and the memorial service too. My mother wrote but I've been on tour and so the letter only reached me today. Such a terrible shock; such a terrible loss. What a horrible thing war is.

I've felt inundated all day by those old memories, especially from the days when Jim and I were boarders at Stambroke College. How I hated that place. It was thanks to him I got through all that.

I know you loved him too and must be suffering from this awful shock. I wish I could have been there for the service. Jim was one of those rare creatures, a genuinely good human being.

With love from
Philip

She stood and walked to the window. It framed an ultramarine sky and row after row of terrace houses stepping down the hill. She opened the sash wider and leant out. By craning around to the right she could just make out the eucalyptus tree three doors away. It was covered in pale yellow clusters of flowers and reminded her of Jingera and the bush by the lagoon.

Philip had blossomed since he left Stambroke College years ago, and that had been thanks to Jim. Holding on tightly to the window frame, she no longer saw the view. Instead she glimpsed the lonely path she would take stretching out before her.

What would Jim have felt when he'd begun his final journey, in the instant between capture and getting a bullet in the head? Or had he been shot in the middle of a battle, with no warning that his life was to be snuffed out? She hoped the latter. No time for fear or regret or pain.

And how was she going to cope, now that hope had gone? She'd have to force herself to get on with her own journey, and to negotiate it as well she could. She'd have to bury herself in her work, and become more and more single-minded. She would seek out the truth, be more willing to take risks, trust in her own judgement. Her career – and she knew she would never marry now – would become a vocation and maybe that would eventually bring her some happiness.

She refolded Philip's letter and put it in her chest of drawers, next to the shoebox full of Jim's letters that she'd accumulated over the years. Then she shut the drawer firmly, as if by doing so she could shut off the past. Wasn't the best way to deal with grief to keep busy? To fill your days, your nights? To leave no time for remembering?

⋯

Not long after dinner that evening there was a ring at the front door. Zidra turned on the verandah light before opening the door. Her old friend Stella Papadopoulos stood there, reeking of Mitsouko. Zidra had first met her during university orientation week when they'd each been trawling around, deciding which clubs to join, and had started talking in front of the Labor Club stall.

As usual Zidra was struck by how narrow her friend's face was, and how emaciated, apart from the wide nose. It was as if all the flesh of her face had been concentrated here, leaving only a thin layer of muscle and skin to clothe the rest. Her body was lean as well; narrow shoulders and hips, and arms that were so slender that her sleeveless dress gaped at the armholes, exposing glimpses of olive skin and a rather ancient-looking red bra. Her eyes were black, as was her gravity-defying hair that nonetheless glowed like a halo under the bright verandah light.

'Come in,' Zidra said. 'I was just about to make some tea.'

'Can't stay long. I'm running late for a meeting. But I've been thinking about your Hank.'

'My Hank? I hardly know him.'

'That's not the impression I got when you introduced me to him at the Gladstone pub the night of the march.'

That was a lifetime ago, Zidra thought as she ushered Stella into the kitchen. She and Hank had spent a couple of hours talking and drinking with Stella and her husband, Nic, before Hank had whisked her out to dinner, his arm around her shoulders as if they were already lovers.

After putting the kettle on, Zidra flung open the window. There was something wrong with Stella's sense of smell if she didn't notice how strong the Mitsouko was. It was making Zidra's nasal passages tingle and eyes water, and any moment now she'd start to sneeze.

'Maybe you should find out a bit more about Hank, that's what I've been thinking. After all if he's working for the US Consulate, he might be CIA.'

'Didn't you once tell me that the trouble with *you journalists* is that you see conspiracy everywhere?'

'Well, Zidra, maybe you're right to see conspiracy everywhere. And you can bet that the CIA and our security people are sharing information. So you need to be a bit careful.'

'I realise that, and of course I'm careful. Anyway, I've hardly seen Hank since I got back from Jingera.' She couldn't bear to say *since Jim's death*. Time was now divided into two periods: before she last went to Jingera and after she got back. She added, 'We've just had lunch a couple of times, that's all.'

'He hasn't come around here again? Sorry, that sounds like prying, but you did tell me you were seeing him a bit before Jim came back.'

Zidra opened a cupboard and got out a couple of cups and saucers. 'Like a biscuit?' she said. The last time Hank had dropped in was the week before Jim returned for that abbreviated visit. It had been late at night, after eleven o'clock, and she'd let Hank into the house reluctantly.

'I've just come from a dinner,' he'd said. 'Work of course. I was passing on the way home and I saw the light on. So I stopped on an impulse.'

I'll bet, she'd thought, but she took him upstairs to her bedroom. Foolish girl – it seemed like a betrayal now. But how could she have known then that her feelings for Jim were reciprocated? What a lost opportunity that was.

Hank's glance that night had been like a movie camera, panning around the room. 'Didn't you have a typewriter here last time?' he said.

'Still do. It's on top of the chest of drawers, behind the clothes.'

'Last time it was on your desk. Don't you use your typewriter at home?'

'No, or only for letters. The typewriters at the office are better. This one's just a clapped-out portable Olivetti.' She'd been glad she'd taken all her work material back to her office in the *Chronicle* building. Only a couple of days had passed since she'd decided to do all her writing there and to keep it locked up in her office filing cabinet at night. She'd added, 'I keep all my stuff in the office. Absolutely everything.'

'Not quite everything. Certainly not your gorgeous body.' And then he'd put his arms around her waist and run his hands over her buttocks, pulling her close.

At this moment the whistling of the kettle returned Zidra to the present. 'Did you say you wanted a biscuit?' she asked Stella.

'No biscuit and I like my tea weak,' Stella said.

'I haven't forgotten.' Zidra poured the boiling water into the teapot.

'You seem distracted. What are the lunches with Hank like? Does he ask you lots of questions?'

'No more than you do.' Zidra managed to smile although she didn't feel like it. Since she'd returned from Jingera, Hank had been kind, had seemed to understand that their friendship had shifted into a new phase, and she'd liked that about him. Yet now she thought about it, his interest in where she kept her work, on that last night they'd slept together, did seem excessive.

'I know how you could check up on Hank,' Stella said. 'Remember Samantha Browning?'

'Yes. She had a room on the same floor as me in Women's College.'

'She's working at the US Embassy in Canberra.'

'Really?' Zidra put the teacups on a tray and led the way into the living room.

'She's a secretary there. She could get hold of Hank's entry in the US Foreign Service Register.'

'Have you kept in contact?'

'Yes. Christmas cards and the odd phone call. We went to Sydney Girls' High together, and she's one of the few girls I keep in touch with.'

'I haven't seen her for four or five years.'

'I could ring her and ask her to get a copy of Hank's entry. All's fair in love and war.'

'I've got absolutely no idea what you mean by that.' Zidra frowned at Stella. Surely she wasn't fantasising about her relationship with Hank.

'I'll call her tonight,' Stella said, ignoring the frown. 'I'll get her to post a copy to me.' She put down her cup and stood up. 'Sure you don't want to come to this meeting? It's the local Labor Party. It would do you good to meet some new people.'

'No, I stay out of all that now. Can't be seen to be partial to one political faction rather than another.' Although she'd started slogging through her contacts in political groups, checking if they'd been infiltrated, she certainly didn't want to be seen at any meeting in Stella's company.

'That's bullshit and you know it. You could be there for your work.'

'Precisely, Stella, and that's just what I don't want people there to think.'

Stella laughed. 'Fair enough. Thanks for the tea. I'll call you when I get lucky with Samantha.'

———•———

Two days later Stella phoned Zidra to say she had the information from Samantha. On the way home from work that night Zidra dropped into Stella's tiny terrace not far from where she lived in Paddington. Stella and Nic had bought the house recently, with a loan from Nic's parents to cover the deposit, and they were slowly renovating it.

'Come in,' Stella said. 'Mind the missing floorboards there. Nic did a bit of rewiring last weekend and he hasn't had time to nail them down again.'

Zidra stepped over the gap, through which she could see rough dirt and some fresh wood shavings, and followed Stella into the kitchen. On the kitchen bench, between the paint pots and unwashed dishes, her friend had placed a photocopied page from the US Foreign Service Register.

'I reckon you'd need special training to tell from this if Hank's CIA,' Stella said. 'He was born in October 1937, so he's older than he looks, and he's not married. He's got an undergraduate degree from William and Mary College in Virginia and a postgraduate qualification in international relations. And he's fluent in Spanish, Portuguese and Italian apparently. Then there are various assignments and promotion dates.'

Zidra inspected the entry. Might Hank's time in military service be a clue? She had an idea that CIA trainees were drafted for longer than usual. Or perhaps it was shorter. To the right eyes this information might indicate if he was deep-cover CIA, but there was no way she could make any inferences without getting advice. Dave Pringle, the foreign editor, was bound to know how to interpret the material. 'I can't decipher any of this,' she said. 'But I know someone who can.'

'How?'

'By checking how long Hank's spent in military service. How rapid his promotion's been. His assignment pattern. That sort of thing.'

'Do I know this person?'

'Just a colleague who used to work in Foreign Affairs.'

'Maybe you'll let me know what the verdict is.' Stella handed Zidra the page with Hank's details.

'Of course, but I'm not planning to see Hank any time soon.' After brushing a few crumbs from the paper, Zidra folded it up and zipped it into the inside pocket of her handbag.

And soon she forgot all about it, for events in her life were to develop a momentum of their own over the next few weeks.

CHAPTER 22

The following afternoon Zidra knocked on Joe Ryan's office door. His feet were resting on his desk. As usual it was littered with papers. In one hand he held a lit cigarette and in the other the telephone receiver. He waved her into the room and she sat opposite him. His side of the phone conversation was limited to the occasional yes. Eventually he banged down the receiver, muttering to himself, 'Useless bloody bloke, that, and a terrible talker too.' After easing his feet off his desk, he stubbed out his cigarette with some vehemence and said, 'What can I do for you, Zidra?'

If only she could return later when he might be in a better mood, but it wasn't possible to back away now. 'There's something I wanted to ask, if you've got a minute.'

'What's that?' He began to shuffle papers around his desk.

'Have you ever faced a conflict of interest? You know, like when you're investigating something that a friend may have told you. And you know that if you pursue it you'll put that friend in danger.'

'All the time, Zidra. It's the journalist's dilemma.' Joe leant forward and rested his elbows on the desk. 'Is there anything in particular you want to discuss?'

'Not really, but maybe I should fill you in a bit about my friend Lorna Hunter.' Not much though; she wanted to firm up the story a bit more before telling him all she knew. And anyway, while craving his reassurance, she also wanted to stay independent.

When she'd finished, Joe said, 'The trouble about reporting, Zidra, is that you're all the time filtering information. You're all the time drawing on stuff people tell you. Following things up. Using people that you know and people that you don't know. Maybe you're exploiting them a bit.'

'Friends as well as acquaintances,' Zidra said. Once more she wished that her best friend wasn't one of her crucial sources; better by far that it had come from some other contact.

'Well, you know I'm here any time you want to talk things over. But seeing you has reminded me of something else I wanted to say.' He began to shove around his heaps of paper again, eventually retrieving a crumpled packet of cigarettes. After pulling one out, he thought better of lighting it and stuck it behind his right ear. He continued, 'You're really good at winkling information out of people, Zidra. They tell you things they wouldn't say to others. It's your empathy, sympathy, call it what you like. Just you remember that when you're feeling low.'

'Thank you.' His kind words brought unwanted tears to her eyes. She stood up; before she was even out of her chair, Joe's left hand was on the telephone receiver, his right hand dialling a number. Once the call was through, the Ryan feet would be up on the desktop again, and the cigarette transferred from behind the ear to his mouth.

———•+•———

Zidra stepped through the door into the Ladies' Bar of the little pub in Darlinghurst. Lorna was the only person in the room and there were two glasses of lemonade already waiting on the table in front of her. After hugging Lorna, Zidra retrieved from her bag an envelope containing the photographs Chris had taken at the march. Both were of Mr Ordinary but it was hard to make out his features. Even though Chris had managed to take one of his face in profile, the image was blurred. 'Do you recognise this man?'

'Yes.' Lorna's face crinkled as she returned the pictures to Zidra. 'It's definitely John.'

'He followed you along the street for maybe fifty metres, snapping you with that ruddy great telephoto lens. Did he contact you again?'

'Yes, a couple of days ago. I wasn't wearing the tape because I hadn't known when he'd get in touch, though I'd kept all the stuff in my bag. So I told him I was running late for a lecture, and we arranged to meet afterwards. By that time I was all wired up.'

'How did you get on?'

'All right,' Lorna said. 'John took the bait. I managed to get him to repeat a lot of what he'd said last time and it recorded okay – I checked it when I got home. I told him I was going to cooperate by letting him know what's going on at the meetings and telling him what my friends are doing, all that sort of thing.'

At this moment Zidra glanced up and saw two women entering the bar. 'It's those two old dears who were here the other day. You'd better keep your voice down.'

Lorna twisted around for a quick look, before beginning to speak so softly that Zidra had to lean forward to hear. 'I've arranged to meet John again next week. Same time, same day, but not in Railway Square. I'm to go to Hyde Park and mill around with the crowds by the war memorial at lunchtime. Then he'll casually come up to me. He's rather good at that. Didn't see him until he was right beside me, although I'd been on high alert the whole time.'

Zidra turned to see where the two women were sitting. They'd chosen a table as far away from theirs as possible. She said, 'What else does he want – any more details on that?'

'It's all on the tape. Advance knowledge of protests, information about demonstrations being planned, information about any unusual sexual activities. "For anyone?" I said. "You can't expect me to get such private information for just anyone."' Lorna took a sip of her drink before continuing. 'Then he said, "I'll tell you who in due course. I'll give you some names and get you to find out if they get up to anything."

'"Oh," I said. "What do you mean precisely, *get up to anything?*"'

Lorna paused dramatically, her wide open eyes expressing innocence. Then she continued in an exaggerated drawl: '"I think you know," he said, "but let me spell it out for you anyway. Fucking the wrong people. Not their wives or husbands if they're married. Fucking underage kids. Same-sex fucking. Fucking their bloody dogs. Get what I mean?"

'"Yes," I said, "I've got the idea now. So what will you use that stuff for?"'

'I reckon we know,' Zidra said.

'But I wanted to get it all down on tape, see.'

'Of course. You're a natural at this, Lorna. Go on.'

'So John said, "You're the law student, supposed to be so clever. You have a guess what that stuff might be used for."

'"Do you mean prosecution if they don't cooperate?" I asked, just to clarify.

'"That's right," he said.'

'This is all on the tape too?' Zidra said.

'Yes, it's all there.'

'Carry on.'

'So then I asked him, "How do I know you'll drop the charges?"

'And he said, "As long as you carry on cooperating, you won't get prosecuted. You've just got to be a good girl."

'"Oh, I will be," I said. "I'll be a very good girl. And nothing will happen to my kid sister either, will it? Last time we met, you said you'd welfare her if I didn't cooperate."

'"I'm a man of my word," he said. "You'll see that, believe you me." And then he left, after telling me when and where to meet next time.'

Zidra took the tape that Lorna held out for her and put it in her pocket. 'Phone me if you need me. By the way, John didn't mention his surname, did he?'

'No, though I did try asking. "You don't need to know that," he said. "Don't call me, I'll call you." Then he laughed, as if he'd said something original.'

'So he's not going to be easy to track down. John Ordinary. He could be anyone.' She stood up. 'You will be careful, won't you?'

'You bet. You know me, I'm always careful.'

——•——

Zidra hesitated on the pavement opposite the building housing New South Wales Police Intelligence. It was an imposing-looking red-brick edifice that probably dated from the turn of the century. The facade of the building was punctured by windows displaying just about every type of arch known to humankind. Did she really want to go inside? Was this the best way of learning what she wanted to know? She took a deep breath, swung her bag onto her shoulder and crossed the street with a gaggle of pedestrians. Once inside the building, she checked the information board. New South Wales Police Intelligence was on the third floor. Avoiding the lifts, she ran up the wide staircase.

For a few seconds she waited by the lift shaft to regain her breath. Through a set of glass doors she could see a carpeted reception area with a large desk, behind which a blonde young woman sat, her head bent over some papers. No one came in or out. She decided to wait for half an hour before opening the glass doors and asking to see John. 'John who?' the receptionist would say, and then Zidra would be stymied. 'How many Johns have you got?' she might ask, and with a bit of luck the woman would list them all. There'd be dozens though, it was such a common name, and anyway John wouldn't be his proper name. Again she wondered why she was wasting her time like this.

Be patient, she told herself. *Give it a go.* She sat on the bottom step of the flight of stairs and took a map out of her bag; if anyone came along, she would pretend to be studying it. Although she could occasionally hear one of the lifts rattling by, none stopped at the third floor. After fifteen minutes or so, a grey-haired woman wearing a blue overall trundled a tea trolley into the reception area. Zidra licked her lips; she could do with a cup of tea herself. Her throat felt dry and her palms clammy. The tea lady and the blonde receptionist chatted for a few minutes before the trolley was wheeled along a corridor at the back of the reception area. The lift shaft hummed again and soon a car stopped with a clang on her level. As the doors were opening, she dashed up the stairs towards the next floor, turning at the dogleg in time to see a couple of burly young men in police uniform push through the swing doors below.

When she was slowly descending again, the door of the reception area opened and a man in a suit appeared. She held her breath and stood perfectly still, back pressed against the wall, barely half a dozen steps above him, her pulse resounding so loudly in her head that he must surely hear. It was Mr Ordinary. He was of average height, average shape, mid- to late thirties. Under the standard grey suit he wore a white shirt with an unremarkable tie. His round face, lacking any striking feature, might have been formed by a child from slightly grubby flour-and-water dough.

After the lift door opened and Mr Ordinary stepped inside the car, Zidra began to breathe normally again. The doors slid shut and the lift rumbled down towards the ground floor. Quickly she ran down the stairs and through the glass doors into the third-floor reception area. The blonde woman looked up and smiled. 'How can I help?'

'I've got an appointment with the man who just left. He got into the lift just as I was getting out and I didn't twig in time who he was.'

'An appointment with Steve Jamieson?' The woman looked up the diary in front of her. 'I don't think so. There's nothing about a meeting here.'

'Oh dear, I must have made a mistake. I could have sworn it was today.' *Steve Jamieson*, she thought. *I've got exactly what I wanted.* Now she could identify in her article precisely who John was.

'Would you like to leave a message?'

'No, thanks. I'll phone tomorrow morning.' Zidra smiled at the receptionist before pushing through the swing doors and running down the staircase and out into Cleveland Street.

While she'd been indoors, the stiff breeze had swept away the earlier haze of pollution. Now it was intent on driving eastwards the few remaining wisps of white cloud. It was a beautiful afternoon and she would mark her success at identifying Mr Ordinary by walking back to the *Chronicle* building. Fast; she'd have to walk fast. Only that way could she keep the pain at bay. Keep busy, always busy, and try not to think of Jim.

The pressure of the headphones hurt the sides of her head but Zidra barely noticed, so absorbed was she in the words she was hearing. Once she'd listened to the cassette Lorna had given her, she pressed the rewind button on the machine. The content of the tape was more or less as Lorna had recounted it in the pub, even down to her imitation of Steve Jamieson's drawl. It was clear he was enjoying exercising his power, enjoying threatening Lorna. But worse than that was the viciousness in the way he sometimes spoke. At first this had made Zidra feel sick, and after a time angry. This fury was good, she knew. Feeling outraged was firing her up, getting her going, giving her the resolve she needed. She hated the way Jamieson was making charges against people who didn't have the resources to refute them, and then using his charges to force them to do what they would never otherwise do. Intelligence was abusing people's privacy in order to pursue their own ends. It had to be exposed.

She spooled into her typewriter a couple of blank pages with carbon paper between and pressed the play button again. There was a faint hiss as the tape started running, and then Steve Jamieson's twang filled her ears. 'G'day, Lorna. Glad you've turned up. I've been watching you.' Zidra began to type, her fingers speeding over the keys. Occasionally she paused to rewind and listen again.

An hour later she'd finished the transcript. She clasped her hands behind her head and arched her back. Since the memorial service, she'd become more conscious of the effort required to breathe, of the effort to stay alive. As she exhaled, she realised she hadn't thought of Jim once while she'd been transcribing Lorna's tape, so involved had she become. But then it hit her like a physical blow to her chest, the realisation that she would never again be able to write to Jim of things that were happening to her.

'Get a grip, get a grip, get a grip,' she muttered to herself. She still had Lorna and she wouldn't let her go. She would fight her cause no matter what.

She put the transcript and cassette in the back of the filing cabinet under her office desk, locking the drawer afterwards. It occurred to her that perhaps she should have another word to Joe about the piece she was working on. After all, anything could happen. If she had an accident, no one would know about the latest tape or the story. Yet if she started telling people about it too early, it might get out and Lorna's confidence – and security – would be breached.

Still undecided, Zidra stuck her head around Joe's office door just before leaving. Feet up on the desk, he was talking on the telephone. Seeing her, he waved. After putting his hand over the receiver, he mouthed, 'See you when I get back from Canberra on Friday,' before resuming his conversation.

So that was that. The matter had been decided for her. She put the filing-cabinet key into her bra cup just as photographer Chris appeared unexpectedly in front of her. 'It's where I keep my twenty-dollar notes,' she said, smiling sweetly.

'Wish I could do the same, Zidra. You girls get all the breaks.'

She grinned and headed for the lift.

CHAPTER 23

Voices shouting, sound reverberating off the hard walls of the café. The coffee machine hissing, the air humid, more people squeezing in from the street to join the raggedy queue at the counter. Zidra was glad that she and the foreign editor, Dave Pringle, had got there early enough to secure a table for two in a quiet corner at the back. 'A working lunch,' he'd said that morning when he'd suggested getting together. 'Joe's told me a bit about what you're up to and I've heard something that will interest you.'

They sat without talking while Dave finished the first of his sandwiches. There was still a whole round in front of him, and an iced finger bun waiting in the wings, when he began to speak. 'Did you know that ASIO's engaging in more spoiling activities, like they did after the Freedom Ride? You know, that bus trip to country New South Wales that was organised by university students and the Aboriginal activist Charlie Perkins?'

'Of course I remember it,' Zidra said. 'It was in the newspapers and on the telly. It's what got me really interested in politics. My mother said the Freedom Riders should have come to Jingera and Burford as well as going to all those northern New South Wales towns like Moree and Walgett.'

'Anyway,' Dave continued, after wiping his lips with a paper napkin, '*The Bulletin* ran a piece called "After the Freedom Ride". It was anonymously written and argued that there was growing Communist preoccupation with Aboriginal affairs. It implied that the Communists were taking over the land-rights movement.' He picked up a quarter of a sandwich and neatly posted it into his mouth. It didn't take him long to process it. 'You know what spoiling is, don't you?'

'Yes: trying to slag off one group you don't approve of by linking them with another group you don't approve of. Raising suspicion about Aboriginal activists by saying they're closely supported by the Communists.'

'That's right. Now here's something that might interest you. My oldest daughter works for Legal Aid in Redfern. And one of her clients is being blackmailed by someone called John.'

'John?' Zidra's voice cracked and her throat suddenly felt dry. She picked up her water glass and took a swig.

'Yes, she only knows his first name.'

Steve Jamieson, Zidra thought, and waited for Dave to continue.

'She had drugs planted on her. Then this John fellow told her the charges would be dropped if she informed on other members of her land-rights group.'

'I've got to meet her. Is she clean?'

'Yes. So my daughter says.'

'What's her name?'

'Wendy Ferris.'

Zidra thought for a moment before saying, 'Can your daughter tell Wendy she can collect an envelope with her name on it from the lobby here next Tuesday? It'll contain details of where and when we can meet. What does Wendy look like, by the way?'

171

'She's Aboriginal and quite young but that's all I know.'

'In that case she'd better leave her photo with the woman at the desk when she collects the envelope. That'll make it easier for me to recognise her.'

'Good girl. She'll have to put it in a sealed envelope, mind. You wouldn't want anyone else checking up on her.'

'Tuesday afternoon, Dave. By two o'clock at the latest.'

'Got it,' Dave said, smiling. 'I thought this would interest you.'

Too bloody right, she thought. *Too bloody right.*

CHAPTER 24

Hands clasped behind his head, Joe Ryan leant so far back in his chair that Zidra feared he might fall over. He'd called her into his office not long after he'd arrived back. So far they'd been sitting on opposite sides of his desk for five minutes and still Joe hadn't told her why. It was unlike him, she thought, to waste time yabbering about whether or not she was happy in her work. Usually he just assumed everyone was; most journalists at the *Chronicle* knew they were incredibly lucky to work in this newsroom.

Through the open window she heard the distant hum of cars from the street far below them and a sudden screech of brakes as someone got caught at the traffic lights. Inspecting Joe's face, she tried to infer from his expression where this conversation was heading. His skin looked redder than usual; it made his eyes seem even bluer. Sunburn rather than high blood pressure, she decided; he must have spent time out of doors and forgotten the zinc cream. But she certainly wasn't going to learn anything from his bland expression. She sighed, but not so that he'd hear. She wanted to get on with her research, rather than sitting about waiting for Joe to get to the point.

At this moment he released his hands and let his chair tilt forward again. Resting his elbows on the desk, he said, 'Are you aware that ASIO used to vet all new reporters to the *Sydney Morning Chronicle*? They did that until I took over as editor back in 1966.'

'I didn't know that,' she said.

'The funny thing is that no one ever told me. I had to find out the hard way. The outgoing editor didn't tell me, and neither did Bolton, the newspaper proprietor. I only found out when I got a call from somebody in Special Projects in ASIO asking why the new reporters I'd hired hadn't been vetted.'

Zidra leant forward in her chair. 'Was I checked?'

'No. I've never had any new reporters checked,' Joe said and grinned at her. 'That was a practice that had to go. You can't have an independent media if its reporters and editors have to be approved by a government-funded body. We're not a police state. Yet.'

'Do you think you were checked?'

'Almost certainly. But you know me, squeaky clean. Anyway, even though I've never asked for any reporters to be vetted, ASIO carry on collecting their own information. And that's what I wanted to talk to you about. This afternoon when I got back I found something had arrived on my desk from ASIO. Something that looks rather serious.' He leant towards her and placed a hand on a folder that lay before him on the desk. 'It's your file,' he said. 'And three other files as well, of people appointed at around the same time as you.'

Zidra gulped. 'You mean it's the file that ASIO have on me independent of anything this newspaper's ever done?'

'Exactly. And for some reason they decided to send me a copy now.'

What sort of material would be in there? Meetings with her various contacts, could they know about those? She doubted it somehow. She was always so careful. Maybe what was in the file wouldn't be all that bad: joining the Labor Club at university; the time a bunch of students tried to flood the state's tax department by flushing all the toilets and urinals at once; the brief marijuana-smoking period; her involvement with the university revue. All harmless things. This file's appearance was surely just a bluff.

Joe said, 'I haven't read it and I've got no intention of doing so. But I did think that you ought to know about it.'

'Why didn't they send you that when you hired me four years ago?'

'Well, I did make it very clear to them that I wasn't going to check out any of my new reporters. They've probably sent it to me now because of the moratorium marches.'

It occurred to her now that there might be some other reason for Joe's revelation. She took a deep breath before saying, 'Is this going to affect the story I'm writing?'

'Do you mean, did ASIO mention anything about that? No, I've had no contact with them. This file was here when I returned. Left at reception, apparently, and with no note. Remember I said I was giving you a bit of a free rein? Well, I meant it. But is there something you want to tell me?'

'Yes.' Quickly she explained what had been happening with Lorna recently and the meeting she was planning with Wendy Ferris. 'Do you think I should change my strategy?'

'Hell no,' Joe said. 'I employed you in the first place because you can write well and you're hard-working, but also because I could see you were a bit of an investigator. Your stuff in the student newspaper *Honi Soit* showed that. You're one of the people I hired to shake up the stuffy atmosphere that used to pervade this newsroom. Okay, you did have to have a trial on the women's pages but I soon got you out of that. And ASIO have sent me files on all of you.'

'Can I read my file?' It might be useful to know if ASIO had been following her recently. Recording her meetings with Lorna. Spying on her other activities.

'I don't think I'm going to let you read it,' Joe said slowly. 'It might change you. I'm going to put it in my safe. You can bet it's only a copy and they're trying to intimidate us. But we'll need to be a bit more careful. Keep the tapes locked up. Keep the transcripts under lock and key.'

'I lock them up already.'

'Good woman. Where?'

'In my filing cabinet.'

'That's not very secure. Anyone could break into that. After you've transcribed them, they can go into my office safe. At any rate, the arrival of this file now can mean only one thing: they're becoming suspicious of you.'

'Do you think there's anything else I should be doing?'

'Well, I reckon you should get your story about Lorna and the rest out really soon,' he said, 'after the fuss about that MP's sex scandal has died down, the randy bugger. A man in his position ought to have more sense. We'll have to think of putting Lorna somewhere safe. Maybe she could stay with us. Bridget wouldn't mind. And I want to consult a lawyer.'

'I might need a bit more time than that,' she said.

'Not too much more time, Zidra. You never know what else might happen.'

You never know what else might happen. In a moment her grief returned, driving away everything else. She stood up, legs shaking, and made her way blindly out of Joe's office.

The ladies' room was empty and she locked herself into a cubicle. She felt cold and alone, but her eyes were dry. The time for crying had gone. She'd done enough of that at Jingera before and after the memorial service. There remained only this cold vacuum inside her. It would be an absorbing state if she let it, but she wasn't about to do that.

CHAPTER 25

The following day Zidra stopped at the *Chronicle* reception desk. 'Was the envelope I left with you this morning collected?' she asked Emma, a pretty girl, in spite of the pancake make-up as thick as a clown's and false eyelashes like furry black caterpillars weighing down her upper eyelids.

'Yes, two hours ago,' Emma said. 'And one was left for you too.' With the thumb and forefinger of her left hand she delicately picked up the envelope. Her bright-red fingernails looked as if they'd been glued on.

The envelope was of poor-quality manila and sealed. Zidra put it into her handbag and ran down the stairs and out of the building. The first bus that turned up was bound for Circular Quay and she hopped onto it. It was only a quarter full and she took a seat at the very back. Ripping open the envelope, she pulled out a black-and-white photograph of an Aboriginal girl who looked about eighteen or nineteen years old. She had a long upper lip, a wide unsmiling mouth, large sad-looking dark eyes and wavy black hair cut in an old-fashioned pudding-basin style. Zidra studied the portrait carefully before stowing it inside the internal compartment of her bag.

At the Quay, she alighted and strolled across to the ferry terminal, where she bought two return tickets to Neutral Bay. There were ten minutes to go before the ferry was due to leave. She ambled along the Quay to the finger wharf from which the Manly ferries departed. A young Aboriginal woman, wearing a nondescript blue denim dress, was waiting next to the turnstile. Zidra walked by and stumbled, knocking into her with her bag. 'So sorry,' she said, briefly resting the hand in which she was holding one of the ferry tickets on the woman's right forearm. The fingers of the woman's left hand closed around the ticket. 'Neutral Bay in seven minutes,' Zidra murmured, before striding off.

The Neutral Bay ferry had just arrived and people were streaming off it. Zidra didn't look behind her to check if Wendy was following. After an elderly couple boarded, she slipped into the front of the queue and surged on board, ignoring the hissing of the woman behind her. Quickly she moved along the side of the cabin and sat on a hard wooden seat on the deck in the bow of the boat. A cool breeze was blowing and she guessed that few people would want to sit in such an exposed position. One of the deckhands unslung the ropes and pulled the walkway on board. Seconds later the ferry chugged away from the wharf. Zidra kept her eyes firmly fixed on the Opera House, its white shells stark against the relentless blue. She watched the two red cranes, slowly shifting, like vast insects straddling the curving construction.

Someone sat down next to her so abruptly the seat rocked. She turned. 'Good to meet you, Wendy,' she said, smiling. 'Is that your real name?'

The girl nodded, her face giving nothing away.

'Thanks for coming. You do know that I'm a journalist, don't you?'

'Yes. That's why I'm here.'

'Good. We haven't got all that much time. Neutral Bay and back, that's all, and we don't know how many people will be getting on at Neutral Bay. We mightn't be able to talk much on the way back.'

'That's all right.' The girl's voice quavered. 'It'll only take twenty minutes at most to tell you what's been happening.'

'Do you mind if I record you?'

The girl looked suspicious. At once Zidra said, 'Okay, it doesn't matter. I'll take notes instead.'

Wendy hesitated before blurting out, 'You can record me if it's easier. Just don't say my name, that's all.'

'Okay. Now tell me how it all began.'

Wendy started to talk rapidly and sometimes so softly that her words were lost to the breeze and the wailing seagulls, and several times Zidra had to ask her to repeat what she was saying. Wendy was involved with an Aboriginal-land-rights movement and had, several months before, moved from northern New South Wales to Redfern, where she was staying with friends in a shared house. The trouble had begun when the house was raided by the police and marijuana had been found, some in her backpack. She knew several of the others smoked it, but she didn't. She'd never touched it, never. She'd seen what ganja and booze and petrol-sniffing did to you. Clearly it had been planted on her.

'You're shivering.' Zidra pulled a cardigan from her bag and spread it around Wendy's shoulders. She sensed that Wendy wasn't as strong as Lorna, who was made of a sterner material tempered by fire.

Wendy explained that, after the police had planted the marijuana, they'd arrested her and in due course they'd let her go, after the man called John said the charges against her would be dropped if she became an informer. The Abos were a bunch of no-good Communists, that's what John had said. After she'd been released, she'd got in touch with Legal Aid in Redfern and that's how she'd made friends with Dave Pringle's daughter. John had recently found out about her visit to Legal Aid, and only yesterday he'd found her and told her to keep away from bloody lawyers or else. The girl now glanced around in great agitation.

'You're okay,' Zidra said. 'No one's seen us together.'

But suddenly Wendy ducked below the gunwale. 'John's there,' she said, her voice breaking. 'He's on the jetty.'

Zidra turned off the tape recorder and stowed it out of sight at the bottom of her bag. Then she stood up and leant on the railing. There were perhaps half a dozen people standing on the wharf at Neutral Bay but she couldn't make out their features from this distance. 'Go inside,' she said but it was to the empty air. She saw a flash of blue dress through the window behind her. After picking up the abandoned cardigan, she moved to the other side of the boat. Sheltered by the cabin, she could nonetheless distinguish the people on the jetty. Her heart skipped a beat as she saw that one of them was indeed Steve Jamieson, alias John Ordinary.

She walked along the deck and slipped inside and up onto the top level. Protected by the cabin, she watched the passengers disembark. Wendy wasn't among them. She ran down the stairs and saw her slipping into the toilet cubicle, and heard the snick of the bolt as it slid across. Running upstairs again she scrutinised the new passengers boarding the ferry. Mr Ordinary was still standing on the wharf, arms akimbo, watching. Just as the deckhand was about to pull on board the walkway, Mr Ordinary dashed over it. She could see him taking a position on the lower deck outside. He was holding up his camera as if he were a tourist taking photographs of the harbour foreshore. It had a telephoto lens, she observed and wondered if he'd seen her and Wendy together.

For the rest of the voyage she remained where she was, keeping an eye on Mr Ordinary. Back at Circular Quay he was the first to disembark and at once he vanished into the anonymity of the crowd. *Probably watching or photographing from somewhere in there*, she thought. As she passed the toilet door, she saw that it was still locked. On the wharf, she waited by the milk bar. The next passengers were about to board and there was still no sign of Wendy. At the last minute Wendy got off and sprinted across the finger wharf and onto the ferry on the other side. *Wise girl, and stronger than she looks*, Zidra thought. She hoped that Mr Ordinary, or another of his ilk, wouldn't be waiting for her at the other end.

Zidra walked over the street and caught the first bus that came along. It was heading for West Ryde. She alighted at the Town Hall stop and flagged down a taxi.

'The *Chronicle* building,' she told the driver before settling herself in the back.

'You look very pale,' the driver said, peering into his rear-vision mirror. 'Feeling okay?'

She succeeded in transforming her frown into a smile. 'Never better,' she said, although the cold emptiness inside her was growing again. She began to tremble and hoped she wasn't going to faint.

Once inside the *Chronicle* building, she made straight for her bolthole in the ladies' room. Perched on the shut lid of the WC pan, she fought the vacuum inside her by counting the mosaic tiles on the floor. When she'd reached three hundred, the void had shrunk to a manageable size and she unfastened the door.

Her face looked ghastly in the mirror above the washbasins. She pinched her cheeks. Fluorescent lighting was terribly draining, she told herself. Maybe a bit more make-up was called for. She opened her bag and pulled out a red lipstick. A part of her had been amputated with Jim's death and the wound gaped still. *When will I heal*, she asked her reflection. *When will I heal?*

Concentrate, said her reflection. *Concentrate on your work and the time will pass.*

Wendy Ferris and Lorna, she answered back. *Focus on Lorna and Wendy. Here, now. They're what you must think of. Their stories, their treatment.*

CHAPTER 26

Zidra's office telephone rang for the fifth time in ten minutes. She picked it up wearily. 'Hello, gorgeous,' said a familiar American voice. 'I've been thinking of you. Wondering if you'd like to meet up for lunch again.'

'I'm busy at work.'

'You still need to eat,' Hank said. 'Couldn't you manage to get away for an hour or so? Or we could have dinner, if that's easier.'

Not dinner, she thought. *Definitely not dinner.*

'There's a great new restaurant I'd like to take you to. My treat.'

'Thanks, Hank. It's really sweet of you but I'm barely holding it together. Too tired all the time. Maybe in a couple of weeks?'

'Okay, gorgeous. I'll call you then.'

'Lunch not dinner,' she said firmly.

As soon as she put the receiver down, it rang again. 'There's a fellow here who wants to see you,' said Emma from reception. 'Are you free?'

'Who is he?'

'Won't give his name.'

'I'll come down right away.' People who wouldn't give their names were either time-wasters or had a story to tell. Mostly the former, and she'd become expert at getting rid of them.

She picked up a notebook and pen from her desk, just in case, and slipped them into her bag. She took the staircase rather than the lift. It was faster and, with a bit of luck, would give her a chance to observe the visitor before he saw her. Pausing on the landing at the top of the last half-flight, she inspected the brown-haired young man pacing around the lobby. He was short and overweight; walking wouldn't be his usual activity. The tweed jacket, blue button-down shirt and moleskin trousers were the uniform of someone from the country, although the briefcase wasn't. He looked vaguely familiar and she wondered where she'd seen him before. Or perhaps it was just the type that she recognised.

She clattered downstairs two steps at a time and saw him turn towards her.

'Zidra Vincent,' he said, his voice light but steady.

When he shook her hand, he held it longer than was customary, as if testing its weight. Taller than him by a few centimetres, she looked down into the glistening yellow-brown pebbles of his eyes – the most interesting feature, she thought, in a pleasant but otherwise unremarkable face. When he released her hand, she noticed that his fingernails were bitten down to the quick.

'You don't remember me, do you?'

'Well, you certainly look familiar but I can't quite place you. Do we know each other?'

'You were three years ahead of me at Burford High. Everyone in my year knew who you were.'

'That's often the way,' she said easily. 'You know the people ahead of you but not the ones behind. Everyone trying to grow

185

up faster than they need to. Always looking ahead.' She wondered if he was fabricating this connection; she could have seen him anywhere. 'What's your name?'

'Malcolm Edgeworth.'

'Oh, Malcolm Edgeworth! You're Jane's little brother.' She recognised him now, though she hadn't seen either him or Jane for years. 'My, how you've grown!' She laughed but noticed he didn't smile. He was tensed up and nervous; she'd have to go carefully with him. 'What are you doing now?'

'I'm in my honours year of Arts at Sydney University.'

'That's great. There weren't too many of us at Burford High who went on to university.'

'No. Three in my year, that's all.'

'And Jane, what's she up to?'

'Married with a kid and living in Eden. Listen, I've got something to tell you, but here's way too public. Can we go to your office?'

'We could, but it's even more public than this. Open-plan. I can take you to a quiet room though, where we won't be overheard.'

In the interview room he sat down opposite her. 'I've got something to tell you,' he said again. 'I think you might find it very interesting.'

'Do you mind if I take notes?'

'No. That's what I want you to do.'

She took out her notebook and pen. He began to talk, so fast that several times she had to ask him to slow down and repeat what he'd said. Three years ago he'd been recruited by ASIO as an agent. Her excitement grew as she listened. She noted he didn't make eye contact but stared at a point behind her head. For the first couple of years he'd felt honoured that he was serving his country, he said. He'd always been deeply patriotic. He'd been told to gradually infiltrate a number of organisations. It had taken a long time. He'd been informing for ages but now he was having a crisis of confidence. He thought what he was doing was wrong. He'd been young and naive when he'd agreed to be an ASIO agent and had made a mistake.

When he'd finished, she thought for a moment. He began to pull at a piece of loose skin next to his fingernail, so hard it must be hurting, and she looked away. *Mustn't reveal my enthusiasm before making a few checks*, she thought. Carefully she said, 'How did it work? Who handled you?'

Malcolm stopped pulling at the loose skin and folded his hands on the desk. He looked at her now, his eyes more yellow than brown under the artificial lighting. 'An ASIO officer called Mr Jones. I met him every third Tuesday in a café in Kings Cross. Then we'd go outside and sit in his car, and he'd debrief me.'

'Why did you do it?'

'For my country.'

'Did you get paid?'

'Yes, quite well.'

'How much?'

'Well it wasn't very much at first. Fifty dollars each month. But then last year it went up to four hundred a month.'

'What did you report on?'

'Members, party meetings, car number plates, home telephone numbers.'

Making it easier for those people to be tracked, she thought. *Cars followed, phones bugged, meetings infiltrated.* 'Which groups in particular?'

'Anything left wing really, and lately the Aboriginal groups.'

'Could I reveal your identity if I wrote you up?'

'Yes. I want this to be an exposé of what ASIO's doing. I think it's wrong. I want my name in the article. I started on this because I was patriotic and I thought it was the right thing to do. Now I know it was wrong but I'm not ashamed that I've changed my mind. I'm still patriotic. I feel that by exposing it I can make up for what I did.'

'Why do you think it was wrong?'

'Last year I did a course in political science and I started to think about things. Like how closely should a security intelligence organisation check on the private lives of ordinary people. And how far is ASIO motivated by other interests that have nothing to do with national security.'

'Good questions,' Zidra said. 'But getting to more practical things, can you name people? Mr Jones doesn't sound like a real name.'

'No. It probably isn't.'

'Do you know a Mr Jamieson?'

'I once met Steve Jamieson. He reports to ASIO.'

Zidra felt suddenly very cold and shivered. 'How do you know?'

Malcolm frowned. 'Mr Jones told me. And I met Jamieson at Jones's flat. He took me there once, for a little party, and Steve Jamieson was one of the guests. I reckon the flat was borrowed, actually. In fact I wouldn't be surprised if it was borrowed from the organisation.'

To conceal her excitement, Zidra pulled out a handkerchief and blew her nose. *So this is it*, she thought. *Now I have both sides of the story*. Until today she'd felt she was getting nowhere as she trawled through her contacts in left-wing groups. All she was finding was suspicion and paranoia about ASIO. Nothing of substance.

'I'm not doing this cloak and dagger stuff any more,' Malcolm said.

'Okay. But tell me, why come to me?'

'I know you and I trust you. And the *Chronicle* is the only small-l liberal newspaper in New South Wales. I certainly couldn't go to your competitor. It's as simple as that.'

She said, 'I won't let you down.'

'I know that.'

'And you feel you're a good judge of character?'

'Yes. I never trusted Jones. It was my own character that I misjudged. I thought I could do this spying stuff and I thought that the end justified the means. But I've changed my mind about that. Now I know myself better.'

'I'll have to verify this, Malcolm. Do a few checks. Can you help me there?'

'You bet I can.' He pulled out a manila folder from his briefcase. 'You can't reveal I've got this though. I don't want to be arrested.'

'Neither do I,' said Zidra. 'I'll have to call in my editor, Joe Ryan, on this next. Are you happy with that? He'll have to deal with the legal aspects.'

'I have to do this, Zidra. I have to make up for the wrong I've done.'

'Good man,' she said, smiling. Already she was thinking of how she would weave this exposé into the narratives of Lorna and Wendy. It was going to make a terrific story.

CHAPTER 27

The Gladstone pub was becoming way too popular, Zidra decided. When Lorna had phoned the day before, she'd suggested meeting there rather than the usual place in Darlinghurst. Zidra circumnavigated the crowded tables around the perimeter of the saloon bar, before threading her way through the dense mass of people who hadn't arrived early enough to bag a table. All the doors and windows were open but there was no breeze, and cigarette smoke hung heavy in the air.

It was when Zidra was wriggling past the scrum in front of the bar that she glimpsed Lorna at the far end. Resting her elbows on the counter top, she was holding a dollar note in her hand. Although facing the man serving, as if waiting to be noticed, she wore a preoccupied expression. Indeed, she seemed to be focusing on something distant, something over the heads of all the drinkers.

Zidra changed direction, narrowly missing the schooner of beer that a burly six-footer with no neck was pointing her way. 'Watch it, love,' was his first response, quickly followed in an altogether different tone by, 'Hello, babe. Looking for anyone?' Smiling, she shook her head. There was no point trying to reply against the noise: raised voices competing with one another to be heard, waves of sound bouncing off the walls and rippling back into the room, myriad conversations in which only the loudest could communicate.

A smile stuck on her face like a Band-Aid, she negotiated a path through the interweaving stories. At last she reached Lorna, who was still staring across the room, seemingly oblivious to what was happening in her immediate vicinity. When Zidra kissed her cheek, Lorna started.

'Hell's bells, you gave me a shock.'

'Sorry, Lorna, but we did arrange to meet. That was a kiss for the Sleeping Beauty.'

'How are you, Dizzy? You look exhausted.'

'I'm coping. Working hard helps me forget a bit.' She felt her eye twitch. This had been happening a lot lately and she hoped it wasn't noticeable. She didn't want Lorna getting needlessly rattled. 'And how are you? You seemed distracted, like you were miles away.'

'I guess I was. Well, twenty metres away, to be precise. I thought I saw someone come in that door.'

'That was me, Lorna. I've just arrived.'

'No, through the far door. You didn't come through that. I've been watching it all the time.'

'What's up? You seem really on edge.'

Lorna bent forward so that her mouth was close to Zidra's ear. 'Give me your hand, would you?'

Almost at once Zidra found she was clutching what felt like another of the microcassettes. Carefully she turned it over in her palm, before slipping it into the pocket of her skirt. She said, 'Do you want to go somewhere a bit quieter?'

'No, this'll do just fine.'

'What was wrong with the usual meeting place?'

'Too close to home. Time for a change, I reckon. But even so, I think I might have been followed here. Not by Steve or John or whatever he's called, but by someone else.'

'Who?'

'You won't be able to see him from here because he's just moved out of sight. He's mid-twenties, average height, ordinary looking, like Steve. I saw him watching me when I was waiting for the bus in Oxford Street. When the bus came, I got on and at the last minute he hopped on too. When I got off, I thought at first he was staying on, but he leapt off just as the bus started moving. So I turned down Queen Street, took a left, then a right, and immediately hid in a doorway. I saw him go by, walking fast. After a minute I came out again, thinking I'd lost him, but two minutes later he was tailing me again.'

Zidra glanced around the room.

'Don't look so obviously, Dizzy. Just relax.'

'How can I, after what you just told me?'

'Well, I've got to head off again in a couple of minutes. You're late, you know. I'd buy you a drink but this bloke behind the bar's never going to serve me, even though I've been waving a dollar note at him.'

'I don't really want a drink, but thanks anyway. I'm going to Stella and Nic's for dinner. Nic always tops up your wine glass when you're not looking, so you can't gauge how much you're drinking. It's best to arrive there cold sober. What's on the tape?'

'Listen to it and see. More threatening stuff, only this time against me.'

'You and not Daisy?'

'Yes. And it's not nice.'

'You'd better tell me.'

'You'll hear it on the tape.'

'Tell me.'

'He says I'm not leaking fast enough. He threatened to plant drugs on me and then arrest me. Said they'd follow that up with a beating in the police station, and worse.'

'That's terrible. And you've got it all on tape?'

'Yes.'

'We'll soon be ready to print the story. Joe's had the legal aspects checked and we're okay. I'll transcribe this new tape tomorrow. Thank God it's Sunday. By the way, Joe thinks you should move into a safe place somewhere, once the story's printed. He offered to put you up at his place.'

Lorna raised one eyebrow and drew down the corners of her mouth.

'Don't look so horrified. The Ryan family's really nice. You'd love his wife, Bridget, and they've only got two boys at home now.'

'I don't want that, Dizzy. Get the story out fast. I just need some peace. I feel like things are spinning out of control. My exams are less than a month away and I'm desperate for some time to study.'

'Give it some thought, Lorna. Let me know in a day or two about staying with the Ryans.'

'Okay. Look, I'm going to have to leave in a minute. Mick's picking me up at the top of Queen Street in five minutes.'

'Who's Mick?'

'My flatmate. You've met him.'

'Oh, that Mick. The incredibly handsome one with the big smile and the nice teeth.'

'That's him. My, you are observant.'

'That's why I'm a journalist. And I saw you with him at the march. He was wearing a T-shirt with the Aboriginal flag on it, like you.'

'What are you grinning about?'

'Nothing. Well, not quite. I'm just very pleased.'

'We're only friends.' Lorna smiled for the first time. 'I'm out of here now, Dizzy. You look after yourself, won't you. Don't come with me. Stay here for a bit.'

Zidra watched Lorna until she was swallowed up by the crowd, and then pretended she was waiting to be served. It was a good place to pick if you didn't want a drink, she thought; not once did the barman glance in her direction. After ten minutes or so, when she saw the burly six-footer heading her way, she left the hotel by the side door.

Outside the humidity hung heavy in the air, wrapping itself around her like a blanket. She stopped in front of the grocery shop fifty metres down the street from the pub. An observer would assume she was inspecting the array of small goods rather than checking to see if she was being followed. Obliquely she looked up and down the road. No one was paying her any attention. The crowds on the pavement in front of the Gladstone were getting more raucous but they were engrossed in each other and the sound of their own voices. A few couples were strolling down the hill in the other direction and a jogger was running along the road as if he had right of way. She watched him pass by, wearing a dogged expression and a sweat-soaked T-shirt and running shorts. He looked to be in his mid-forties and anyway was too tall to be the man Lorna had described.

Although Zidra had planned to go home before Stella and Nic's dinner party, there was nowhere near enough time now. She remembered a short cut, a long narrow lane running between the backyards of the rows of terrace houses. This would take her straight to the street in which her friends lived. For an instant she hesitated at the corner. The lane was empty, apart from a few garbage bins that hadn't been claimed since the last refuse collection and a supercilious-looking white Persian cat. Glancing around, Zidra saw that the jogger had gone and only the self-absorbed crowd in front of the Gladstone remained. Apart from the cat, no one was interested in her. She ran a hand over her skirt pocket, feeling the microcassette tucked securely away, before turning into the lane.

After several metres the cat altered its expression to one of enquiry, and she bent down to give it a quick pat. When she was straightening up, she heard footsteps behind her. Revolving quickly, feet poised ready for flight, she was relieved to see that there was no one in sight. The sound she'd heard must have been a resident of one of the houses pottering about in their backyard or about to reclaim their garbage bin. Someone called out, 'Pussy pussy pussy.' At this the cat abandoned its dignity and Zidra, and leapt onto the top of the paling fence and down the other side.

Zidra began to stride along the lane. The light was fading and the way was longer than she'd thought. When the single street light was switched on, she flinched; it was almost as if someone were watching her progress. Her nerves were going to pieces. What was she thinking of to take short cuts through deserted alleyways in the evening with an important tape in her pocket? Her palms became clammy and her pulse sped up. Quickening her pace, she once more heard footsteps behind her. Firm steps, leather slapping down on bitumen.

She stopped and the footsteps stopped too. Again she turned. There could have been a person crouched behind a garbage bin twenty or so metres away, or it could have just been a shadow. The sudden screaming of an ambulance made her jump. She broke into an adrenalin-charged sprint to the street at the end of the lane. The ambulance sped by, its siren wailing and light flashing. At this instant she bumped hard into something and gave a little yelp. It was a couple, whose features she barely registered, so intent was she on peering behind to see who was trailing her.

The lane was empty.

It was her imagination, nothing more.

'So sorry,' she said to the woman standing next to her. 'I thought I was being followed.' As her heart rate slowed and her panic abated, the features of the couple became more clearly focused. An elderly pair, their faces lined with the passage of years and too much sun, their expressions as anxious as hers must have been.

The woman took Zidra's arm. 'There's no one there that I can see, dear. But you really shouldn't walk down lanes like that on your own, in the daytime or the night-time. Where are you going? Do you want to walk with us?'

'Yes, thanks. I'm only going a short way. To that white terrace house with the red front door.'

The elderly couple waited with her until the door was opened by Nic, his shoulder-length black hair as unruly as ever. After she'd thanked them, Nic ushered her inside.

'What's up?'

'Nothing. Apart from the fact that I thought I was being followed.'

'That's unlikely, unless you mean those old folk you came with. This place is as safe as a country town.'

As safe as Jingera, she thought. But she hadn't always felt safe there.

'Mind the floorboards, they're a bit rickety. I haven't had time to nail them down properly but at least the wiring's done. We're going to eat in the kitchen. The dining room's still full of boxes.

Follow me and I'll get you a glass of wine. Is red okay? We've just opened a bottle.'

Now she could admit that she felt desperate for a drink. As she followed Nic along the hallway, she wondered if she was losing her grip. She patted her skirt pocket. The cassette was still there. But there was no point taking any more risks. She would get a taxi home that night.

CHAPTER 28

The next morning Zidra woke with a start and looked at her watch; it was ten minutes past nine. How had it got to be so late? She'd gone to bed before midnight and had planned to go to the office to transcribe Lorna's new tape this morning as well as work on her article. She sat up and reached for the notebook and 2B pencil on the bedside table. After adjusting the pillows behind her back, she began to make a list of points. ASIO were violating their charter and reporting to the Liberals; ASIO were endeavouring to fabricate links between Aborigines and Communists to wriggle out of land-rights issues and to satisfy vested interests and lobbyists; ASIO were blackmailing young Aborigines, using threats to get them or their families welfared or jailed if they didn't toe the line.

She chewed the end of her pencil. The ideas she wanted to get across were the warp; they would hold the article together. But the weft was the important thing, the human stories that would bring colour to the tapestry. After some thought she began to write, her pencil skipping over the pages. She stopped only to sharpen the pencil and flex her aching fingers. By noon the new draft was done. All she needed to do next was listen to Lorna's latest tape.

After a shower she looked for some clean underwear. There was nothing. Everything was in the dirty-linen basket. She pulled on the knickers and bra she'd worn the day before, and retrieved from the basket some crumpled trousers and a shirt. They would do for today. She'd drive to the laundromat and come home for a quick lunch before heading off to the office with Lorna's cassette.

———

It was mid-afternoon before Zidra opened the drawer in which she'd put the cassette the night before. It wasn't where she thought she'd left it, under her tights. Maybe it had slipped to the back of the drawer, but it wasn't there either.

Could she have put it in another drawer? After all, she'd been pretty tired last night. She sifted through the other drawers. No sign of the cassette anywhere.

Maybe she'd left it in her handbag, although surely she wouldn't have been that careless – she never left anything really valuable in there. Her irritation with herself was beginning to turn to anxiety as she fumbled through the compartments of her bag. She found the pink lipstick she thought she'd lost a few weeks ago but the cassette wasn't there. Now her apprehension was starting to metamorphose into panic.

Had someone broken in while she was out? She glanced around the room. Everything looked much as it had before she went out. Or did it? The papers on her desk were misplaced and the portable typewriter had been shifted. Had she done that? After all she hadn't really been concentrating on anything apart from her article and how much more work she still had to do on it. Keeping her depression at bay, that's what she'd been concentrating on.

And yet she didn't think she'd been anywhere near her desk. Someone must have come into her room and taken away the cassette.

She ran downstairs and knocked on Joanne's bedroom door. After the second knock Joanne opened it. Her hair was tousled and her face marked from lying on creased sheets. 'Sorry to wake you,' Zidra said. 'Have you been here all morning?'

'No.'

'When did you get back?'

Joanne looked at her watch. 'Maybe an hour ago.'

'When I was at the laundromat?'

'I suppose so. You weren't in, that's for sure.'

'I think someone's been through my room when we were all out. Lisa wasn't here today, was she?'

'No, she's staying at Ross's place. She always does that on Saturday night.'

'And she didn't come home?'

'No. As far as I know, she'll be back around eight tonight, as usual. What's missing?'

'Just something from work. A little cassette.'

'Maybe you left it in the office. You've been pretty distracted lately.'

'I know I didn't leave it in my office. I brought it home last night.'

'But Zidra, the house was locked when I got back. Both the front door and the back door.'

'I'll check there's nothing missing anywhere else.'

They went through the house together, including a quick inspection of Lisa's room. It was a tip, with clothes everywhere and the bed unmade, but that was nothing new.

'Perhaps you should call the police, Zidra.'

'I don't think so. Anyway, what could I say? Nothing else is missing. They'll say what you said: "I expect you left it in your office. You've had a lot on your mind lately."'

'Sorry. I didn't mean to sound patronising.'

Zidra decided to phone Joe Ryan. An hour later she was sitting in his office, telling him of her suspicions about the cassette. When she'd finished, Joe sat in silence, frowning so hard his eyebrows met in the middle. She tapped her foot on the leg of the chair. Maybe he'd want to hold the story back, and then everything she'd worked for could be lost. Even if he agreed to run with it, if anything else happened – another massacre in Vietnam or Africa, or some sex scandal – the story might be lost or displaced, at best a tiny paragraph hidden away between the advertisements for David Jones and Gowings.

'We'll run with the article,' Joe said, rubbing the back of his neck. 'We'll put it out on Tuesday. You've got it just about finished, haven't you?'

She swallowed. The draft she'd done this morning was pretty good, she thought, but it needed more work. Could she do it in time? Of course she could do it in time. Rising to the challenge was all that was keeping her going *after Jingera*. 'Yes,' she said. 'It's well on the way. I was going to add that extra stuff Lorna gave me though.'

'What did it say?'

'I think it was more of the same. Lorna couldn't tell me much – the pub was really crowded. But she did say that Steve, the cop from intelligence, is starting to put more pressure on her. Threaten her. She seemed pretty rattled. She reckoned she was being followed. I reckon I was too.' She told Joe of the footsteps she'd heard behind her as she walked down the lane.

201

'You need to take care of yourself, Zidra. But it sounds as if losing the tape won't make much difference to your story. Let me see the draft, will you? You could give the article a final polish tomorrow. Having the cassette go missing could work in our favour. But if someone's been into your bedroom to steal it, now's the time to get Lorna shifted somewhere. She mightn't be all that safe at her place until this is out. Bridget and I would be only too happy to have her stay with us for a few days until things quieten down, like I said to you the other day.'

Zidra stood up. She felt in control of her life for the first time in weeks. After all, the story she'd wanted to tell was roughly in place. Another few hours' work this afternoon and evening and it would be ready.

It would have been good to have Lorna's extra material, but she knew that sometimes you just had to make do with what you'd got. That's what she'd been struggling to teach herself. Make do with what you've got.

CHAPTER 29

Zidra decided to drop in to see Lorna. It would be easier to persuade her to accept Joe's invitation personally rather than by phone. She hadn't visited Lorna's house for ages; they'd thought it best that she didn't. Though there was space right outside Lorna's place, she parked fifty metres away. Before getting out of the car, she checked in the rear-vision mirror to make sure she hadn't been followed.

The road was as deserted as a small country town, although she could hear the hum of traffic from the main thoroughfare a block away. The night was moonless and Lorna's single-storey terrace house in a pocket of darkness between street lights. Zidra peered up and down to see if she was being watched. Not a soul in sight, though she could hear voices raised in argument from a house over the road and the sound of a television from next door.

The low gate to Lorna's verandah was shut, and she fumbled with the catch. The roof of the verandah was in need of replacing; several sheets of corrugated iron were missing and another one was loose and clanged as the wind worried at it. Becoming aware of the doormat only after tripping over it, Zidra fell hard against the front door, bumping her elbow. A syncopated crash from the verandah next door startled her, and a second later she heard a cat meowing and an empty milk bottle rolling across concrete. This announcement of her arrival went unnoticed by anyone. She knocked on the door.

No one answered. Through the obscure glass panel in the front door she could see that a light was on somewhere inside, and she could hear the sound of a radio or a television. She knocked again, more loudly this time, and at last heard footsteps.

The door was opened by an Aboriginal man of around her age and height. Lorna's new flatmate, she guessed, who'd moved in a month or so ago.

'I'm Zidra,' she said. 'Lorna's friend. Is she in?'

'I'm Jeff. I've heard a lot about you. Lorna's not back yet but she shouldn't be too much longer. Do you want to come in? You're shivering.'

Zidra followed Jeff down the long narrow hallway and into the kitchen at the far end. A radio was playing country music. On the table was a plate with a few abandoned baked beans and next to it was a can of beer. 'I'm sorry,' she said. 'I've interrupted your dinner.'

'It's okay. I've just finished. Would you like a cup of tea?' As Jeff spoke, he turned off the radio before clearing the table and filling the battered aluminium kettle with water from the tap over the sink.

'Do you mind if I use your bathroom? I know where it is.'

She went out to the tiny backyard and into the lean-to bathroom at the back of the house. Over the old-fashioned rust-stained bath a couple of Lorna's shirts and a white plastic curtain were suspended from the shower rail. As she was drying her hands, she heard a loud knocking from the front door. *Lorna home at last*, she thought, before common sense told her that Lorna would have a key with which to let herself in.

She turned off the bathroom light and stood for a moment on the uneven brick paving outside the kitchen. A sweet scent, orange blossom perhaps, or jasmine, overlaid the faint odour of drains. Through the open doorway she could hear Jeff unlocking the front door. The kettle was simmering on the stove but something made her hesitate rather than moving at once into the kitchen to turn it off. Now she heard footsteps thudding along the hallway. She stayed where she was, out of sight, as first one policeman and then another erupted into the kitchen. They were too big, or the kitchen was too small. Solid men, both of them. Their short-sleeved blue shirts strained across their chests, and bulky tooled-up belts encircled their waists. Next to these big blokes Jeff looked as puny as a fifteen-year-old.

'Any idea where Lorna Hunter is now?' The larger of the two policemen, with the closer-cropped hair, leant towards Jeff as he spoke.

Jeff stood his ground. 'No.' His face could have been no more than twenty centimetres away from the policeman's collar.

'Having a cuppa, are you?' the second policeman said. 'I thought you said Lorna wasn't here.'

'She's not.'

'What have you got two mugs out for then?'

'For a friend.'

'A friend, eh? I don't see any friends here, do you, Keith?'

'No. There aren't any friends here,' Keith said. 'Unless you count the two of us. But maybe there's some more friends behind those doors we passed on the way down the hall. Don't mind if we have a squiz in a minute, do you, mate?'

'You've got no right to come barging in here without a search warrant.'

'We make the rules, mate, not you. Any idea when Lorna will be back?'

'No.'

'Maybe we'll just have a seat here and wait. You don't mind, do you? Maybe Lorna'll be in for that mug of tea in a minute, that's what I reckon.'

At this point Zidra opened the back door and stepped in. Both men swivelled around in triumph. When they saw her, their expressions altered. Disappointment that she wasn't the one they'd been looking for, but predatory as well, their eyes moving up and down her figure as if she were up for sale. Yet she was pleased with this reaction: they hadn't recognised her as Lorna's contact; they were viewing her only as Jeff's girlfriend.

'Is this mug for you?' Keith said, grinning.

'Which mug do you mean, mate, the cup or this fellow here?' the smaller policeman said, and both of them laughed.

'What are you doing here, love?' Keith moved close to her as he spoke.

Perhaps there was something wrong with his sense of distance or else he was trying to intimidate her. Looking up at him, Zidra was close enough to see a few blonde whiskers on his neck that had escaped the morning shave. 'I'm just visiting,' she said and stepped back a pace.

'Well, so are we. But maybe it's time for us to go.'

On the way out the larger policeman, Keith, stopped at a closed door. 'Where does this door lead, mate?'

'A bedroom.'

'Sure there's no one in there?'

'Positive.'

'Don't mind if we have a look?'

Before Jeff had a chance to reply, Keith opened the door, flicked the light switch and stepped in. Zidra wriggled past the smaller policeman obstructing the doorway and watched Keith closely as he looked around the bedroom. His fists were balled on his hips, exposing dried sweat-stains in the armpits of his shirt. Though he might have been poised to punch someone, at least in this pose his hands were clearly visible; she could spot right away if he were to dig into his pockets for little packages to plant. Or to pick up an object that wasn't his.

'You can't do this without a search warrant,' she said.

'Can't do what? We're not doing anything.'

'Can't search.'

'Well, there's no independent witness here now, is there?'

'I'm an independent witness.'

'I don't think so, love.'

You'd be surprised, she almost said, and then thought better of it. Sometimes it was wise to keep your mouth shut.

He shepherded her out of the bedroom and stood in front of the next door. 'And what about in here?'

Though the smaller policeman moved to block her way, Zidra was too quick and followed Keith into the next bedroom. This was Lorna's. The bed was neatly made but had garments strewn across it, as if Lorna had been trying on clothes for an evening out. On her desk were piles of law books and a couple of folders. Keith bent down to look under the bed and stood up again with a struggle and a grunt.

Jeff was ahead of them into the third bedroom. Zidra observed the men from behind. No little gifts, no little plants, and she sighed with relief. After this the policemen thundered to the front door. They opened it and banged it shut behind them.

Zidra and Jeff stood in silence while they listened to the receding thump of police boots on the footpath. Soon afterwards came the slamming of car doors, and the sound of a car being started up and driven away.

'They'll be back,' Jeff said.

'They may be too late,' Zidra said, more confidently than she felt.

Only now did she realise that neither she nor Jeff had asked why the police were looking for Lorna. She thought of her last conversation with her friend, in the Gladstone pub on Saturday. There'd been more intimidating stuff, Lorna had said, only this time against her. Threats to plant drugs on her and then arrest her. Threats to beat her up in the police station.

Zidra felt that the two policemen who'd just visited would relish that sort of thing.

'Lorna and Mick will be back soon,' Jeff said. 'Lucky they didn't return while the pigs were here.'

'She needs to get away from here,' Zidra said.

'Too bloody right,' said Jeff.

CHAPTER 30

Since arriving at work that morning, Zidra hadn't had a moment to herself. It may have been a long day but it was rewarding too, for now the Tuesday-morning edition of the *Sydney Morning Chronicle* was spewing out of the printing machines, with Zidra's article on the front page. Piles of newspapers were being parcelled up and fed into the distribution network; they would travel into the heart of Sydney, into the suburbs, and on to the more distant towns of New South Wales. Bundles of papers were being loaded onto vans, onto trucks, onto trains, absorbed into the network connecting the communities of this vast state.

And once Zidra's piece had been read, other media would take up the story: radio and the television networks, and the press agencies, who would distribute it to all the other states and territories, including the federal capital. There it would cause an uproar, Zidra knew. For it was the coalition government that had allowed this police state to develop, that had used the security intelligence organisation as a tool for its own political purposes.

Although Zidra's article did not prove this, it was what she suspected. It was what Joe Ryan suspected. It was what thousands of others like them suspected. Her article dealt only with the

209

specifics. It made clear the type of blackmail in which the intelligence arm of the New South Wales Police was engaged, and the Special Projects Section of ASIO too.

Time and time again Zidra inspected the front page of the *Chronicle*, which was spread out on the table next to her desk. Though she knew her article off by heart, it gave her a glow of pride just looking at it and at its continuation on page two. Occasionally, when no one was looking, she ran her hand over the newsprint and each time felt a thrill of excitement. To think that she could have written that, the girl from Jingera, a place no one from Sydney or Melbourne had ever even heard of.

'It's dedicated to you, Jim Cadwallader,' she whispered. 'To your memory. To my very best friend, and the love of my life.'

She retrieved a handkerchief from her handbag and blew her nose loudly before inspecting her face in the compact mirror. She looked exhausted but she certainly wasn't going to miss the celebrations in the pub across the road. 'My shout,' Joe had said. 'You deserve it.'

I deserve it, and so too does Lorna, Zidra thought as she absent-mindedly powdered her nose. While Lorna wasn't her only contact, she was the most important one. It was Lorna who'd taken all those risks to obtain hard evidence. Lorna who'd recorded Steve trying to blackmail her and more. Lorna who'd recorded him saying explicitly that the goal of his activities was to damn the Aboriginal-land-rights movement. Few people would like this. Certainly not the Aborigines, certainly not the growing number of Labor Party supporters. For different reasons the coalition government wouldn't like this either, for there was to be an election next year. *The prospects don't look good*, Zidra thought, *for the prime minister or his government.*

This country was becoming a police state, she reflected as she ran her fingers through her unruly hair before peering again at the tiny mirror in the compact. It was the Labor government who'd set up the security organisation after the Second World War, prodded by pressure from Britain and the United States. But how far should this surveillance go, she wondered. What should it be used for? Would it ever be feasible to monitor whoever was drawing the line between surveillance for national security and surveillance for political purposes? What was clear was the necessity of stopping misuse of all the information that was accumulating, hour after hour, day after day, week after week.

She put her powder compact into her handbag before calling Lorna's house. The phone rang and rang but no one answered. After this she made a half-hearted attempt to tidy her desk. Was it going to be possible in the longer term to limit the amount of information collected by the authorities? Probably not. Technology would change, new methods of snooping would be devised.

She picked up the telephone again. After dialling Lorna's number, she listened to the ringing while she hummed the theme tune from *The Avengers*, her favourite television program. At the ninth ring, the phone was picked up.

'Hello?'

'Hi, Jeff. Is Lorna home?'

'She's gone out. It's Zidra, isn't it?'

'Yes, sorry, I should have said.'

'It's okay, I recognised your voice.'

'Did she get back all right last night?'

'Yes, but not till very late.'

'Thank heaven. I was worried. Have you had any more visits from the cops?'

'No.'

'Thank God for that. Can you tell Lorna to phone me when she gets back?'

'You bet, though not if it's after midnight.'

She laughed and hung up.

———•———

By the time Zidra unlocked the front door of her house, it was well after eleven o'clock. Lisa and Joanne were in bed and the house was in darkness. Although she still felt on a high, fatigue and disappointment that she hadn't seen Lorna were starting to creep around the edges of her euphoria.

The sausage roll she'd eaten at the pub wasn't much of a dinner and her stomach was growling with hunger. As she put some bread into the toaster, she saw the note on the writing pad next to the phone. Her heart jumped. It would be from Lorna, surely. She picked up the pad: 'Zidra, your mother rang and wants you to phone back.' A glow of pleasure briefly drove away fatigue. But it was too late to phone Ma now, and anyway she didn't want to be on the line if Lorna called.

After eating two slices of toast and cheese, she crept upstairs and cleaned her teeth. Too tired even to wash her face, she stripped off her clothes in her bedroom, leaving them where they fell on the floor. She tumbled into bed and, a moment later, into oblivion.

———•———

Tuesday morning in the newsroom. Phones were ringing, voices shouting, fax machines whirring, people rushing around the office, pats on the back, a senior politician on the line to Joe.

While Zidra was speaking to an anchorman from a television news program, the receptionist handed her a piece of paper. Zidra glanced at it, her attention elsewhere. 'Your mother phoned. Ring back today.' She put the slip of paper on her desk. She'd phone her later, as soon as there was a free moment.

The day wore on. There was talk of a parliamentary enquiry. There was talk of a Royal Commission. The government was embarrassed; the opposition was exultant. Activists were enraged; the organisers of the moratorium marches gleeful. There were phone calls of congratulations, phone calls of opprobrium. Letters to the editor were already arriving, some hand-delivered to reception.

It was a good day, her best ever at the newspaper.

At around nine o'clock that evening Zidra decided to drop in to Lorna's house on the way home. She found a parking space right outside.

The door opened as soon as she knocked. It was Jeff. 'Zidra, our paper girl. That was a beaut article in the *Chronicle*.'

'Thanks. Is Lorna in?'

'No. She hasn't been back since yesterday.'

'You mean she didn't come home last night?'

'No. She hasn't contacted you?'

'No. And Mick's not home either?'

'He was here this morning and went out later. Looking for Lorna, he said.'

'So you don't know where she is and Mick doesn't either?'

'That's right. Mick thought she might have been with you. He tried to reach you at work.'

'It's been impossible today. The lines have been busy all the time.'

After giving Jeff her Paddington phone number, she drove home. Her stomach was churning with anxiety. Confidence in the success of her scoop was disintegrating. It was surely no coincidence that the police had been seeking Lorna two days ago and that Lorna had disappeared at the same time as Zidra's article had been published in the *Chronicle*.

But where on earth could she be? Could she have been picked up by the police? Zidra carried on along Oxford Street after the junction in Taylor Square. If the police could fabricate some charge against Lorna at the Third Moratorium March, they could do so again. It would be easy. Plant some drugs on her, or some subversive material: fictitious donations to the Vietcong, that sort of thing. Or allege that she'd assaulted a policeman, or caused a disturbance in the streets. Rough her up a bit, or have her disappear altogether.

But it was too late for all that stuff. Surely the police would never dare to pick her up after the story in today's newspaper. Or would they? She shivered. You could never know what they would do, or what they might be ordered to do.

From the phone in the kitchen she called her mother. The Ferndale number was engaged. It was a party line, so this signified little about her mother's whereabouts. Next she tried some mutual friends. Although full of congratulations, they didn't know where Lorna was and promised to ring her as soon as they had some news. Feeling sick with anxiety, Zidra rang Joe. 'She'll turn up,' he said. She thought he didn't sound all that convinced, or perhaps the flatness in his voice was simply fatigue.

Again she tried phoning Ferndale, and still the line was engaged. After toying with the idea of calling the police, she looked up their number and dialled it. If either of the policemen who'd muscled their way into Lorna's house picked up the phone,

214

she'd just hang up. The phone was picked up by someone whose voice she didn't recognise. She told him she was calling about a missing person, Lorna Hunter.

'How long has she been missing?'

'Over twenty-four hours.'

'Not long then. She'll turn up, don't worry.'

'Have you arrested anyone of that name?'

She thought the man hesitated for a moment before saying, 'No, love.'

Next she decided to ring St Vincent's Hospital and eventually managed to get transferred to someone willing to talk to her. Lorna Hunter hadn't been admitted. After this she tried all the other Sydney hospitals. Nothing. But how could Lorna just vanish like this? No one had heard of her. No one knew where she was. It was as if she didn't exist.

By now it was nearly midnight and way too late to try phoning Ferndale again. There was nothing else she could do tonight. When she went to bed, she found it hard to sleep. Eventually she dozed, disturbed by dreams in which she was chasing someone whom she thought was Steve, who was pursuing Lorna through labyrinthine streets, streets that seemed to twist and turn forever, until at last she wrenched herself awake, body sweating, face wet with tears.

She switched on the lamp and looked at her watch. It was not even four o'clock. She sat up and had a sip of water from the glass on the bedside table. Afterwards she picked up a novel and struggled through a couple of pages. It was impossible to concentrate. *I've pushed Lorna too hard*, she thought. *Wiring her up was dangerous. It's left her exposed.* Worse, her bloody article had compromised Lorna and now she'd be paying the price. And it was all her fault. How stupid she'd been. Blinded by ambition, kidding herself she was doing Lorna a service, when all the time she'd been endangering her friend.

The ground beneath her had gone with Jim's death, and an abyss lay yawning in its place, with only a few bare roots to grasp in order to stop the plunge. For the last few weeks she'd been clutching at these but now that her article was finished, and Lorna had vanished, even those bare roots had gone. There was nothing to halt her fall.

Where was Lorna? If only she knew. Murder could be made to look like an accident. Lorna could be lying dead on a road somewhere, deliberately knocked down by a car. Or incarcerated in a police cell, abused and without hope. How could she continue if she lost Lorna as well as Jim? She would be to blame and her life wouldn't be worth living.

CHAPTER 31

At seven o'clock Zidra dialled the Ferndale telephone number. As she listened to the ringing of the unanswered phone, she bit off a ragged piece of fingernail with her teeth, too impatient to get an emery board or the nail scissors. It tore off too far back and would hurt for days. She cursed softly. Still the phone purred on like an oblivious cat. Surely Ma hadn't left the house this early. Why the bloody hell didn't she answer after five rings the way she usually did? After thirteen rings the receiver was picked up and she heard her mother's voice.

'Sorry, Ma. Did I wake you? You're normally up and about by now.'

'I was outside. I'm so glad you rang. I've been trying to reach you for ages. Congratulations, darling! That was a wonderful piece in the *Chronicle*. We're so proud of you.'

'Thanks.' Her voice cracked. The article was nothing without Lorna to share it with.

'Did you get my messages?'

'Yes, and I did try to call you several times. Listen, something's happened to Lorna. She's vanished, days ago now.'

'Lorna vanished? No darling, you're wrong.'

'Of course I'm not wrong.' Zidra's anxiety was now overlaid with annoyance. Carefully enunciating her words, she said, 'Please help me find her. I'm so worried something awful's happened to her.'

'She's fine, Zidra.'

Her mother's calm voice maddened her. The voice of reason, as if Zidra were some crazy person fabricating anxieties. Controlling herself with some difficulty, she said, 'Lorna's gone. She's not at her house. No one knows where she is. I've got to find her.'

'But that's why I was ringing you. You won't have to look far. Lorna's right here, at Ferndale.'

'At Ferndale?'

'Well, not quite here. She's in the manager's cottage. She turned up a few days ago with a portmanteau and a whole lot of books. Said she needed somewhere quiet. A safe house. She said you'd told her to find one.'

'You mean she's been there all the time?' Relief served to fan her irritation rather than souse it. She snapped, 'Why the hell didn't you tell me? You could have said that in your message. And it's not a bloody *portmanteau*, it's an overnight bag.'

'There's no need to swear at me, Zidra. If you'd called me when I first phoned, you would've known. Lorna asked me not to put it in the message. Think about it, it makes sense. She didn't want the police to know where she is after all that's happened to her.' Zidra's mother was talking fast, the way she did when she was upset, and her Latvian accent was more pronounced. 'I wanted Lorna to stay in the house with Peter and me but she said she'd rather be in the cottage. You know what she's like, incredibly independent. More so even than you. The cottage was terribly dusty but she and I cleaned it out in a couple of hours, and then Peter shifted in the folding bed and an old card table and a couple of chairs. She's been working in there ever since. Her exams are really soon, you know. Shall I get her for you?'

'Yes, please.'

'I'll phone you back in about five minutes.'

'Ma?'

'Yes?'

'Sorry I was cross.'

'No worries. She'll be right.'

Ma indulging in Aussie-isms was always a good sign. After replacing the receiver, Zidra sat cross-legged on the landing floor. Through the open bedroom window she could hear noisy miner birds screeching as they gathered in the palm tree several houses away. When the phone rang a few minutes later, she picked it up at once.

'Hello, Dizzy. Really glad you called.' Lorna's voice was so gay she couldn't have known she was a missing person. 'We've been trying to reach you for days.'

Zidra visualised her friend sitting comfortably in the Ferndale hallway next to the telephone table. She said, 'Why didn't you tell me where you were going? You could have got a message to me. Didn't you trust me? Was Steve following you?'

'I was worried he might be, or one of his minions. And Jeff told me the police had been looking for me. Anyway, you did say I should go somewhere safe.'

'But why didn't you tell me where you were going? Mrs Ryan was expecting you. She had your bed made up and everything.'

Lorna laughed. 'Oh, Mrs Ryan made the bed – what an effort. Honestly, Dizzy, you sound so bloody suburban sometimes. Remember that I couldn't contact you. God knows, I tried. Your line was always engaged. You knew I was being followed in Sydney.'

You knew the phone was being tapped. It probably still is. Mick borrowed a mate's car and drove me down to Nowra and then I got on the bus. I wanted to come south to my country. To come home. I couldn't go to Wallaga Lake Reserve though. I thought the police would have someone watching that, and so I came on to Ferndale. I knew your parents would look after me.'

Lorna paused, and then said in a rush, 'That was such a terrific article you wrote. Really terrific. And it was especially courageous of you to run with it after all that happened. I know you've been grieving for Jim and yet you still managed to do all that work. You've been so brave.'

'Brave?' Zidra couldn't imagine that this word would ever apply to her.

'Yes, brave. Brave and courageous.'

'Not me. You're the brave one,' Zidra said, her voice unusually high. 'Always have been, all the time I've known you.'

'You mustn't underestimate yourself, Dizzy. Never. I'm incredibly lucky to have you as my friend.'

Zidra's vision blurred. She wiped her eyes with the back of her hand. 'Me too,' she said. She might have told Lorna that she loved her if she hadn't feared she would break down altogether. She managed to say, 'I'm so glad you're safe.'

'Thank you for everything, Zidra.'

Only as she put the receiver down did she notice that Lorna had just called her Zidra rather than the usual Dizzy. It was because Lorna was hanging out with Zidra's parents, she told herself, nothing more than that. Their friendship was the same. Hadn't Lorna just told her she was lucky to have her as a friend? It seemed that these days she was looking for conspiracy everywhere.

All things conspire.

And yet anyone with an ounce of rationality must know that much of her life was just one damned random event after another.

Jim would know that more than anyone. She sat on the floor and began to sob as she hadn't done since Jingera.

All things conspire to hold me from you. All things conspire.

PART V

Mid-November 1971

CHAPTER 32

Walking up the hill towards Oxford Street, Zidra tripped on a lager can that someone had left on the ground. The can clattered across the pavement and glittered in the sunlight. She picked it up and looked about for a bin. The street was dirty. Gusts of wind lifted up food wrappers and plastic bags, and tossed them around like small kites dancing along the pavement. At the pedestrian crossing beyond the supermarket, a small stooped woman in a long black coat waited for the lights to turn green. The coat was too large and hung almost to the ground. A huge black beret framed like a halo the woman's dried up brown face, paradoxically possessing the expression of a small child looking out at the world with intense wonder. Then the lights changed and the traffic came to a stop. The woman picked up her torn plastic holdall and began the struggle to walk across the road, every step an agonising effort. When she reached the opposite kerb, she put down the bag so that all her energy could be directed towards climbing the step to the footpath.

Zidra's heart ached. *That could be Ma in twenty years' time,* she thought, *and me in forty years, sooner probably.* When the pedestrian lights turned green again, she crossed over Oxford Street.

At the entrance to Centennial Park, she joined the trickle of people moving through the gates. She found herself behind a couple pulling along a reluctant silky terrier on the end of a tartan lead. The man was shorter than the woman by a good head. He had an arm around her waist, and her arm was resting on his shoulders, her hand caressing his neck. After overtaking them, Zidra looked back and saw the man's head lolling into the woman's caress. She felt a stab of envy. No one loved her like that.

She knew what the trouble was. She was in a state of limbo. Now that her mission was finished and her article published, she'd have to find some other issue to investigate. It wouldn't be hard; there was plenty wrong with this city and this country. But in the meantime she felt beached and alone. She wanted, with a desperation that shocked her, to feel someone's arms around her. She wanted comfort. Physical comfort.

Get moving, get cracking, you're not here for soul-searching, she told herself fiercely, *you're here for some exercise*. After running a few hundred metres, she slowed down. All of a sudden she thought of Hank. She didn't even have his telephone number, though she had asked him for it.

—◦—

'I'll miss you,' Hank had said that night over a month ago now, the week before she and Jim had travelled to Jingera. 'Do you mind if I phone you at Ferndale?'

'Of course not,' she'd said, even though she'd wondered if this was wise. They were simply two people whose lives were briefly intersecting before arcing away on different trajectories. Yet she'd added, 'I must get your home phone number too. I looked it up in the directory the other night but it wasn't listed.'

Ignoring her comment, he'd glanced at his watch. 'It's time I went home. I can't believe it's nearly one o'clock. I've got a busy day tomorrow. Today, rather.'

'So have I,' Zidra had said lightly. Hank had an exasperating tendency to assume that he was the only busy person. 'You'd better get going.'

He'd climbed out of bed and begun to dress quickly. She'd got up too and pulled on her kimono. After tearing a sheet of paper from her notebook, she'd written on it her parents' phone number. Hank had carefully folded it into a small square before tucking it into his wallet.

As she'd opened her mouth to ask him again for his phone number, he'd leant down and kissed her parted lips.

Later, before she unlocked the front door, they'd kissed once more. It was only as the door clicked shut after him that she'd remembered he still hadn't given her his home phone number.

———◆———

Ever since Jim's tragedy, she hadn't wanted to see Hank. Though she'd met him twice since Jim's memorial service, that was only for lunch. In a way she'd enjoyed seeing Hank; he was lively and quick-witted, and could make her laugh. Yet at the same time he was too much of a distraction from what else was happening in her life.

But she was no longer so sure. She started running again and almost fell over a large black Labrador dog dragging its owner along on the end of a leash. *I would welcome seeing Hank now,* she thought. *But there's something I must do first.*

The next day she waited until Dave Pringle was relaxing with a cup of coffee before asking him, 'Could someone working at the US Consulate be with the CIA?'

'You mean the consulate rather than the embassy?'

'Yes. The Sydney consulate.'

'It's possible,' Dave said.

'But presumably only intelligence coordination with Australian officials?'

'In principle. Nothing focused on Australia or anything internal. There are agreements forbidding that.'

Zidra handed him the photocopied page from the US Foreign Service Register that Stella had given her. 'Is this man likely to be working for the CIA, do you think?'

Dave pulled a pair of glasses out of his breast pocket and put them on. After reading the page several times, he said, 'Henry Fuller. Military draft shorter than it would've been for a CIA recruit. Consular affairs track, and he's got all the right credentials for that. His promotions haven't been suspiciously fast and so far he hasn't spent any time in unstable Latin American or Eastern European fringe states.'

Dave pursed his lips before adding, 'Mind you, this isn't from the latest register. It's at least three years old, I reckon. Most embassies have the yearly copy. Every time a post has a vacancy coming up, they get a list of everybody bidding for that job. Then foreign-service officers can use the register to get an idea of an applicant's assignment pattern and background and can pinpoint anyone who's deep-cover CIA. But anyway, based on what's here, this bloke looks pretty straight to me.'

That evening Zidra wrote Hank a note and posted it to him care of the US Consulate. She kept it short and innocuous:

Dear Hank,
Let's meet for dinner.
Best wishes,
Zidra

———◆———

Zidra was too early. She and Hank had arranged to meet at a fancy restaurant that had recently opened in downtown Sydney. Although it was raining, people were thronging the pavements. She alighted from the bus at Market Street. The wind blew the rain up under her umbrella and threatened to turn it inside out. In high-heeled shoes that she hadn't worn for weeks, she tip-tapped around leaves and rubbish skittering hither and thither, driven by a wind that couldn't make up its mind where it was blowing from.

The blustery weather exacerbated her nervousness. When meeting Hank was a prospect and not a reality, she'd been quite looking forward to it; but the closer she got to her destination the more unsure she was becoming. Perhaps she was mistaken about Hank being fun. After all, she hardly knew him.

She heard someone call her name. There he was, shouting at her from the other side of the street. His cream trench coat flapped as he ran between the cars, revealing khaki trousers, blue shirt and navy tie. He had no umbrella and his hair was dripping wet. A metre away from her, he stopped and held out his arms. 'Great to see you, gorgeous.' He leant under her umbrella and kissed her on the mouth. 'Serendipity. Now neither of us will have to wait for the other at the restaurant.'

While maintaining his hold on her shoulders, he beamed at her. He'd just come from a consular do but she didn't really take in the detail of what he was saying, so surprised was she by her pleasure at seeing him again.

'You're all wet, Hank,' she said. His eyes looked darker than she remembered, as if the grey evening had absorbed some of their colour.

'Say that again.'

'You're all wet.'

'No, say my name.'

'Hank.'

'I love the way you pronounce it.'

She smiled. 'You haven't been listening to enough Australian accents.'

In the restaurant they were shown to a quiet table for two by the window. She sat facing the room and Hank sat opposite, the candlelight illuminating his face. She watched him obliquely while he studied the menu. After ordering, they talked about the success of her article until her attention began to wander.

'What are you thinking?' he said. 'You look miles away.'

She hesitated. She longed to ask him how seriously he was taking her but knew this wasn't really fair, when the last thing she wanted was for him to turn the question back to her.

Hank broke the silence by saying, 'I hoped you'd agree to see me again. I was so happy after you sent that note.' Although his face was impassive, he leant towards her and looked her straight in the eye. 'And that's why I'd like to go home with you tonight. God, I've missed you so much, Zidra.'

Her laughter sounded artificially high. Without thinking, she said, 'Have you ever been married?'

Though he began to play with a fork, he kept his eyes on hers. 'Yes. What do you expect? I'm thirty-five, after all.'

I might have guessed, she thought. *He's really too good to be true.* She wondered why that hadn't shown up on the register that Dave Pringle had examined so closely. He must have got married after that entry.

'But we're separated,' he continued. 'Julia works in the States. We broke up when I was posted here two years ago. We'd been married less than a year.' Looking down at the tablecloth, he began to sweep some stray breadcrumbs into a neat pile. 'We're going to get divorced. She's found someone else.'

'That's tough.' She wondered why he hadn't told her before. Perhaps she simply hadn't given him a chance.

Still he didn't look at her but transferred his gaze to the single white rose in a silver vase in the centre of the table. She glanced at the bloom. Although its petals were tightly furled, they were beginning to wither at the edges.

'Do you blame yourself?' she said.

'No. It wasn't anyone's fault.'

There was a pause, during which she could hear the conversation at the adjacent table. Three men dressed in almost identical dark suits appeared to be discussing the plot of a play but after a couple of seconds it became clear it was the outline of a TV commercial.

'And have you had many affairs since you separated?' she said. A normal person, she thought, might have asked these questions ages ago, when they'd first met and certainly before they'd first slept with each other.

'Are you interviewing me?' He sat up straight in his chair and looked mock-serious. Then he took her hand and said, 'I've had one affair since, and that's with you.'

'Was that an affair? It was very short-lived.'

'I remember every minute of it. I know you've just lost someone you loved and it must be hurting like hell. Don't frown, Zidra, I do understand, and I don't want to wound you or to rake up the past. But don't lock me out, please.'

'No lockout. You make it sound like an industrial dispute.'

He laughed, and the conversation turned to lighter matters.

Dinner was soon over, the coffee cups cleared, the waiter hovering restlessly nearby and the restaurant starting to empty.

Hank insisted on paying, on the grounds that it was his idea to eat at an expensive place. While he was dealing with the waiter, Zidra found the ladies' room. As she was washing her hands, she wondered how you could want someone so much when you still loved another. And was she being fair to Hank? She'd never given him much of a chance. She'd been wrong to think he'd been snooping that first time he visited her house. Perhaps he'd simply fallen in love with her.

It was then that she decided to invite him back to her house in Paddington.

———

Having Hank's warm body close to her all night, waking with him next to her, would surely keep the blackness away. His arms were around her still. Though his breathing was slow and steady, she guessed that he wasn't asleep. 'Are you awake?' she whispered.

'Yes.' He kissed the top of her head. 'I'm your guardian angel keeping watch over you.'

She laughed and stroked his cheek, remembering his earlier tenderness, that touch of skin upon skin, and, best of all, that banishment of self, that oblivion. She would have oblivion again if only Hank would stay the night.

He kissed her neck and then her collarbone. 'It's amazing how one little action that we repeat so many times over a lifetime can have so much meaning.'

'I haven't repeated it enough over my life,' she said.

Afterwards she closed her eyes and listened to Hank's regular breathing. Not since before Jim's death had she known such peace. She drifted into sleep with Hank's arms around her.

Later she woke to see him standing with his back to the bed, pulling on his trousers. 'Aren't you going to stay the night?' she asked.

He knelt by the bed and kissed her lips. 'Next time. I have to go home for a change of clothes.'

'But it's Saturday night.'

'I know, but we've got an important visitor arriving early in the morning from Washington and I've got to take him into the consulate. I won't have time to go home if I stay here overnight.'

'When will we see each other again?'

'I'll call you. I love you, gorgeous. Truly madly deeply.'

Shock and confusion warred within her. The words came easily to Hank. He was generous with his feelings, and open. Was it possible that Hank might fill the gap in her life and keep her from the abyss? But wouldn't that bring responsibility? She wasn't ready for that, but nor did she want to hurt him.

He kissed her again, before saying, 'I promise I'll stay the next time. Maybe tomorrow night? I'll call you.'

The bedroom door clicked shut behind him and she heard the creak of the staircase as he made his way out. Although she'd managed to sleep earlier, with his arms around her, now she felt wide awake.

What was it about making love that could make her forget everything? With my body I thee worship. Religion and sex, were they one and the same? She thought of what Hank had said in her bed: 'Oh God. Oh God. Oh God.'

Turning her face into the pillow, she inhaled the fading scent of him. The trouble with life was that nothing ever lasted. Everything was evanescent: sex, love, security, friendship.

She sensed she would always fail at a game whose rules were beyond her comprehension. And now that she was alone, she felt again those waves of dark despair sweeping towards her. All the hard work of the past few weeks had been little more than a dyke – a temporary dyke – to stem the rising tide. With the article finished, the furore nearly over at least until the Royal Commission, she had no more defences at her disposal. She had no higher ground to run to, and yet still the breakers were rolling towards her.

CHAPTER 33

Six o'clock in the morning. Zidra rolled over for the hundredth time and adjusted the folded-up T-shirt that was supposed to be supporting her lower back. If she could ever muster the energy to go shopping again, she'd replace this lumpy old mattress, though maybe it wouldn't make much difference.

Opening her eyes, she saw golden light fingering the edges of the curtains. Already she could hear the racketing of the noisy miner birds from their colony in the palm tree several houses away. At this moment the telephone rang. She staggered onto the landing.

'Hello?' The line was terrible and the static so bad that she couldn't tell if it was a man or a woman speaking. 'Hello. Who is it?'

There was more crackling on the line.

'Who is it?' she repeated, more loudly this time. 'Hello?'

The line hissed some more. She said slowly and clearly into the mouthpiece, 'I think you'd better hang up and try dialling again.'

After putting the receiver down, she waited by the phone. No one she knew would call this early unless it was an emergency.

A minute later it rang again. On picking it up, she was irritated to discover that the static was almost as bad as before. She wondered if something might have happened to her parents. 'Hello,' she articulated carefully. 'Zidra Vincent speaking. Who is this?'

At last she could distinguish several words. A man with a French accent wanted to speak to Sandra, or perhaps it was Alexandra.

'There's no one here with that name,' she said.

'No, no. I need to speak to Sandra.'

'You've got the wrong number,' she said wearily before putting the phone down. Feeling dizzy with fatigue, she took the receiver off its cradle again and left it lying on the floor, before lurching back to bed. She lay face down, confused by the emotions she was feeling. Did she want Hank or didn't she? She didn't want his declaration but she didn't want to be alone either. Being alone gave her too much time to think. Too much time to think of all she'd lost since losing Jim.

After a while she rolled onto her side and put a pillow over her face. For nearly an hour she lay still, unable to move. Just before seven o'clock she reached out for the dial of the radio on the bedside table. With a bit of luck, after the news was over, the commentator's voice would lull her back to sleep, or at least distract her from her thoughts.

For a moment she hesitated, hand on the radio dial. Depression washed over her, so that even the act of turning the knob seemed like a struggle. She knew with the rational part of her being that the days would pass and her anguish would slowly diminish. And maybe her affair with Hank would help. Yet, underneath it all, that yawning abyss would still lie. At any moment she could go plunging into it. Down, down, down, into the desolate black depths.

After switching on the radio, she rolled onto her back. It was impossible to concentrate. If asked what the news was about, she wouldn't be able to report a single detail. All she could hear were words jumbled randomly together. None of them made sense at all, until a particular name seized her attention: *James Cadwallader*.

James Cadwallader! Perhaps it was an obituary. Or maybe another journalist had been killed or captured. She sat up too quickly and her head began to spin. No, this was no obituary, and no more correspondents had been captured either, at least not this weekend. 'The Australian correspondent, James Cadwallader,' the newsreader announced, 'had phoned United Press International from Kampong Speu late yesterday.'

This must have been some cruel mistake, a vicious hoax. Jim was dead, his body cremated.

Yet in measured tones the newsreader was describing how four journalists had been released by the Vietcong after weeks spent in the Cambodian jungle. Picked up on Highway Four, they'd been taken by helicopter to Phnom Penh airport. The news summary ended and the weather report began.

With shaking hands Zidra fiddled with the tuner, trying to pick up another radio station with a longer bulletin. There was nothing but music, a Sunday church service from St Botolph's, sports commentary, a program about exchange rates. Maybe she'd dreamt the news item. No, no; that wasn't right. She'd been wide awake for hours. Or perhaps someone else had turned up on Highway Four and she'd heard Jim's name because it was always on her mind. That had to be the most likely explanation.

She stumbled onto the landing and picked up the telephone receiver. Her trembling hands made dialling difficult. It was only on the third attempt that she managed to get through to a colleague at the *Sydney Morning Chronicle* whom she knew was on the night shift.

'What's come in from Cambodia?' Her voice sounded calm but she could hear blood pounding in her ears. 'Anything on Jim Cadwallader?'

'Yes, something came in a couple of hours ago.'

'What did it say?'

'He and three other journos were picked up by the South Vietnamese Army on Highway Four. They'd been prisoners of the Vietcong, who decided to release them. Lucky it wasn't the Khmer Rouge is all I can say. They're all okay apparently. Two have got malaria.'

Malaria was treatable, unlike death. 'Where are they now?' she said.

'Somewhere in Phnom Penh. Do you know them?'

'I know Jim.'

'Great tale, I reckon. Lazarus arising from the dead, eh? Of course the press were everywhere when they were Medevaced to Phnom Penh airport, even though the air-force people tried to keep them away. So there'll be pics as well as stories in all the newspapers. They'll have a few yarns to spin, you can bet.'

After Zidra rang off, she lay face down on the bed and buried her head in the pillow. Now she began to feel a deep and extraordinary calmness. Time was ticking away, the earth rotating, the oceans bulging with the pull of the moon, waves pounding inevitably on beaches. But for an instant she was at peace, a fixed point of stillness.

The moment passed. She stood up and looked at her smiling reflection in the glass. Jim was alive and she was a different woman now. Quite how he would have been changed by his weeks of capture she had yet to find out.

———•———

Standing next to the phone on the landing, Zidra willed it to ring. The calls she'd received earlier must have been about Jim's release. She might have missed countless messages about this when she'd had the phone off the hook. After a few moments she picked up the receiver and dialled the Cadwalladers' number in Jingera. It was answered right away by George.

'You know,' he said, recognising her voice.

'Yes. It was on the news just now.'

'We tried to ring you earlier but your line was engaged. The embassy called us. It's so amazing I still can't quite believe it. Eileen keeps saying it's like a resurrection.'

'It is indeed.' But she didn't want Jim ascending into heaven quite yet. 'Have you spoken to him?'

'No, not yet. He's asleep now. Apparently they were all exhausted and there was a bit of a media circus in Phnom Penh, the embassy cove said. We'll be talking after lunch today and he'll be phoning you then too. All we know is that he's been a prisoner of the Vietcong for the best part of a month.'

'This is the most fantastic news ever. Do you know why they were released?'

'Not yet. The embassy did say that it was probably because the Vietcong worked out they weren't from the military.'

'Whose body was found then?'

'It could have been anyone's. The fact that the Cambodians cremated it so soon made it hard to tell. It was a Caucasian male, that's what the Cambodians said, but they could have made a deliberate mistake. It was someone who had a gold tooth like Jim's. Apparently that's how they identified the body. That and the civilian clothes.'

239

After they'd hung up, Zidra continued to stand on the landing. Jim's sentence – and her own – had been miraculously reprieved. If she believed in a god, she would find a church and offer up thanks. As it was, she believed only in the forces of nature and she knew that Jim's salvation had been due to luck.

But still she would pay homage to the sky and the spinning earth and the blazing joy of the day.

CHAPTER 34

Although it was early, the sky was already an enamelled blue. The leaves on the trees lining the street, washed by the rain of the previous day, fluttered like victory flags in the light breeze. Zidra drove to a secluded park on a narrow promontory overlooking the iridescent harbour.

I'll swim, she thought. *There's no one around and what better way to mark the morning?* After peeling off her dress, she flung it onto the grass. Wearing only her bra and knickers, she ran to the harbour's edge. Rippling waves formed by the westerly breeze flirted with the incoming tide. She dipped one foot, then the other, ankle-deep in the water that slid over her warm skin, as tender as a lover's touch. A few more steps and she was submerged up to her thighs. Bending her knees, she felt the silky caress of the water sliding up to her waist. Abandoning herself, she lay on her back, feet tilting upwards as her head settled back onto the buoyant surface. The whole length of her body was supported now; she was at one with the water the ocean the sky.

She scissored her feet and was gently propelled backward. Deliberately she raised her right arm, elbow straight, and stretched it behind her. Sweeping it down, fingers and palm aligned into a blade, she felt the resistance of the water as she pushed hard against it with her hand. Then back with the other arm, and she was starting to pick up speed. Faster she scissored her legs; she was shooting backward now. The sunlight glanced off the drops of water falling from her raised arm, an arc of sparkling crystals that made her heart sing.

Jim had died and risen again. He was alive and all Sydney was celebrating.

The sun on Zidra's skin warmed her damp body and began to dry her soaked bra and knickers. Sitting on the coarse buffalo grass, she listened to the morning's jubilant chorus. The triumphant slip-slap of the waves against the shore, the joyous cries of seagulls circling the rocks, the gleeful pulsing of cicadas in the shrubbery behind her, the laughing voices of runners jogging by the water's edge.

The park was starting to fill with people, none of whom took the slightest notice of what she was wearing. After her underwear had dried, she pulled on her dress before strolling along the path to the street in which she'd left the car. As she passed through the park gate, she almost collided with a tall man. They both stopped short, apologising. At this point she recognised him. Smiling, she said, 'Well, if it isn't Hank! What a nice surprise to see you in these parts.'

'Hi, Zidra.' Hank's voice was cool, his embarrassment almost palpable. It was only now that she noticed he was holding the hand of a brunette with a smooth pageboy bob. Like Hank, she was wearing a navy jacket, white shirt and beige cotton trousers. *I can't believe it*, she thought, and in the next instant, *I might have guessed. And what a preppy pair.* Involuntarily she raised her hand to her tousled damp hair and flicked out of her eyes the fringe that she hadn't had time to have trimmed.

'I'd like you to meet my wife, Julia,' Hank said. 'She arrived back this morning.'

'Julia, how lovely to meet you.' Zidra held out her hand. She felt nothing but relief tinged with curiosity.

Julia extended her hand. On her wrist she wore a thick gold chain and on her left hand a wide wedding band. Zidra continued, 'I've heard so much about you from Hank.'

'Is that so?' Julia might have been looking at her rather suspiciously or perhaps it was just that she had the sunlight shining into her eyes. 'And you two know each other from where?'

'I'm a journalist,' Zidra said. Avoiding the question was a trick she'd learnt from interviewing politicians. 'Well, I must dash. It was lovely to meet you, Julia, and so nice to see you again, Hank.' With that, she proceeded along the path at a cracking pace and turned into a side loop through the shrubbery, where her body shook with hysterical laughter. She had no need to give another thought to Hank's feelings or how she was going to get rid of him. And he was a double liar, deceiving her as well as Julia.

After she'd stopped laughing, she began to feel sympathy for Julia. She looked lovely – just the sort of woman you might pick for him if you were arranging the perfect marriage. Zidra shrugged and sauntered on. When she'd almost reached her car, she heard him calling her name.

'Well, if it isn't Hank again,' she said. 'What have you done with your wife?'

'She's waiting in the car. She's just got in today, as I told you. We've had a trial separation.'

'I don't believe anything you say. Especially what you said last night.' Then he'd been lying to her with his words for sure, but had he also lied to her with his body?

'I didn't tell you any lies. It was all the truth.'

'Was there truth in the words, or in the actions?' she said.

'In both. How can you think otherwise?'

She thought again of that oblivion, that loss of self that she'd experienced with him. For half an hour she'd forgotten herself. Did it matter with whom? Yes, of course it did, or at least to her. The oblivion came with the trusting. She said, 'You didn't tell me the truth about your visitor from the United States.'

'Of course that was the truth.'

'Your visitor, was it Julia?'

'Yes.'

'You said it was a he.'

'Did I? A slip of the tongue.' He smiled.

'Do you tell me what you think I want to hear?'

'Sometimes. Doesn't everyone?'

'No, Hank. I don't think they do,' she said. But she didn't care any more. Nothing about Hank concerned her any more.

'It's not like you think it is.'

'I don't want to hear any more lies.' Of course it was possible that Hank hadn't told the truth about anything. Again she wondered who'd broken into the Paddington house and stolen the cassette that Lorna had given her. She never had learnt what had happened to it, though she could guess it was either in the hands of ASIO or else had been destroyed by Steve. That tape didn't matter though, not now that Lorna's story, and those of others like her, were in the public domain. But there was something else that Zidra wanted to clear up with Hank. She said, 'Why did you take photographs of me at the Fourth Moratorium March?'

244

'Because you're gorgeous and I wanted to go to bed with you.'

'You must take photos of a lot of women if that's your rationale.'

He laughed again.

He thinks he's charmed me, she thought. 'What did you do with the photographs?'

'I keep them in the drawer of my office desk.'

'Did you give a copy to ASIO?'

'No, why on earth should I? They'll have their own people following you, you can bet on that.'

'They have a file on me.'

He looked interested. 'Have you seen it?'

'No. They gave it to my editor but we decided not to look at it. It was only a copy of course.'

'They'll have an even bigger file on you after your piece in the *Chronicle.*'

'Do you mean the one that's likely to result in a Royal Commission?'

'Yes.'

'I should think they'd be shredding stuff in my file now rather than adding to it.'

'I wouldn't know about that sort of thing. I only deal with passports and visa applications.'

Was he telling the truth about this? She would never know. And did it matter? Probably not. She said, 'Why did you say you were separated from your wife?'

'Because I was. And anyway, I didn't think you'd care. Ages ago you said you were a free spirit and didn't want involvement with anyone.'

'Did I? Does that translate into an invitation to be dishonest?'

'Would it have made a difference if I'd told you the truth?'

She shrugged. 'That's not really the point.' She didn't want to admit, even to herself, that earlier today she'd been hoping for more from Hank.

'Can I see you again?' he said.

'No.'

'I heard the news about your friend Jim. You must be thrilled.'

'Oh, I am.' But she had no intention of discussing Jim with him. She said, 'Goodbye, Hank. It's all over now. Your wife looks lovely, by the way. Appreciate what you've got instead of hankering after what you haven't, if you'll pardon the pun.'

He grimaced before saying, 'She only returned today. She travels overseas a lot. You and I, we did have some fun, didn't we?'

'We did, but maybe we both knew it couldn't last. And it's all finished with now.'

He didn't look too pleased, and she guessed that he was usually the one who did the dumping. She watched expressions flit across his face: annoyance, followed by resignation, followed by what might even be wry amusement. 'See you around, Hank,' she said.

CHAPTER 35

Never before had slouching in an armchair felt this good, and it had been a long time since Jim had felt this clean, although it had taken three baths to wash away all the ingrained dirt. Dominique's Phnom Penh apartment was sparsely furnished but that was one of the reasons he liked it; that and her black and white photographs adorning the whitewashed walls. Opposite him she was stretched out on a cane chaise longue, reading a book. Several packets of Gauloises and an overflowing ashtray lay on the wicker table next to her. After an afternoon of interviews and the night of celebrations at the Hôtel le Royal, he'd been delighted to take up her offer of somewhere to stay. She'd missed the revels the night before and would soon want to hear of his experiences first-hand, but with her usual tact she read on, giving him the peace he needed. His own place was his no longer, and his few possessions gone. The clothes he was wearing were borrowed from a Canadian photographer, who was his height. His feet and legs were painful, the sores throbbing still.

A light breeze shifted the curtains of the open French windows. The sound of the traffic seemed alien after weeks of hearing only jungle noises interrupted by artillery and bombing raids. He sipped a glass of orange juice and stared vacantly at the newspaper on his lap, struggling to adjust to his new surroundings. Eventually Dominique interrupted his reverie, evidently deciding that half an hour was sufficient to provide the peace he'd said he was searching for.

'When did they tell you they'd be letting you go?'

'Four days ago.' He still couldn't believe that they'd made it safely back to Phnom Penh.

'And how did you find out?'

'The bloke who usually gave us the daily re-education lecture turned up but instead of the lesson he told us we'd be released the following day. We were stunned, though we'd been hoping. Anyway, what he actually meant was that there'd be a release *ceremony* the next day. That was a strange experience. They began by taking photographs of each of us, in the new green military clothes they gave us. Then there were group photographs, standing with all the soldiers.'

'What do you think they're going to use them for?'

'Propaganda, I expect.'

'What happened next?'

'They sat us down on benches and an old fellow, who seemed to be someone from high up, read out a statement in Vietnamese. It was translated by an interpreter. "According to the humane principles of the Liberation Armed Forces, the journalists are today released and given safe passage to the agreed release point." After that there was a whole lot of stuff that I had trouble following, and then they gave us a signal to clap. And we did. Enthusiastically. Then we had to sign.'

'Sign what?'

'The speech, and a piece of paper listing our belongings. They kept all the cameras though. "Now the tools of the imperialists and their lackeys will serve the Liberation Front," they said.

'We each had to make a statement and they tape-recorded the whole thing. We were hoping the recorder wouldn't work. The last thing we wanted was to feature on Radio Hanoi. Then Kim asked if we could take back news of the nineteen other journalists like us who'd been reported missing. The old chap looked a bit annoyed and began another long speech. "Foreign journalists shouldn't travel with Lon Nol troops. In battle anything can happen. It's impossible to tell what will occur. No other journalists have been captured in this area."'

Probably the others had been captured by the Khmer Rouge, Jim thought. After a brief pause, he continued. 'Anyway, the old man said he wanted us to write the truth about them but not to reveal their position. We promised to do that.'

'That's a standard rule for any journalist embedded with an army: never reveal your position.'

'Well, we weren't exactly embedded voluntarily.'

'*D'accord*. You lawyers love to split the hairs. Go on.'

'That night we set off with six men escorting us. They gave us bundles of rice and our civilian clothes. And we each had a toothbrush and a tube of Lucky toothpaste.'

'That is very appropriate,' Dominique said, lighting another cigarette.

'So off we went, flip-flopping along in our rubber thongs.' Seeing Dominique's puzzled expression, Jim added, 'That's Australian for what the Americans call shower sandals.'

'Ah, thongs for the feet and not for the bondage.' Dominique smiled and flicked some ash in the direction of the ashtray.

'In each village Cambodian kids were lined up to stare at us and, behind them, rows of adults.' That was a sight he'd never forget, Jim thought, all those faces illuminated by kerosene torches. Expressionless faces, closely watching them march by escorted by the guard of Liberation soldiers. What the Cambodians would have made of that was anyone's guess. Their loyalties must have been torn apart. Would they have been supporting the group that hassled them least or most? The US bombers hassled them the most, destroying their crops, their livelihood, their communities. Yet the Liberation Armed Forces were wreaking havoc too. The Cambodian peasants would have been confused, frightened, weary of it all and wanting all the invaders out.

'How I wish I could have photographed you.'

'Kim and Michio were wishing that too.' That night they'd barely slept. Short naps punctuated by distant phosphorus flares that lit up the darkness. In the end he'd hauled himself awake and listened to the drumming of machine guns and the deeper explosions of artillery fire.

'And then?' Dominique asked.

'I reckon each of us was wondering why the Liberation Armed Forces would risk the lives of their men to get us out. And all the time we heard bombing and artillery. Not actually on us, but awfully close – so we were starting to feel more and more nervous.'

'*Agité*. And then what?'

'Eventually we reached the bitumen road near the release point and our guards left us. It was strange. I felt like we were losing old friends.' Especially Anh Tu, Fourth Brother. He was the only one of their captors who'd remained with them until their release.

'You were. They did accompany you all that way without killing you.'

'All the time we were worried that the town we were heading for might now be in Khmer Rouge hands. We found an abandoned house and we changed out of our army garb there. Kim had been given a piece of white parachute silk and we tied it to a stake. Then we saw a bunch of government soldiers heading towards us. Kim waved his white flag. I recognised the officer in charge at the same time he recognised me. "You're dead," he said.

'"No we're not," I said.

'He shook my hand so hard it almost fell off. Then he got us into an escorted jeep and helicopter transport to Phnom Penh. The rest you know.'

'Not quite. *Peut-être* you will, some time, tell me more.'

'Since then I've been wondering if our escort made it back safely. I hope they did. They were good people.'

'There are good people on both sides. And bad, *mauvais. Très mauvais.* This is what being here has taught me.'

––––•••––––

To clear his head before making the phone calls to Australia, Jim took a short walk down to the Mekong River. Ahead of him was the glistening white spire of Wat Phnom, a Buddhist temple on a small rise. Although surrounded by open spaces fringed with trees, it would be swarming with people. Turning into a side street, he made his way down to the riverfront. The park alongside the water was crowded too. More and more refugees were thronging into Phnom Penh. Even after just a few weeks' absence he could notice the difference.

He sat on the grass and leant against the trunk of a palm tree. How could you ever measure the human cost of war? Not only all those lives lost so senselessly but all the other myriad destructions. The disparate countries of Indochina had been pushed around by colonisers, from the time of the Chinese, then the

French, and now the Americans. And how would the new types of warfare affect future generations? The outcomes of this war would be horrific: the displacement of millions of people, rural poverty, destabilisation of societies, of families, of institutions.

And what was he doing in Phnom Penh? He'd always upheld that noble aim of reporting the truth, chronicling both sides of the conflict. But was he really any better than the swarms of journalists who thronged into Saigon and Phnom Penh to thrive on adrenalin and booze? Nearly seven hundred of them, according to that report he'd read, and the vast majority were probably covering the war from the bars in Saigon. It was all too easy to get a press card. All you had to do was turn up at the US Army Press Centre with a visa and a letter from your employer or, if you were freelance, from your agency.

Was this the best way for him to use his intellect? His talent wasn't for journalism or even for writing, although he could do both reasonably well. But these activities gave no real meaning to his life. He wanted to reach out to help people, not in the medical sense but in fighting for basic human rights. Sure, that's what America and her allies, the Australians and New Zealanders, thought they were doing in this screwed-up war. But they weren't. They were making things worse. They were destroying Indochina and it would take years, decades, for it to recover.

He would go home and take up the job in the Human Rights Centre, and would feel his way forward to a better use of his life than he'd been making of it so far.

He stood up, abandoning his introspection. In a quarter of an hour it would be time to phone home. At this moment a legless man in his early twenties rolled by. Perched on a trolley – a crude thing, no more than a piece of planking on four small wheels – he managed to stop using his bare hands. He said something in a Cambodian dialect that Jim didn't understand. The man's intention was unmistakable, as was his need. Jim dug into his pocket. Pulling out all his change, he placed it on the proffered palm. The man grinned and nodded before wheeling himself off.

Slowly Jim made his way along the crowded boulevards and back to Dominique's flat. He was fortunate to know precisely where he wanted to go and to have the means of travelling there.

CHAPTER 36

To fill in time while she waited for Jim's phone call, Zidra began to tidy her bedroom. She picked up some clothes she'd left in an untidy heap on top of the chest of drawers and tossed them onto the bed. After pulling open the top drawer, she tried to lift out the shoebox in which she kept Jim's letters. She'd decided to reread the most recent, even though she knew it almost by heart. A week ago she'd tied the lid onto the box with a hair ribbon, and now this caught on the side. As she tugged, the drawer twisted and then came out with a rush. All its contents spilt onto the floor. She picked up the drawer and pushed it into the recess. It refused to glide back into place. She wriggled and shoved it, but it wouldn't slide all the way in. Something had to be blocking it – perhaps a pair of knickers or those navy-blue tights that had gone missing a few weeks ago.

She removed the drawer again and ran her hand over the slightly splintery wood that partitioned each layer of the chest. At the back she touched a small object that felt like plastic. She lifted it out.

Lorna's missing microcassette was missing no longer. It had been in her room all along.

She began to laugh and was still laughing two minutes later when the phone rang. She picked up the receiver on the top landing.

'Hello?' Jim's voice was unmistakable.

'Jim!' She let out a yelp of joy. 'This is the most fantastic day of my life!'

'Mine too. I've been really looking forward to talking to you, Zidra. By the way, I gave your number to a journalist friend last night. He was supposed to ring you to let you know.'

'Someone did call, twice. He asked for Sandra. Jim, I can't believe you're alive! We thought you were dead. Everyone did, what with your body being found and everything. Or what they said was your body. And now you're back. It's a miracle.'

'Yes, it's a miracle.'

'It's terrific to hear you.' Abruptly she was seized by a shyness she hadn't felt for years. Though she longed to say that hearing his voice was what she'd been dreaming of, the words that came out were simply, 'I got your letter.'

'Which one?'

She felt surprised. Surely he'd know what she was talking about. 'The one you wrote on the plane. It was postmarked Saigon.'

'Oh, that letter.' His voice sounded strained.

At once she guessed that he was regretting sending it. Embarrassed, she said, 'It was a lovely letter.' Perhaps it was understandable for him to be having second thoughts. After all, he'd written that ages ago. His world had altered dramatically since then. Those weeks with the Vietcong were bound to have changed him, in ways she could only imagine.

'That trip back home seems like a long time ago now,' he said.

255

There was a brief pause. In the background Zidra heard a woman's voice, French, Dominique perhaps, and then an American man speaking. 'What's going on?' she said, fighting back a twinge of suspicion.

'I've moved out of the Hôtel le Royal. I'm staying in Dominique's flat. Some guy wants to interview me again. Now's definitely not the time.' Jim's voice sounded even more tense, or maybe he was simply distracted. 'About that letter . . .'

'It arrived late.'

'You didn't reply?'

She was unable to speak for a moment. How could she have replied when he was already dead? She swallowed before saying in a strangled voice, 'I only got it the day before the memorial service.'

'Nothing was waiting for me when I got back to Phnom Penh,' he said. 'No letters, nothing. Even my typewriter had gone. They reckon my flat was broken into after I was reported missing.'

There was another pause. Dominique and the American man were talking again, their accents unmistakable although it was impossible to pick out the words. After they faded out, there was only silence. She said, 'Did you have anything else valuable there?'

'No. My typewriter was pretty ancient. I'll buy another one.'

She wondered what had happened to all those letters she'd written to him over the years. Weren't they valuable? She'd hate to lose the shoebox containing all his letters to her.

Suddenly she heard the American man's voice on the other end of the line. 'Just five minutes of your time,' he was saying, and then Jim said quite impatiently, 'No interview now, I'm on the phone to Australia . . . Sorry, Zidra, what were you saying?'

'Something riveting about your typewriter,' she said, struggling to keep the frustration out of her voice. To calm herself, she grabbed at the first thing she could think of and said, 'I suppose you'll have job offers from everywhere now. And I'll bet that the CIA and ASIO mobs will be wanting to cosy up to you.'

'The US Embassy people in Saigon want to debrief me. I refused. I told them that after I'd spent all those weeks with the other side denying any involvement with the CIA, I certainly wasn't going to change that position. Anyhow, I've agreed to meet with the ambassador after I finish writing some pieces for the UPI, but there won't be any debriefing. Then next weekend I'm coming home.'

'Coming home?' She might have leapt for joy if she hadn't at that moment heard Dominique's voice murmuring in the background, '*Du café, mon cher?*'

'Yes. I'm giving up my UPI job.'

'Are you really?' She sat down on the top stair tread. Was it even remotely possible that he could still mean the words he'd written in his last letter? But if he did, he would surely be telling her so now. And why was Dominique calling him *mon cher* if they were just good friends?

'I've had enough of being a foreign correspondent. Being a prisoner makes you see things clearly. What matters, what doesn't.' At this point Zidra heard Dominique saying, '*Le voila, mon chouchou,*' and Jim's reply, '*Merci,*' followed by the clink of a cup. Zidra spoke as calmly as possible. 'What'll you do?' Her question would give him the opportunity to reassure her, assuming he hadn't changed his mind about her.

'Take the human-rights job at Sydney University if it's still open,' he said at once. 'There are human-rights issues all through South East Asia.'

'There'll be even more once the fighting in Indochina ends.' Delight that he'd be returning to Sydney tussled with disappointment that he hadn't reiterated his love for her.

'How are you, Zidra? You sound different.'

'No, I'm the same,' she said, speaking with forced calmness. 'By the way, did your parents tell you what I read at your service?'

'No. I haven't spoken to them yet. I'm going to do it next.'

That he called her before his parents must show that he still cared. She might have felt exultant if she hadn't heard again Dominique's voice and the murmur of Jim's reply. He must have put a hand over the receiver, for she was unable to discern his words. 'Good,' she said, her response inadequate to express the emotional turmoil she was experiencing.

'It's so weird that people think I've risen from the dead. I feel terrible I've put everyone through all this. What did you read at the service?'

'The poem by Judith Wright you sent me. "All things conspire to hold me from you."'

'"All things conspire to stand between us – even you and I."'

Especially you and I, she thought. After a pause, she said, 'Are you okay, Jim?'

'I'm two stone lighter and I've got one or two ulcers on my calves.'

This sounded like jungle rot to her but of course he would play down any injury. 'What's the treatment?'

'Antibiotics and mercurochrome. Plus lots to eat. Preferably not rice. Dominique's been a real godsend.' He laughed. 'She's such a brilliant cook.'

Zidra squashed down her jealousy at the thought of Jim and Dominique eating delicious French food together. Whenever people had the chance, they'd get up to all sorts of things; you only had to consider her and Hank to see that. Even if Jim was going to withdraw his marriage proposal, she told herself sternly, all that mattered really was that he was still alive. 'I missed you so much,' she said, picking her words carefully. 'I can't wait to see you again.'

'Nor I you. We've got a lot to discuss.'

She hated the businesslike way he spoke those words; he might have been talking to another lawyer rather than to someone he'd once written a love letter to. Choosing to ignore his brusqueness, she said, 'Would you like me to collect you from the airport?' She stood up and took a couple of paces around the landing.

'Yes. I'll call you again in a day or two with the details.'

She remained still for a moment, gripping the phone receiver in her hand, her finger pressed down on the button. She was feeling light-headed and confused, as if she could float right up to the ceiling if she didn't hold on tightly to something. After a few moments the dizziness went, and she put the receiver back in its cradle. Even now she had trouble believing that Jim's return wasn't simply a dream.

Mon chouchou. She didn't know what that meant but it certainly sounded like an endearment.

She ran downstairs to the bookshelves in the living room and pulled out Lisa's French–English dictionary. '*Chouchou (informal)* pet, golden boy, blue-eyed boy.' That pang of jealousy returned. She really had to get a grip, she told herself firmly. Jim was alive; he was returning home. That was all that mattered.

CHAPTER 37

George was marching around the kitchen waiting for his turn to speak to Jim. For a good ten minutes Eileen, who usually had little to say on the phone, had been talking to – or, more precisely, interrogating – Jim about the state of his health. Having established that he wasn't one of the two journalists who'd been reported with malaria, she was asking about his feet. His feet! Certainly they were important, but what George really wanted to find out was his state of mind.

'Jungle rot,' Eileen was saying. 'You mean like they had in the trenches in the First World War? Surely not . . . You were lucky not to get that. You've still got all ten toes? . . . What are they treating the ulcers with? . . . Mercurochrome, is that all? . . . Yes, yes, I see. Antibiotics too. Good, glad to hear it. Your father's pacing around the kitchen, wearing a track in the linoleum, so I'll put him on in a minute. When are you coming home? . . . Next week, did you say? You know we're longing to see you again. Will you carry on staying at the Royal Hotel till you leave? . . . Pardon my French' – and she was laughing now – 'The Hôtel le Royal . . . You're staying at Dominique's flat? . . . Okay, I'll get a pen to write down the number while you speak to your father.'

Once George had the phone in his hand, those words that had been queueing in his brain suddenly vanished, and all he could get out was, 'Good to have you back, son.'

'Back from the dead, that's what people are saying,' Jim said. His voice was the most beautiful thing George had ever heard, resonant and clear. 'There was a wake for me at the Gecko Bar apparently. And I heard about the memorial service at St Matthew's. I'm really sorry you had to go through all that, Dad. It must have been terrible for you.'

Terrible was an understatement, George decided. He felt a momentary pang of remorse about holding the memorial service too early. After all, it wasn't like a funeral, where you had to rush in to bury or cremate the body. The cremation had already occurred, or so they'd been advised. But on the other hand, everyone thought Jim was dead and they'd had to observe the rites of passage. Eileen especially had wanted that.

'It was a big turnout,' he said. 'Half the town was there and many from further afield.' With Eileen hanging about in the kitchen, he judged it wouldn't be politic to mention the incident of the handbagging of the Reverend Cannadine. He added, 'It was a very moving service.' He coughed to cover his feelings. He was on an emotional roller coaster and had been for weeks. The last thing he wanted was to start blubbing again on this, the day of Jim's resurrection from the dead. Once his fit of coughing subsided, he said, 'Yes, it was terrible, but your capture must have been too.'

'After my first interrogation I was sure they were going to kill me,' Jim said, his voice tense. 'I even heard the click of the pistol's safety catch being released but the guy didn't fire it. Maybe he did that deliberately, or maybe I just imagined it. I'll never know the truth about that.'

A pistol at your head, the belief that your life was over. How would you deal with that? And then, a moment later, realising your life continued: would you feel euphoric or afraid? If George hadn't wanted to protect his son, he might have asked what that was like. Instead he enquired how the Vietcong had treated them.

'They looked after us pretty well.'

'Why do you think you were released?'

'Well, I'm not sure really, but I've got a few theories. I'll tell you about them when I get home.'

George was pleased to hear that, in this regard at least, Jim was unchanged by his experiences. Much of his life had been spent searching for explanations and, when there weren't any, devising hypotheses.

Jim continued. 'But I think the main reason they let us go is that Hanoi's starting to see foreign journalists as a propaganda tool. Since the My Lai Massacre the media's sympathies are increasingly with the north, and Hanoi knows that.'

'I suppose reporters are a propaganda tool if you report what you're told,' George said. Believing you were about to be executed would have to leave a legacy, he decided. Not to mention what-ever else had happened to Jim in his weeks in the jungle. Things that perhaps they'd never learn about.

'We had lots of discussions with the Vietcong,' Jim said. 'I wouldn't say it was a re-education exactly, although they intended it to be. I reckon they thought it would serve their cause better to treat us well, knowing we'd spread the word.'

'You're not bitter?'

'On the contrary. It was a way of seeing what's happening on the other side.' Yet Jim's voice sounded strained as he spoke these words and George wondered how much of what he was saying was bravado. 'All I'm sad about is the hell you must have gone through.'

'Yes, it was hell,' George said. There was no point pretending otherwise. 'But it's over now.'

'Did you and Mum throw out my stuff?'

'We kept everything as it was. Not that you've got many things here anyway. A few books, some old clothes, that's all.' George was glad he'd left Jim's box of treasures in the garage exactly as he'd found it.

Now Eileen was hovering at George's elbow, trying to retrieve the receiver from him. As he handed it over, fatigue hit him like a blow to the head and he knew he'd have to spend the afternoon in bed.

It wasn't often that an ordinary cove like him experienced a miracle.

CHAPTER 38

Jim saw Zidra standing by the barricade as soon as he came through the swing doors from the customs and baggage hall at Sydney airport. Dressed in a black linen dress, she looked more elegant than he'd ever seen her, as if she were off to a party. When she saw him, she grinned and waved. He put down his bag and held her close. 'I'm so glad to see you.'

When she moved back a pace, he wondered why. He could do with a shower, he decided, though he'd had a thorough wash and brushed his teeth in the tiny toilet area on the plane. To fill the rather awkward silence, he said, 'Are you sure it's all right for me to stay at your place?'

'Yes, it's fine.' She looked tired and there were dark smudges under her eyes, but she was smiling. 'Joanne and Lisa don't mind in the least. They're dying to meet you. I borrowed a folding bed and we'll put it in the dining room. We don't use that room much, so it's no imposition. This is such a fantastic day! It's hard to believe you're back at last. I thought we'd go to the TV station first, for your interview. It's lucky you're back on a Saturday and I've got the whole day off. And then after that I think you've got some more interviews?'

'Yes, just a couple today and they won't take long. Then I've got a few more lined up for Monday.' There'd been so many interviews since his release he no longer needed to prepare beforehand. The questions were always the same. Why did the Vietcong let you go? What was it like with the enemy? Did they mistreat you? He could answer these even when only half-awake.

'Stella and Nic Papadopoulos are having a lunch party at their place. Are you happy to go to that? Any time after twelve noon, they said. I hope you're not too tired for all of this.'

'I slept on the plane for the entire trip. I feel terrific.' In fact he felt exhausted but he didn't want to spoil the day by mentioning this. 'Zidra, I really do need to talk to you.'

'Can it wait?' Her voice cracked slightly. 'We've got a tight schedule.' As she bent to unlock the car door, her hair fell forward and obscured her face.

'Okay.' He put his bags down on the bitumen and waited.

'Maybe we can go for a walk after the party,' she said. 'Through Centennial Park or somewhere like that. Then you can talk to me. There's so much I want to tell you. And to ask you.'

'By the way,' he said, remembering the present he'd bought for her at the duty-free. 'This is for you.'

'How lovely.' She took the bag and smiled, her golden-brown eyes glowing.

'Dominique suggested this brand would suit you. I've told her all about you and she said you sound just like a Chanel No. 5 girl. French women seem to know these things somehow.'

'Is that so?' Her smile vanished and a tiny frown appeared. Perhaps she hated Chanel No. 5. Or maybe she'd given up wearing scent and he might have done better to buy chocolates and whisky or cognac instead.

'Aren't you going to look in the bag?'

'Sure, although you've already told me what's in it.' After removing the sticker holding together the sides of the carrier bag, she gave the contents a cursory inspection before saying, 'Thank you, Jim. That's really lovely.'

'I'll hold the perfume,' he said. 'You seem to have your hands full, what with your handbag and the car keys.'

'My handbag's tiny and anyway I've nearly got the key in the lock.'

'Tiny? It's enormous.'

'It's my briefcase too.'

'An enormous handbag but a tiny briefcase.'

His laughter must surely have sounded as forced to her ears as to his own – a perverse and unnecessary addition to his words. However she acknowledged neither. All her efforts were directed at opening both doors of the car, an activity that seemed to require an unusual amount of concentration. After this achievement she tossed her bag onto the back seat before tackling the boot.

'You look beautiful,' he ventured. 'That's a lovely dress.'

'Thank you. It's what I wore to your memorial service.'

'A dress for all occasions,' he said and regretted it immediately. Disappointment washed over him, at his own performance as much as Zidra's. For so long he'd been wanting to see her; he'd never imagined their meeting would be awkward. Anticipation of their reunion, and a conviction that his love was reciprocated, had kept him going through those weeks of suffering in the jungle. Into his head slid the memory, quickly suppressed, of those seconds that he'd thought were his last, when he'd been so sure he was about to die. Zidra had been foremost in his mind then.

But why should their conversation be this complicated when he had so much to say to her? Perhaps he should have telegraphed from Phnom Penh, straight after that first phone call last week. Why was it so much harder to express your feelings verbally than in writing? Probably it was that extra layer of protection you gained by not being able to see or hear any reaction. After a moment inwardly rehearsing his words, he said, 'I'm pleased you chose to wear that dress today.' Yet in spite of his preparation the words were like awkward pebbles that he had trouble spitting out.

Perhaps it was fortunate that she didn't hear. As she opened the back of the car, she said, 'Have you heard about my ASIO story?'

'Yes. Congratulations. That was fantastic.' Of course he should have mentioned it before, as soon as he'd seen her. No wonder she was a bit irritated. He placed his bag in the boot, together with the unwelcome bottle of Chanel No. 5.

'I'll tell you all about it in the car,' she said, locking the car boot before putting on her sunglasses.

CHAPTER 39

The sun was low. Though Zidra would have liked to take Jim's arm as they strolled across the rough grass of the park, she felt as if there were a glass wall separating them. He seemed tired and distant. Perhaps the day had been too much for him. *I really do need to talk to you.* That sentence had been fermenting in her mind ever since she'd collected him from the airport that morning. Filling her with foreboding and almost spoiling the day. Her anxiety was accumulating and she struggled to calm herself with the mantra she'd been repeating to herself a lot lately. *Remember he's alive. Remember that his altered feelings can never take that joy away.* She kicked with her sandalled toe at a tussock of grass, hard enough to express her apprehension but not hard enough to hurt.

'You did that a lot when you were a teenager,' Jim said and laughed.

She used to hate the way he would sometimes invoke the past like this. It had seemed to distance them rather than bring them closer, as if that difference in their ages gave him an advantage that he didn't deserve. Yet now she felt touched by his comment and their shared memories, and she smiled back. For a few minutes more they walked in silence. In her head she began to formulate the words she would say. *You said you needed to talk to me about something.* Yes, that would do. They had to get this unsaid thing out into the open. She couldn't bear the thought of not knowing where she stood. Or maybe she'd just say, *What did you want to talk to me about?*

But in the end it was Jim who broke the silence. 'You didn't reply to my letter.'

'The one you wrote on the plane?' She glanced up at him. The cruel glare of the sinking sun hurt her eyes and she quickly turned away to avoid it.

'Yes.'

'I only got it the day before the memorial service. I told you that on the phone. There was no point writing to a dead man.' Her words came out far more harshly than she'd intended. It was too late to snatch them back again. They hung solidly between them in the still air.

'I didn't mean it like that, Zidra. I meant that you haven't answered that question I asked you.'

'Which one?'

He didn't reply. His attention was directed to the buttressed trunk of a Moreton Bay fig tree some twenty metres distant. 'Did you know those figs are strangler plants?' he said. It was as if he'd forgotten the point of their conversation. 'When a seed lands in the branch of a host tree it sends down aerial roots, eventually killing the host and standing alone. I saw an amazing *ficus* in the jungle. It was completely covering some ancient Cambodian temple. It looked like lava trickling down the sides and oozing over the ground.'

The crumbling temple covered with molten lava appeared to her like a vision glimmering in the greenish jungle light. 'Where did you see it?' she said gently.

'I can't remember where it was. I got very confused with direction. But I can tell you when. It was when I was being asked a lot of questions. My last interrogation.'

Her heart skittered and she was about to speak when he said, in a choked voice, 'Do you care for me, Zidra?'

She turned to look at him, shifting her position slightly so that his head was no longer silhouetted against the sun. His eyes were obscured behind dark glasses, and his face was expressionless, if you didn't count the tension around the mouth. He meant friendship, that was all.

'Of course I care for you.' She'd make it easy for him to withdraw his proposal if that was where this conversation was heading. If only he'd take off those bloody sunglasses she might have a better chance of gauging his thoughts. 'Do you still care for me? Even after all your time in captivity?'

'Yes.'

She felt a flicker of hope. 'Didn't that change you?' Yet even as she spoke, she knew what the answer must be. How could his experiences not have altered him? He'd gone into the jungle and come out again. He'd faced the enemy and found that they weren't so different from the allies. He'd faced the possibility of his own death, had known there was a pistol being held to the back of his head. How could you possibly be unaffected by that?

And then there'd been Dominique waiting for him when he'd returned to Phnom Penh.

'Yes, but it hasn't changed my love for you. Just think, Zidra, have the reports of my death changed your affection for me?'

'No, of course not.' But she knew they'd changed her in other ways that she didn't yet fully comprehend. Made her more anxious, made her less trusting, and that was probably the least of it.

'Well, the same with me. I still mean everything I said in that letter. Absolutely everything.'

'Everything?'

'Yes. Every single word, every phrase, every sentence, every paragraph. Every feeling.'

'I thought you'd changed your mind,' she said hesitantly.

'Is that why you were so abrupt on the phone when we spoke?'

'*Me?* It was you. You sounded distracted, almost like it was a chore to ring me.'

'Well, Dominique had just come into the room with some journalist friend that she couldn't keep out. That's why I might have come across as distracted.'

'You haven't fallen in love with Dominique, have you?' She looked into the distance as she spoke; she couldn't bear to face the answer she was dreading. '*Mon chouchou, mon cher*: I couldn't help hearing her call you that when you rang me.'

'Dominique calls everyone that,' he said. 'It means nothing. Of course I'm not in love with her. How many times do I have to say it, Zidra? It's you I love. Why can't you believe it? Or have you fallen in love with that American with bad taste in books?'

She laughed. 'You mean with Hank? No, I haven't. That's all over. And I do believe you now, Jim.'

'And what's your answer to that question?'

'You mean the one asking me to marry you?'

'Yes, that one,' he said.

'Yes, I'd love to marry you, Jim Cadwallader.' Her voice cracked and gave away her feelings, but that didn't matter any more. After reaching up and removing his dark glasses, she said, 'I've missed you so much. More than I ever thought possible.'

He pulled her to him and she rested her head on his chest. 'Me too, Zidra. More than I thought possible.'

'I think we might forget about that folding bed tonight,' she said. 'I reckon you'll find it more comfortable upstairs with me.'

'I reckon I will too,' he said and began to kiss her.

PART VI

Late November 1971

CHAPTER 40

Zidra opened her eyes and saw, only centimetres away, Jim's green eyes staring at her. She said, 'How long have you been awake?' It had been Jim's idea to break their journey at Gerringong on the drive to Jingera. His first few days in Sydney had been filled with radio and television interviews, with everyone wanting to know about his time as a captive of the Vietcong. And endless interruptions. Friends dropping around, the phone ringing incessantly, the Paddington terrace house always full of people.

'Half an hour. It's only seven o'clock. I've been watching you. You look so young and innocent. Very misleading.'

She laughed and rolled over so that her ear was resting on his chest. The morning light filtering through the ugly floral curtains was absorbed by the clinker-brick walls of the barn-like room of the motel. Jim's heartbeat formed a soothing accompaniment to the keening of seagulls and the slower rhythm of breakers crashing onto the beach to the north.

'I wonder who else has been watching me,' she said.

'No one, I hope, now that the Royal Commission's been decided on.'

'I'm probably being watched all the more closely, and Lorna too. I don't understand how the government can have a largely unchecked surveillance system and yet view itself as the custodian of democracy and personal privacy. Who on earth is observing the observers?'

'People like you.'

'People in the media? You can't trust the press too much, you know that, though the *Chronicle*'s a bit of an exception. The media picks up something, distorts it a bit for effect and then drops it.'

'That's a blessing. I don't want to do any more interviews.'

'What, don't you want to be like Coleridge's Ancient Mariner, repeating your story forever to everyone who'll listen?'

'I don't need to do penance and I don't want to think of it at all,' Jim said, gently running his forefinger down the bridge of her nose and tracing out the contours of her lips.

She smiled at him and pulled his face down to her own.

Some time later she woke again, with a start. She reached out for Jim, but he was no longer beside her. She sat up too quickly and saw through oscillating waves of dizziness that he was seated at the desk at the far end of the room. Wearing only boxer shorts, he had a pile of papers in front of him. Deeply absorbed in what he was reading, he hadn't noticed that she was no longer asleep. His head was tilted at an angle. He looked peaceful; he looked unshakable. He looked lost to another world, one in which he belonged to himself and had no need to assume a protective mantle. She caught herself smiling at his exposure and turned her head away, forgetting for an instant that she no longer needed to conceal the tenderness she felt towards him.

Presently she sat up and perched on the edge of the bed. Although she thought such happiness was more than deserved, she wasn't going to let it get away from her. Quietly she stood, not wanting to disturb him, wanting to creep up on him.

At once he looked up. He smiled; he stood. She remained immobile, unwilling to change anything, unwilling to spoil anything. As he walked towards her, she watched his face, kind and reliable. He didn't say anything; he put his hands on her shoulders and gently tilted her towards him as if she were a cardboard-cut-out doll, so that her hips were resting against his and her head was against his chest. They stood together for a long time, his warmth against hers, his hands holding her bare back.

Suddenly there was a click as the small hatch door to their room opened. He manoeuvred her around so that her nakedness was concealed, and they smothered their laughter. The breakfast tray slid onto the bench by the door, pushed by an anonymous hand that withdrew immediately before the hatch snapped shut again.

As Jim turned to retrieve the tray, she noted again how badly pitted was the calf muscle of his left leg. The scar tissue looked pink against his tanned skin; the tiny craters would be permanent reminders of his time as a captive. There were scabs too, from the slower-healing sores, and there were other wounds that she could not see. He was a lot thinner than he used to be. Each vertebra was clearly visible, making him look somehow defenceless.

She remembered how, as a girl, she'd first noticed how beautiful he was. An image returned to her of Jim sitting on the beach at Jingera in the late afternoon, during one of those summer school holidays that used to seem endless, day after perfect day. Perhaps it was around four o'clock, the day-trippers already gone, the surf advancing with the incoming tide and the air not yet cool enough to make them want to put shirts on over their swimmers. After she'd shaken the sand out of her towel and spread it on the sand near Jim, she'd fought back an impulse to touch his tanned and vulnerable shoulder blades. How old would she have been? Thirteen or fourteen, no more.

She no longer had to repress those memories of Jim that were crowded into her head. He was tightly woven into the fabric of her past, and he would be tightly woven into the fabric of her future. They would grow up – and grow old – together.

Chapter 41

Jim watched Andy striding ahead, across the cemetery on the top of the headland above Jingera. He marched between the faiths. Catholics on one side; Protestants on the other. For the first time Jim noticed that the Protestants had the better view, of the ocean and the little township below.

Jim knew where his brother, back home for a week now, was heading. Beyond the white painted fence bordering the graveyard, a narrow track led under twisted shrubs and along the cliff edge, before dropping to a ledge. This was the place they used to go to when they were young. This was the place where Andy could smoke out of sight of anyone who might report him to their mother.

Jim followed Andy, just a few paces behind. His brother had changed. He'd become broader, more muscular. When he was older, he might have a tendency to gain weight. His straw-coloured hair was cut so short that his ears seemed more prominent, and the back of his neck was red, like beef jerky. And the changes to Andy were not just physical. There was a new hardness about him. His larrikinism was still there but it was not as spontaneous as it once was. There was something forced about his boisterousness.

They sat on the ledge, their backs against the eroded sandstone cliff. The ocean lay spread out in front of them, its endless regiments of waves rolling towards the shore. The sky to the east was pale and washed out above the darkening blue of the sea.

Andy pulled a matchbox and a crumpled packet of cigarettes out of the pocket of his trousers and lit a cigarette, sucking hard at it. After its end began to glow, he said, 'Do you remember, Jimmo, that time we sat here when I was deciding to apply to the Army Apprentices' School?'

'Yeah, I do. And I remember the fuss at home afterwards.'

'Who'd have thought that would lead me to Vietnam, eh? Though I remember you saying, "What if there's another war?" and I thought nothing of it.'

'No one would have predicted it.' Yet Jim didn't really mean these words; they were untruths to soothe Andy. Taking the long view, he felt that his country was always moving in and out of wars. Britain's wars. America's wars. There might be no end to it.

'Anyway, I've served my apprenticeship now,' Andy said. 'I've done my time and more. Now we're withdrawing from Vietnam, I could stay on in the army for a bit, but I've had enough of it. Can't wait to get out, in fact.'

'What'll you do?'

'What I've always wanted to do: set up a carpentry and joinery workshop. Only I'm going to do it in Burford, not Jingera – there are more people there. Then I'm going to find a nice girl. Make some nice furniture and, after a while, nice babies. And I'll surf on Saturday mornings with my mates. You know, the funny thing is that I used to want to get away from this place but now I can't wait to come home.'

'Mum and Dad will love that.' Jim gazed at the four headlands to the north, layered like stage scenery and receding into a distant haze. This had to be one of the most beautiful places in the world, he thought.

'Yeah, they're pretty stoked about it.'

'They know?'

'Yes.'

'They've kept quiet about that. I've been back for three hours and they haven't mentioned it.'

'That's because they've been too busy celebrating your return.'

Was there a trace of bitterness in Andy's voice? No, he was imagining it. Andy stubbed out his cigarette and soon after took another from the pack. While he was struggling to light it, Jim said, 'What was it like?'

'What was what like?'

'What was it like for you over there?'

'Grim. You'd know that, after your experiences. And grim coming back too. You should have seen the reception we got when we docked at Fremantle and Adelaide. Anyone would think we'd committed crimes instead of simply doing what the top brass told us we had to do.' Andy was jiggling his leg up and down – something he never used to do. 'The pollies got us into the bloody war and the pollies are taking us out of it, and we're none the wiser about any of it, apart from its stupidity.' He took another hard drag on his cigarette and sucked the smoke deep into his lungs. After exhaling, he said, 'Anyway, I don't really want to talk about it. Except I'll tell you one thing that's really stuck in my mind.'

'What's that?'

'It's what's happening to the kids. We visited a couple of orphanages, me and one of my mates. Thought it was the least we could do. We went with loads of toys but the kids were mostly too far gone for that.' After stubbing out his half-smoked cigarette, Andy flicked it over the cliff edge. Leaning forward, he rested his elbows on his knees. 'There were starving kids lying three to a cot. There were hopeless-case kids abandoned to dying rooms.' For a moment Jim thought Andy was crying but he was wrong: the emotion in his brother's voice was anger. 'There were kids with injuries from claymore mines. Kids with napalm burns that they weren't ever going to recover from.'

'We've got to make sure it doesn't happen again.' Even as Jim said these words, he felt their futility. Was making war – and suffering from it – the inescapable human condition? At his most optimistic he hoped not, even though his reading of history suggested otherwise. Even though he planned to spend the rest of his life working for human rights, because warring *was* the human condition. More and more often since his time in captivity he thought of the moral dilemma of killing in war and not killing in peace: how did people manage to turn that ethical switch on and off? It was impossible to do so without triggering inner conflict of the sort that Andy was clearly struggling through. War made monsters and victims out of us all.

'How can we possibly make sure it doesn't happen again, Jimmo? We don't run the bloody show.'

'We draw attention to it. We vote. We have demonstrations. Look what the moratorium marches are achieving.'

'All they're doing, from my perspective, is drumming up hatred for the soldiers. Makes us feel like shit. Makes us feel we were responsible for those kids.'

'You weren't.'

'You wouldn't know the half of it, Jimmo.' After another pause Andy said, 'Once, years ago, Roger and I talked to his dad about what it had been like in the Second World War. "What's it like to kill someone?" That's what Roger wanted to know. "I never saw anyone close up," his father said. "I was in the artillery, the big stuff, no face-to-face combat. We fired at a target and never saw the casualties." Then after eighteen months his dad was injured and sent home. He was the bloody lucky one.'

Andy's leg was jiggling up and down worse than ever and the fingers of his right hand were worrying at the matchbox. Eventually it broke, and he stuffed the fragments into his pocket. After this he said, 'Some things I can't get over. Like Roger O'Rourke's death, for instance. He was blown to pieces, you know. They bundled up as many bits of his body as they could find, but that wasn't enough, so they added a sandbag to make the weight right. Then they flew the coffin home. His parents don't know about the sandbag, of course, but all his section knew.'

Andy stood up on the narrow ledge so abruptly that Jim automatically reached out to steady him. 'Don't worry, Jimmo,' Andy said. 'I'm not going to jump. Life's much too precious to throw away like that.' He bent down to pick up a pebble; perhaps that was his intention all along. After tossing it from palm to palm as if testing its weight, he flung it over the cliff edge.

When he turned to face Jim, his lips were smiling but not his sad and bloodshot eyes. 'No more of this morbid stuff, eh?'

'Time for a schooner or two at the pub before tea,' Jim said. 'What do you reckon?'

'Bloody good idea. You've been back a whole afternoon and you still haven't shouted me a beer.'

Jim led the way through the cemetery. Past the Catholic precinct, where a part of Roger O'Rourke lay buried together with a bag of sand from a distant land. Briefly Jim struggled to think of who it was who wrote, 'There is some corner of a foreign field That is forever England.' It was Rupert Brooke, he remembered. Now there was a corner of a Vietnamese field that was forever Australia. And so too, right here in Jingera, there was a little corner – a bag or two of sand – that was forever Vietnam.

He carried on, past the Protestant precinct, past the graves of the other Jingera casualties from all the wars in distant lands that Australia had been involved in. Just before the gate, he waited for Andy to catch up.

A sea hawk sailed into view. Wheeling around the cemetery, it was gliding on some updraft. Slowly it floated south, over the long white crescent of Jingera's beach and the bushland dividing the ocean from the river, and towards the distant headland barely visible in the late-afternoon haze.

Without warning the peaceful afternoon was shattered by the roar of a mortar attack. Jim flung himself to the ground. Face in the grass, arms crossed over his head, eyes firmly shut, he knew the drill. His heart was thudding and sweat was beginning to trickle down his back as he waited for the hammering of the helicopter engine that was heading their way. At any moment it would begin to swoop overhead. At any moment he would hear the sound that he dreaded, that he'd heard so often: the staccato burst of machine-gun fire.

Instead he heard the liquid notes of a bird calling and the regular pounding of the surf, and he opened his eyes. He was lying face down on the sweet-smelling grass in Jingera cemetery, thousands of kilometres away from the jungles of Cambodia. The mortar attack that he'd heard was the sound of a car backfiring, that was all. The helicopters would not come again. The impermeable green jungle was not imprisoning him. Slowly he inhaled and exhaled, and soon his heart rate slowed. With unsteady legs and trembling hands he struggled to his feet.

Andy was nowhere to be seen. Presently Jim spotted him, metres away, crouched behind a tombstone. He might have been tempted to help Andy to his feet if their shared past hadn't taught him the value of looking the other way. This didn't prevent him hearing though. So harshly was Andy's breath rasping in his throat that you might think he was suffering from an asthma attack if you didn't know better.

To distract himself, Jim looked at the tilting gravestones and afterwards at the cobalt sky overhead. His eyes slid over the unrelenting blue, towards the paler haze to the east and the smudged rim of the shimmering indigo ocean. As soon as he could no longer hear Andy's breathing above the thump of breakers, he opened the cemetery gate and waited.

He didn't mention the car backfiring and the mortar attack, and neither did Andy. Side by side they walked down the hill, past the primary school and into the sphere of raucous laughter drifting out from the pub.

Here Jim saw Andy straightening his shoulders, saw him bracing himself, saw him shrugging on insouciance as he might don a jacket. When it was done, they walked together through the open doorway and into the bar.

Chapter 42

Standing in the hallway at Ferndale, Zidra peered at her reflection in the mirror. She was pleased that she hadn't thrown away the black linen dress after the memorial service. She'd only got as far as bundling it into a carrier bag, together with those frivolous black sandals, and stuffing the lot in the bottom of her wardrobe ready to take to Vinnies. The dress was gorgeous, she now decided, and she didn't look too bad either. Maybe her hair had gone a bit fluffy, but that was the sea air for you.

She walked out the front door and stood on the top step of the half-flight leading down to the gravel drive, dotted as always with weeds. Golden light saturated the landscape. The afternoon sun, percolating through the pine trees, cast long shadows. A light breeze fingered the pine needles and made the shadows dance across the drive, as if they too wished to take part in the evening's celebrations.

From the shed came the cough of the car engine as it started and then a splutter as it stalled. A moment later it started again, and Zidra saw her mother slowly backing the Armstrong Siddeley out of the shed. She seemed oblivious of Peter, who was standing nearby with his arms outstretched to demonstrate distance from the corner post. They had been performing this pantomime for as long as Mama had been driving, for almost as long as they'd been married. They would carry on doing it all their lives, moving side by side through the years that remained to them, always connected but often moving independently. Peter would forever demonstrate distance from the corner post as she backed his precious car out of the shed, his car that he hadn't driven himself for years, ever since he'd got vertigo driving down the escarpment. Some legacy of his bailout from a burning plane during the war, Ma had said. And just as reliably she would ignore him. She would back out as if he were not there and would miss the corner post by a few millimetres, no more – so close you would be left breathless if you didn't know how perfectly judged it was.

The moment concentrated, it hardened, it passed. The image crystallised into a structure that Zidra would carry with her all her life. It had meaning; it had clarity. The stability of her parents' marriage and, at the same time, the independence of each: this was what she wanted with her own marriage to Jim next April.

Just as Zidra was about to shut the front door, the Ferndale telephone stammered into life. She hesitated for an instant, wondering if she should leave it. At the third ring she put her handbag on the floor inside the hallway and ran to pick up the receiver.

'Hello,' said a male voice that she didn't recognise. 'I'd like to speak to Zidra Vincent please.' He pronounced her name to rhyme with 'cider'.

'Zidra speaking,' she said, emphasising the short first syllable of her name.

'Vance Butterworth here.'

Her heart skipped a beat. Though she'd never met him, she knew who Butterworth was: a retired businessman, on countless boards, and trustee for umpteen charities.

'Joe Ryan gave me your parents' number. Said you'd be staying there for a few days. I'm really glad to have got hold of you. I expect you can guess why I'm ringing.'

There was a pause in which she swallowed so loudly Butterworth could surely hear the gulp. Leaning her elbows on the hall table, she wondered if she was about to faint: the walls were shifting about in an alarming way.

'I'm phoning to tell you that you've won the Wheatley Award,' Butterworth said. 'The committee agreed unanimously. That was a quite splendid piece of work you wrote on internal security. Splendid, we all thought. So congratulations, Zidra!'

Surely there was a mistake; someone was pulling her leg. She slid her back down the wall and sat on the floor with her legs stretched out in front of her. Only thus supported did she try to speak, managing a small croaking sound.

'Are you all right?' Butterworth said.

'Yes,' she succeeded in saying at the second attempt. 'But can you repeat that? There's a lot of background noise.' The pounding of blood in her eardrums was louder by far than the tooting from the Armstrong Siddeley outside.

After Butterworth had finished, she said in a rush, 'Thank you so much, Mr Butterworth. This is a great honour. I'm astonished, of course, but absolutely delighted.' She was wittering on, she knew, like one of those society matrons she used to interview for the social pages, but she couldn't stop herself.

When at last she paused for breath, Butterworth managed to interject. 'Call me Vance. And of course we'll expect you to come to the award ceremony.'

Nothing would keep her away from that, she thought. Nothing. After a few more words they hung up. Outside her mother was impatiently honking the horn again. Ignoring this, Zidra dialled Joe Ryan's number. One of his sons answered and went to find his father. While Zidra waited, she did a little jig up and down the hallway as far as the phone cord would allow her. She'd won! A woman like her, a woman everyone but Joe Ryan thought would be unable to hack it off the social pages.

'Vance Butterworth has reached you then,' Joe said without any preamble. 'Or is this just a social call?'

'Yes and no. Did he tell you why he wanted to talk to me?'

'No, Vance is much too discreet to let a seasoned old editor like me know before telling you. We journalists can't be trusted to keep a good story to ourselves, can we?'

Zidra laughed.

'That's the girl. It's good to hear you laughing again. There were times I thought you'd forgotten how, before a certain Jim Cadwallader came back from the dead. But are you going to tell me why Vance was so keen to reach you? Or do I have to guess that you've won the Wheatley Award?'

'You have to guess,' she said, laughing again. 'You have to guess which one.'

'Well, I know it's not for photography because Chris won that. So let me see, what else do you do? Maybe a news story. Best news story. For your exposé. Am I right?'

'You're right, Joe.'

'Bloody hell, Zidra. This will give us something to skite about in Monday's paper! I'm so pleased.'

'I want to thank you, Joe. For everything you've done for me.' Her voice caught; her damned vocal cords always gave away her emotions.

Yet there was a catch in Joe's voice too when he answered, 'No worries, Zidra. This is what makes our newspaper good. Stories like yours. People like you.'

'Editors like you.'

'Well, blimey, don't get too carried away. But I reckon I might crack open the champers tonight to celebrate. Enjoy your engagement party, Zid, and mind you're back here before too long. You'll have a bit of catching up to do.'

'It's not an engagement party, Joe. It's a welcome-home celebration for Jim.'

'Call it what you will, I'm drawing my own conclusions.' With that he rang off. She pictured him standing in the hallway of his house in Randwick, smiling in that lopsided way of his, before going off to pull out the champagne from the fridge in which he would have placed it hours ago. 'Be prepared', he often said. 'For the good as well as the bad'.

Collecting her handbag, together with a measure of composure, she stepped outside into the late-afternoon sunshine.

'Hurry up, Zidra. We don't want to be late for the party,' her mother called.

'We won't be.' After opening the back door of the car, Zidra sat on the battered leather seat. 'I was on the phone,' she said quietly. 'I've just heard I've won the Wheatley Award.'

'That's nice, Zidra,' her mother said as she negotiated the driveway, which had become rather potholed after the heavy October rains.

'You've what?' said Peter, swivelling his head like an Aunt Sally at a fairground.

'I've won the Wheatley Award,' Zidra said, rather more loudly this time.

Her mother braked suddenly and shrieked, 'You've won the Wheatley! My daughter's won the Wheatley Award!'

'Take it easy, Ma,' Zidra said, as the car veered off the drive and onto the rough grass.

'I knew you'd make a fantastic news journalist, didn't I always say that, Peter?'

'You did, Ilona. You've always said that.' Peter was laughing and at the same time gently turning the steering wheel so the car drifted back onto the drive before coming to a stop.

But you never said it to me, Zidra thought, although at the same time she was thrilled with her parents' faith in her. At this moment she remembered the folder of cuttings she'd discovered under her mother's sewing basket the night after the memorial service. Of course she wasn't going to dwell – or not for long – on why her mother chose to tell Peter of her pride in her daughter rather than herself, or why she kept the file of clippings hidden. Maybe you became secretive if you survived what her mother had, or maybe she just hadn't wanted to pressure her daughter.

The reasons didn't matter though. What mattered was that her mother was now out of the car and opening the rear passenger door, and hugging Zidra hard enough to squeeze the air right out of her chest. This pride Zidra found so touching that she discovered she was crying too, in spite of her happiness. Because of her happiness.

CHAPTER 43

George Cadwallader stands in front of the medicine cabinet in the bathroom and inspects his reflection in the speckled mirror. The orange and brown tie is a bit garish but Eileen bought it for him specially for today's celebration, and leaving it off isn't an option. He opens the cabinet door and takes out his bottle of Hair Restoria. After unfastening the cap, he tips a few drops of liquid onto the palm of one hand and wipes it carefully over his scalp and through what remains of his hair. That bare patch of olive skin on the crown of his head is growing day by day, he's convinced of it, but the Restoria does at least help keep the remaining strands in good condition. They shine with a lustre almost as great as his bald patch.

'Hurry up, Dad! What are you doing in there? We're going to be late.'

'I'm contemplating.' George washes and dries his hands before opening the bathroom door. 'You do look smart, son.'

Andy grins. He slides past his father and stands in front of the mirror. George inspects his son's square shoulders and blonde hair. Even the military haircut can't disguise its luxuriance. Staring hard at Andy's face reflected in the mirror, George realises for the first time that it's asymmetrical. This mirror image strongly resembles but isn't identical to the face that he loves. 'What happened to your nose?' he says after a moment.

'I broke it. Didn't I tell you? That was ages ago now.'

'In conflict?'

'You might say that. It was in a game of footy.'

At this moment Eileen calls out from the lounge room, 'Don't you want to wear your uniform to the party, Andy?'

'Are you joking?' Andy bellows. 'No one wants to see a man in a uniform these days. I'm surprised at you for suggesting it, Mum.'

Eileen totters down the hall in her new high heels and stands next to George. It might be the shoes or her happiness at having both of her boys at home that makes her a bit unsteady. At any rate something prompts her to thread her arm through George's and rest her head for an instant on his shoulder.

Andy says, laughing, 'You might have handbagged Cannadine, Mum, but I don't think you want me to get in on the act. I don't want to be roused on by any clergymen.'

'You won't be,' Eileen says smoothly. 'I haven't invited the Reverend Cannadine this time.'

———•———

Jim pulls out of the wardrobe the new tie his mother presented him with the evening he returned to Jingera. 'To celebrate,' she said, and he decoded this to mean that he is to wear it for the party today. The tie is patterned in purple and mauve flowers that, with a leap of imagination, you could think of as bauhinia. It reminds him of the morning before his capture, when he sat on the flower-strewn balcony of his flat in Phnom Penh, thinking of Zidra.

Now he turns up the shirt collar of the pale-blue shirt he's wearing and slings the tie around his neck. All those years at boarding school mean that he never needs to look at what he is doing when knotting a tie. He can do it blindfolded; he can do it in his sleep – probably has done it in his sleep.

In a few days' time he and Zidra will drive back to Sydney. He hasn't told his parents that they will be living together right away, in the tiny Annandale house that they viewed last week and have arranged to rent for a year. He has told his parents only that they will be married next April at St Matthew's Church in Jingera. Although he'd expected that Zidra would want to be married in a registry office, it was she who'd chosen the church wedding. 'We're doing it for your mother,' she said. Her usually pellucid eyes gave nothing away.

He knows that his parents have been changed by his captivity, changed by his reported death, but he cannot quite clarify in what way, nor does he want to probe. He knows only that they mourned him, that they metaphorically buried him. His mother's eyes follow him whenever they are in the same room. It is as if she doesn't quite believe that he is really her son. While he understands her feelings, it makes him a little self-conscious. She notices him too much – more than she's ever done in the past. And she is thinner; her clothes hang on her. He is responsible for this. His father looks older as well, much older than he did when Jim was last home.

And Jim too has been scarred. You do not slough off, like an arthropod discarding an exoskeleton, an experience such as the one he went through. The capture, the expectation that at any moment you might be shot, the fear also that you might be killed by bombing sorties or artillery fire. He wakes up at night, sometimes trembling, sometimes shouting. Occasionally he awakens only when he is banging on the closed door of whatever room he's sleeping in. Yet his experience is what the people of

Indochina have been going through every day, every week, year upon bloody year. Now he understands much more of what that must be like.

At this moment he hears his mother calling to Andy, and Andy's response: 'No one wants to see a man in a uniform these days.'

He smooths down the tie before taking his navy linen jacket out of the wardrobe. While shrugging his arms into it, he thinks of the new – and to him surprising – bond that exists between his parents and Zidra. When she dropped him off two days ago, she stayed for dinner and he noticed the empathy between them. This didn't exist before, he is sure of it. *My capture has brought them a new daughter*, he thinks. That she wants to marry him in the church to please his mother touches him immensely and so too does his mother's fond expression when she looks at Zidra.

——◆——

The late-afternoon sky is a brilliant blue so deep you could drown in it. From the gable of the church hall is hanging a white canvas banner emblazoned with large red letters: 'WELCOME HOME, JIM AND ANDY'. Crowds of people are standing on the lawn in front of the hall. People Zidra knows. People she's never seen before. New people into the area. Old families from the area. Farmers and fishermen and forestry workers. The men in smart clothes, the women in vivid dresses and shining hair. All keen to take part in this celebration to commemorate the return of the two Cadwallader boys.

Not everyone who went to Indochina has come back though. There are new names picked out in shiny untarnished brass on one side of the war memorial in the middle of the town.

Returning to the car park to collect her forgotten handbag from the back seat, Zidra is overjoyed to see Lorna, in a yellow dress and high-heeled red sandals, walking down the hill towards her. Though she said she might come, Zidra attached a low probability to this, for Jingera is a long way from Sydney, a long way even from Bermagui if you don't have a car.

'I'm staying at Wallaga Lake. I got there last night.' Lorna smiles broadly, her special grin that puts all her teeth on show and makes her skin glow.

Zidra guesses there's a reason for this illumination and says, 'Has something happened? How are you?'

'Good.'

'Just good? How were your exams?'

'Very good,' says Lorna. 'And I've got a job with the Land Rights Commission.'

'Fantastic, you clever thing! I'm so pleased for you.' Zidra gives Lorna a big hug and for the second time today finds her eyes brimming with tears.

'There'll be big battles ahead,' Lorna says, although she is laughing.

'I know,' Zidra says. 'But you'll win them.'

'We'll win some and lose some. That's what we've got to expect.' Lorna leans against the top railing of the fence marking the boundary of the nature strip. Her smile has vanished and her face is serious.

Zidra perches on the fence next to her. 'But you're happy, aren't you?'

'Yes.'

'You look a bit sad all of a sudden.'

'Do I? It's only that things are coming to an end.' Lorna stares at her red sandals. They are shiny, and probably new, and Zidra is

deeply touched by Lorna's pride in them. She remembers the day
she first met Lorna, all those years ago, when she'd been hiding
in a hedge not far from where they are standing now and Lorna
crawled in to join her. She was wearing sandshoes without laces
that day.

'What things are coming to an end?'

'The years at university. The years of being free.'

'Do you feel you've been free?'

'Yes, in spite of everything.'

'But you'll carry on being free.' Turning her attention to a tiny
black beetle labouring along a blade of grass, Zidra wishes she
had more to offer.

'Not free of responsibility though.'

Zidra looks at Lorna, whose smile once more displays all her
teeth. Reassured, Zidra says, 'You've got a vocation.' Lorna is strong
and will travel far, and Zidra feels honoured to be her friend.

'A mission,' Lorna says, laughing now.

'You've had one for years.'

'Ever since Gudgiegalah Girls' Home. You've got one too,
Dizzy. And should I be congratulating you?'

'You know about the Wheatley?'

'Joe Ryan called me. Some bloke from the award committee
was trying to reach you, he said.'

'When? I've only just heard myself.'

'Joe phoned me just before I left Sydney. He said he'd got a
tip-off it might happen but he couldn't be sure. He asked me not
to tell anyone and I haven't. He wanted to know where you were
likely to be, or that's what he said.'

'I didn't know you were such good friends.'

'We're not but he phoned me anyway. He thinks he knows
me because of all you've told him about me, he said.'

'It's your story as well as mine, Lorna.'

'Joe said that's what you think. It *is* partly my story but it's your telling. You ran with it and crafted it and added more stories to it. And got it exposed. I'll always be grateful for that, and very, very proud of you.'

'I feel you should be getting this award as well.'

'That's complete nonsense, Dizzy, though I love you for saying it. Now here's your feller, look!'

Lorna takes Zidra's arm and together they watch the Cadwallader family advance up the hill, the parents flanked by their two sons. Jim catches Zidra's eye right away. He grins and waves.

'The boys are back,' someone says, and cheers and clapping ring out from the throng of people waiting outside the hall.

Glancing around the smiling faces, Zidra notices a shaft of light reflecting off the telephoto lens of a camera. It is held by a rather nondescript figure standing to one side of the crowd. The lens is directed towards her and Lorna.

Her face tenses, her smile becomes a scowl.

It is Mr Ordinary, taking photographs again.

But now the figure turns, the light shifts. She recognises Rod Bigelow, the photographer from the *Burford Advertiser*.

She relaxes, she smiles. She walks towards Jim, whose life has been so miraculously restored to her, and folds herself into his embrace.

HISTORICAL NOTE

Australia's participation in the Vietnam War began in 1962, at a time when there was a deep fear of Communist expansion in the Far East. Commencing with a small commitment of thirty military advisers sent to South Vietnam, Australian involvement in Vietnam expanded to a battalion by 1965 and to a task force by 1966. By the time the last of Australia's forces withdrew from Vietnam in 1972, the war represented the longest major conflict in which Australians had participated.

The conflict in Vietnam spread into neighbouring Cambodia, which is the setting for some of this novel. The North Vietnamese and the Vietcong set up base camps in Laos and Cambodia, with the approval of those countries, along the border with South Vietnam. Their troops were supposed to stay in that corridor close to the border. However, as the troops became more active, Cambodia's Prince Sihanouk allowed the United States to make bombing raids over Cambodia. After a military coup in Cambodia in March 1970, Sihanouk's successor, Lon Nol, called for more active support against the Communists, and in April 1970 Cambodia lost its neutrality when United States President Richard Nixon decided to invade Cambodia.

Initially Australia's engagement in the Vietnam War had widespread public support. However, as Australian deployment grew, conscripts began to make up a large proportion of those being sent to Vietnam and killed. Moreover there was a growing perception that the war was being lost, and reports of atrocities on both sides – including the My Lai Massacre by United States soldiers – further alienated public support. In parallel with the strong anti-war movement developing in America, opposition within Australia grew. In 1970 and 1971 thousands of Australians marched through the streets in three anti-war demonstrations, known as moratorium marches. These demonstrations were closely monitored and some of the organising groups infiltrated by the security services.

By this time Australia was winding down its commitment in Vietnam, while the United States was withdrawing its troops and progressively handing over to South Vietnamese forces responsibility for the conduct of the war – a process known as 'Vietnamisation'.

Engagement in the Vietnam War cost five hundred and twenty-one Australian lives, while around three thousand Australians were wounded. New Zealand forces were also involved in the Vietnam War.

ACKNOWLEDGEMENTS

Research for this book took me to a number of different historical sources, including browsing through newspapers in microfilm format in the National Library of Australia. I am particularly indebted to Paul Ham's meticulous history *Vietnam: The Australian War* (HarperCollins, Sydney, 2007). The letter of condolence I included in Chapter 19 is an actual letter, taken from Ham (p. 431), whose source was the Australian War Memorial, 2904/R237/1/1 Part 1, Correspondence – General – Letters of condolence. For information about the Vietnam War, I also found useful the Australian Government website: http://vietnam-war.commemoration.gov.au.

For background information on internal security and the role of the Australian Security Intelligence Organisation at the time of the moratorium marches, I am indebted to David McKnight's book *Australia's Spies and Their Secrets* (Allen & Unwin, Sydney, 1994). The chapter about Zidra's ASIO file landing on the desk of an editor of a major newspaper – and the editor choosing not to look at it – is loosely based on fact (see McKnight, p. 185). Of course the context, newspaper and characters in my novel are entirely fictitious.

When I first conceived this book, I had not yet discovered two accounts written by war correspondents about their time in captivity in Cambodia during the Vietnam War. Once I found these sources, it was impossible not to be influenced by them. These books are by Richard Dudman, *Forty Days with the Enemy* (Liveright, New York, 1971) and Kate Webb, *On the Other Side: 23 Days with the Viet Cong* (Quadrangle Books Inc., New York, 1972). I am grateful to both authors for the detail they provided of their journeys behind the lines in Cambodia. I owe a special debt to Kate Webb's account. My chapters about Jim's capture and interrogation are loosely based on her experiences as reported in her book, although of course the characters and settings involved in this novel are again fictitious.

Readers of history will know there was no Fourth Moratorium March. The one referred to in the novel is entirely fictitious, as are all the characters, although the quotation at the end of Chapter 1, 'Democracy begins on the farms . . .', is from Jim Cairns, who was an important player in the moratorium marches. The quotation comes from the House of Representatives, April 1970.

Although the Aboriginal Land Rights Commission did not exist in 1971, I have invented in the final chapter another body of a similar name.

For their invaluable comments on an earlier draft, I am grateful to Kathy Mossop and Evie Wyld. Special thanks to Maggie Hamand for her plotting advice when I was at a crucial stage of the first draft, and to David McKnight, who generously discussed with me journalists, exposés, newspapers and ASIO. Thanks also to Tue Gorgens and Tim Hatton for their careful reading of the manuscript at its more advanced stages.

Particular thanks are due to Karen Colston at Australian Literary Management, who has helped in so many ways over the years, and to my publisher, Beverley Cousins, for her always insightful and sensitive suggestions. Once again it has been a real pleasure to work with them, and with copy-editor Kevin O'Brien and the rest of the team at Random House Australia. Last but not least, I thank my family for their support and encouragement.

Alison Booth was born in Melbourne and grew up in Sydney. After over two decades living in the United Kingdom, she returned to Australia in 2002. A professor of economics at the Australian National University, she is married with two daughters.

Alison Booth's website address is www.alisonbooth.net.

A Distant Land is the final volume of the Jingera trilogy.

READING GROUP QUESTIONS: A DISTANT LAND

1. The book's prologue is written from Jim's perspective and provides information about what will happen to him. How different would the pace of the novel have felt to you if the prologue had been removed?
2. Zidra's life is in turmoil for much of the narrative. Do you think she copes well with the events that overtake her? What do you think she learns from her experiences?
3. What role does George Cadwallader play in *A Distant Land*? Why do you think the author chose to write some of the book from his point of view?
4. How do Jim's experiences affect his attitudes to war and to human-rights issues?
5. What is the significance of the Vietnam War to the narrative? Do you think any of the issues raised in the novel are relevant today?

READING GROUP QUESTIONS:
THE JINGERA TRILOGY

1. Why do you think the author decided to situate the final volume of the Jingera trilogy in 1971?
2. In *Stillwater Creek*, the town of Jingera was the main stage on which the action occurred. This location expanded to include Sydney in the second novel, *The Indigo Sky*. By the last novel, *A Distant Land*, the action has moved further afield. Why are the characters so drawn back to Jingera long after they've grown up? What part does the small township of Jingera play in the trilogy?
3. One of the concerns of the trilogy is the effect of war on those who are involved in action as well as those left behind. Which of the characters bear the heaviest burdens of the wars represented in the trilogy?
4. Abuse is another concern of the trilogy. How well do you think the main protagonists deal with abuse in its various forms?
5. Why do Armstrong Siddeley cars last so long?